MAN ALONE

MAN ALONE

George Agnew Chamberlain

South Jersey Culture & History Center

2026

MAN ALONE
By George Agnew Chamberlain
First published by G. P. Putnam's Sons, New York and London, 1926.

This 100th-anniversary edition published in 2026
Design, layout, and additional material Copyright © 2026 by
the South Jersey Culture & History Center at Stockton University
Foreword Copyright © 2025 by F. James Bergmann

Printed in the U.S.A.

stockton.edu/sjchc/
ISBN: 978-1-947889-30-9

Cover photos of glass blowers courtesy of the Library of Congress.

FOREWORD

Before *Man Alone* was published as a historical novel, it appeared as a serial in the *Saturday Evening Post*, 1925–26. The *Post*, on January 25, 1926, sent Chamberlain a letter concerning *Man Alone*. The editors informed Chamberlain that "Burt M. McConnell of the *Literary Digest*" had asked if they were receiving a "high amount of mail as a result of *Man Alone*." McConnell went on to write "I have heard people talking about it wherever I go in the most enthusiastic terms."

The cover of the original dust jacket is suggestive, featuring an "aristocrat blower" holding his blowpipe topped with a large bottle being formed. The inside back leaf explains the bitterness Thomas Strayton held towards women because his wife had run "away with another man." In reaction, Strayton and his young son Torquay journeyed from North to South Jersey to start a new life. When they reached South Jersey, the father's rage against women manifested itself one day when Thomas broke open an apple to show Torquay the "black core" to which he added "these be women" and "this is how you find out what they be like inside." The lesson for Torquay was that women were "rotten at the core." It would take long years—the length of the novel—for him to see women differently.

All of this is woven into the "romance of an industry" and Torquay's quest for a "glass that shall be flexible and unbreakable."

This was Chamberlain's third novel based in southern New Jersey. It is a historical novel about Thomas' dream of owning a glassworks in Hopetown, a fictionalized version of Bridgeton, New Jersey, famous for its glassworks. After a time in sand mining, Thomas—ever enterprising—built the Pine Tree Glassworks on the Cohansey River.

Chamberlain was friends with several owners of glass factories in Bridgeton. They were his card playing buddies. With their knowledge he was able to weave together the evolution of glass making. By the turn of the twentieth century, glass companies like Cumberland Glass Manufacturing Co. were leasing automatic bottle machines, thus forever changing the need for artisan glassblowers. The timeline of the novel mirrors this development. As the glassworks passed to Torquay, the son, he continued to build the works while experimenting with the possibility of "shatter-proof glass" and the possible use of an "infusion of gelatin." Chamberlain's research and dynamic writing brought life to the industry and the men who worked there.

There were numerous reviews about *Man Alone* in newspapers nationwide. One reviewer, Lucile Gulliver, called it a "Study in Misogyny" She then posed the question: "How would such a man and boy conduct themselves, the one as he approaches old age, the other as he grows to maturity?" Gulliver continued, "in pursuing his answer Mr. Chamberlain has achieved a work of extraordinary elements and qualities."

Gulliver thought the novel had "three heroes—two men, the laconic shrewd father, and the son fashioned after the paternal frame and mind, yet qualified by a tenderness which his astounding force keeps crushed and ineffectual . . ." while the third is the "glass industry which grows from the humblest beginning into a flaming monument, dominating the lives of its founders and the country-side, a being inanimate, yet like its masters."

Never has a novel about Bridgeton been so complimentary to an industry that was the life-blood of the community. Even with the advent of glass machines, the reviewer could not have foreseen the enigmatic end to the "flaming monument."

Gulliver saw how Chamberlain turned Torquay into a "pathologic study" who in the end found a "regenerating faith" through a fearless woman.

Her closing remarks praised *Man Alone* and the character of Torquay as an "acquisition to American literature." Her thoughts continued: "The sheer force of his personality, living in words alone, presents another standard of literary manhood and draws admiring thoughts to the author and the art of life and narrative which he commands."

A headline in the Cleveland *Plaindealer* reads, Chamberlain "Writes Romance of Glass Maker." An unnamed reviewer wrote, ". . . [this]

novel is so far his masterpiece." The reviewer saw Torquay as a "hero" who because of his father's misogyny, bore much grief during his lifetime.

The story is not only about glassmaking but also what made Bridgeton unique. The concluding, climactic scene takes place in the "Old State Street Church," Chamberlain's renaming of Bridgeton's Old Broad Street Presbyterian Church where he and several other relatives are buried in the graveyard. He describes the edifice:

> . . . sheltered by towering trees, it stood in the center of a graveyard a block square. It had long since been condemned as unsafe; but the true reason for its abandonment probably lay in its worn red-bricks aisles, awkward rectangular pews and precarious birdnest pulpit (also known as a wine glass pulpit), perched high against the front wall. It was still sturdy and by far the oldest (1795), most airy and loveliest house of worship in the city. Oddly enough it faced away from the street (Broad) and the town, which added to its aloofness. Only the oldest inhabitants know that this strange position was due to the fact the geography had changed while the church had remained fixed. The roadway which now forms a right angle at the back and side of the edifice once passed directly before its front door.

There is the "colored" woman who worked for the owner of the Pine Tree Glassworks, who came from a settlement of colored folk, historic Gouldtown, whose origin was already crowded in the obscurity of a long past. In spite of a missing link of three generations, its inhabitants claimed descent from the disowned kinswoman of John Fenwick, a British founder of Salem, New Jersey.

As a historian, Chamberlain also mentions other South Jersey glassworks. These include Wistarburg, the first successful glass factory in the state (1739) owned by Caspar Wistar. It was known for its fine craftsmanship of hand blown bottles. There is also the mention of the Whitney Brothers in Glassborough.

There were reviewers, and then there were "fans." Fan mail for *Man Alone* was sent from all parts of the country. A former resident of Bridgeton who now lived in Florida had worked in the glass industry, and had first-hand knowledge of the industry. The writer called the novel an "epic on glass and glassmaking." The writer went on about "glass sand" and "glass talk" and that the "older glass workers seem, in past days, to have been men apart." Towns were "different" and people had a "glass psychology." To the workers "it was only a means for a living." Separated from this attitude were the "aristocrats, the blowers" who "did strut, and how their wives did queen it over those of the lesser paid workers," and how they, not the " 'blowers' envied the $20 cash allowed these favored ones every payday." How "every ambitious mother planned for her daughter to marry a 'blower.' "

This knowledge continued with recollections of the "young chaps" who were joyful to enter into "long years of apprenticeship" and how "sad the older chaps were when they had to step off the bench to a sit down job." The wives "dreaded the weeks of night work that alternated with the weeks of day work."

The letter also stated child labor was a given in the glass industry at that time. The writer remembered the "pride and anticipation with which small boys looked to the day when they could quit school and go to the factory." There was agitation against child labor and its effect on these children. This was balanced against the "older men" who proudly spoke against ending child labor, since they boasted of the fact that they left school at eight or ten and began their glass career at a tender age.

Next came the topic of the "blowers" and included a description of these men. He said the way you could tell a "blower" was in "face contour." They appeared as "hollow cheeked men whose face muscles had collapsed soon in the blower's apprenticeship," and developed what was known as "lantern jaws."

There were also women "fan mail" writers. One woman from Florida wrote to Chamberlain that she enjoyed *Man Alone* and it was "one of the best stories I have ever read." What do you suppose was the "best" part for her?

The sesquicentennial anniversary of the founding of America, its 150th birthday, was celebrated in 1926. The Bridgeton Chamber of Commerce planned to celebrate the occasion by sending local memorabilia to Washington, D.C., as a representation of the best of the city. When not in Europe or New York City, Chamberlain gave his address as 99 West Commerce Street, Bridgeton. This was his mother's home and connected him as a resident. Some of the items the Chamber delivered to Washington included a framed photograph of the Bridgeton Liberty Bell and a translucent lamp shade that featured Bridgeton City Park scenes. The third item was the book by Chamberlain, *Man Alone*. Inside was an inscription that read, "Presented to Mrs. Coolidge as a background for the Bridgeton Liberty Bell—Hopetown, in the story, being no other than Bridgeton." It was signed "George Agnew Chamberlain, Bridgeton, NJ, November 1926." The book was to be delivered to Mrs. Coolidge. Chamberlain was unable to deliver it himself due to a prior commitment.

In all Chamberlain wrote thirteen novels and numerous short stories about South Jersey. In 1927 Chamberlain purchased Lloyd's Landing, a home on the Alloway Creek in Quinton, Salem County, New Jersey. During the twentieth century, he was South Jersey's preeminent author.

Note:

The author of this Foreword has been a glass lover since grade school when he first saw a glass "blower" produce a bottle. He had relatives in the late nineteenth century who were in the glass industry. Two great uncles were "blowers" while his grandfather worked packing the finished product. Chamberlain's novel, especially the description of blowing the glass and the "flaming monument," brought back to life his childhood experiences and his journey through the years as a collector of South Jersey glass.

F. James Bergmann

MAN ALONE

CHAPTER I

THOMAS STRAYTON was a native-born Cornishman. Bringing his wife with him, he emigrated to the United States in 1848, started in as an ore miner in Northern New Jersey and did so well that the gold rush of the following years left him unmoved. When a child was born to the couple, he insisted that it be named Torquay in honor of the only holiday its parents had ever enjoyed. His wife fought against calling her son after a locality, not even a place mentioned in the Bible; but he cut her short, ruling her out without argument. Torquay was to be the name.

Three years later Thomas Strayton was blown from the rut of daily routine by a domestic explosion as sudden and effective as an unexpected blast in the mine. His wife went away to live with another man. She did not ask for a divorce, nor had words passed between herself and her husband foreshadowing her desertion. Taking a leaf out of Thomas' book, she had ruled him out without argument. One day she was looking after his home and their boy; the next she was gone.

The explosion shook something inside his powerful frame to pieces. He could easily have broken the other man's neck, and undoubtedly would have done so had he been more of a lover and less of an individualist. To him, each man was a tower and every man's business was to keep his tower standing. All he could think of was himself; that he was stunned, reeling, and that his only hope of avoiding a crash was to stagger along until he could get his innards to working again. Air was what he wanted more than anything else—a new air that he could breathe. In the face of that need, revenge shriveled into insignificance, becoming just one of the many things which could not help to set him upright again on his foundations.

He took his savings from the bank in two one-thousand dollar bills and started southward on foot, carrying his son.

There is only one person living who remembers when he first arrived in what was then known as West Jersey; Benn Furness, the ninety-year-old blacksmith of Lower Hopetown is not the sole surviving eyewitness of that event, but he is the only one on whom it made a lasting impression. To hear him tell about it, however, is like listening to ghost stories or tales of the mythical Jersey monster. Instead of giving a clear-cut idea of Thomas Strayton in the prime of his manhood, Benn paints a picture of an apparition stalking through the countryside, frightening women and horses. Nor has Benn's mind ever been able to bring itself to accept a link between this phantom and the master of the Pine Tree Glassworks, even though it knows the link exists.

It could not be any other way, for seeing a man as he is always makes it hard to remember him as he was, especially if he has climbed in the meantime from the foot of a ladder to its topmost rung. Even back in 1900, a good many years, much money and a lot of power had stepped between two legends—the legend of Old Man Strayton, founder of the Pine Tree Glassworks, and the legend of that other Strayton, seen now only mistily through Benn's faded eyes, looming on many a sky line with his three-year-old son perched like a steeple on his shoulder.

It is easy to realize why Strayton, the wanderer, lingered in the region around Hopetown, for it is a district richer in byways than any other equal portion of the globe. To this day no map has ever been drafted showing the amazing network of roads laid like a spider's web on that portion of New Jersey which lies west of a plumb line dropped from Trenton to Cape May. For a man set on walking away from towns, thirsty for solitudes, and glad of the gritty hold of hard sand under his feet, it was an ideal locality.

The calendar sets one date for our birth, but memory chooses quite another. Thus it happened that life for Torquay Strayton, already three years and two months old, began as an endless pilgrimage on a hundred hidden roads. As long as he lived he was to recognize as if by instinct every dip, every rise, every long hot stretch and every sheltering barn within a radius of twenty miles of Hopetown. He was never to drive a buggy along any roadway, however grass-grown and obscure, without instantly connecting its vistas with the beginning of all things.

Most babies come up out of nothing into nurseries or kitchens or walled gardens, but for all these he substituted a web of lonely roads. No height was ever to seem greater to him or more perilous than his father's shoulder under sweeping boughs; no support, on the other hand, was ever to give him more confidence than his father's shaggy head and beard, both ready to hand in moments of danger. Hardship did not come to him in carefully graduated doses. Hours of sun, drenchings of rain, pangs of hunger and thirst were his baptism, poured all of a sudden as from a bucket.

To the day of his death he could not look from the Salem Pike across the Barrens, mile after mile of somber woods stretching away like a fallen black cloud to meet a low horizon, without feeling a strange puckering of the muscles of his stomach. Through those woods ran the treacherous and endless Buckhorn road, direct and tortuous as a corkscrew is direct and tortuous. His father had plunged into it with the sun low at his back and come out only at dawn, after the most desperately wearying and hungry night Torquay was ever to know.

Dozens of side roads had fooled them, promising a near-by dwelling and delivering only wilderness. But at gray morning they had broken out from the woods squarely in front of the brick house at Babylon. It was a huge building, three stories high, with solid white shutters and a slate roof. It was lonely even at that time, but not half so lonely as it is now, stranded by itself miles away from anywhere, and gone to rack and ruin.

A woman came to the side door at Thomas Strayton's knock. She was fully dressed, although the sun had not yet risen, and behind her was a table already set with steaming dishes. To all practical purposes, this was the first of all women to Torquay. Of course, he had seen and been petted by many others, including his mother, but none of them persisted as a live person. In his mind women began

13

with the mistress of the great house at Babylon, perhaps because of the amazement in her eyes, perhaps because he could remember what was said.

No wonder she stared. What she saw was a great hairy man dressed in coarse tweeds which had the effect of adding to his bulk. Brambles had unraveled his clothes in spots and they were splashed above the tops of his boots with the black mud of the Barrens' bogs. The back of his right hand and its wrist were bleeding from being held up to ward off branches from hitting the child, who seemed anchored to his shoulder as if he had put down suckers like a mollusk. Both of them—man and boy—were unkempt, filthy, unappealing.

Torquay was dressed in a tight-fitting jersey, blue flannel pants and a knitted woolen cap, thickly rolled at the bottom and rising to a sharp peak. His face was badly scratched and there was a drooping look about his eyes and the corners of his mouth which told of exhaustion and hunger. He was looking unusually small that morning, but what surprised the woman most of all was that the man appeared unaware of the child on his shoulder. He did not raise a hand to hold him there; he stood and talked as if he were alone.

"Can I pay for food?" he asked.

"Not here," the woman answered promptly, "but you can have all you want to eat without paying."

She flushed as if the first words to come from the man's mouth had made them enemies.

"I'll take no food unless I can pay," he muttered, and turned away so abruptly that only long practice saved Torquay from a fall.

"Starve then," cried the woman; "but you'll give me that child to feed before you go."

She sprang forward, seized the boy and snatched him from his perch, but not from a quick handhold in his father's hair and beard. She pulled; the child held fast. Strayton braced himself. Without deigning to lift his hands or so much as bending his head, though the pain made water trickle from the corners of his eyes, he took a step, dragging the woman with him. But pity for the man was far from her heart. She held on until quite suddenly Torquay relaxed his fingers. She gathered him in her arms and started back toward the open door. Before she reached it he was sound asleep.

Torquay's next recollection was of being fed hot milk from a spoon; then came real food in tantalizing morsels, and after that a wash in a great wooden bucket of warm water. The ignominy of this last proceeding was increased by the presence of several persons he had not yet seen. The farmer and his two helpers were men; that was all right. But there was another woman, and quite half a dozen children, one of them a girl smaller than himself. Fortunately, all these people seemed exclusively interested in his father, who stood as still as a tree outside the open door. Even so, Torquay was not content or passive. He spit on the dress of the woman who was scrubbing him. She pretended not to notice. She was listening to what her husband was saying to Strayton.

"Why don't you come in and eat? The roads'll wait."

There was a long pause.

"He said he wouldn't eat unless he could pay," explained the woman when she realized Strayton did not mean to answer; then her lips set in a straight line as she held Torquay's face away from her and went to work on his ears. The farmer turned and gave her a troubled look.

"Perhaps it's a religion or a bet, mother, that makes him like that. Besides, we know he ain't right, walking the way he does without going anywhere."

"Do as you want," she answered.

"He sure ought to eat."

"Do as you want, I say."

"Come on in," said the farmer, turning toward the door. "A quarter will pay for all you can stow away."

"A quarter apiece," said Strayton as he entered, sat at the table and began to eat slowly, then voraciously.

The other woman served him, filling and refilling his cup with boiled coffee, placing dish after dish beside his plate and cutting great slices of bread from a homemade loaf. The farmer tried to make him talk, but he paid not the slightest attention to questions, direct or indirect. By the time he had finished his meal Torquay was dried and reluctantly dressed by the woman in his soiled clothes.

"They ought to be washed—boiled," she murmured.

"What's that, mother?"

"The boy's clothes—they ought to be boiled and scrubbed."

Strayton arose, plunged his hand into his trousers pocket and felt around for change; then he remembered. He had no money left except the two one-thousand-dollar bills. His weather-beaten cheeks turned a deep red.

"I haven't any change," he muttered.

"Now that's interesting," said the farmer, suspicion flashing across his face. "It was you made all the fuss about paying."

"All right," replied Strayton, laying one of his bank notes on the table. "Take it out of that." He started toward the door. "Come on, Torque."

The farmer stared with widening eyes at the thousand-dollar bill. He had never heard of such a thing before, much less seen one. Perhaps it was a hoax, but what if it were real? He thought instantaneously of the two farm hands at his side, and of what other people might say or do when word got around that such a sum had been left in his charge. He snatched up the note, ran after Strayton and thrust it in his pocket. As he turned to come back he collided with Torquay, who had eluded outstretched hands and was rushing to join his father.

"Hold him!" cried the woman, appearing in the door. Then she called to Strayton, "Will you leave the boy with us?"

"Tell her, Torque," commanded Strayton.

Torquay turned in the farmer's grasp and stared straight at the woman standing in the doorway with curious children grouped around her, the smallest girl clinging to her skirts, and peering out.

"Go to hell," he called in a shrill voice.

The words had some magic power. The farmer let go of him at once. The faces of the woman and her children took on expressions of horror. As a group, they seemed to freeze. Only from the depths of the kitchen came two loud guffaws, the farm hands—men—

laughing at what he had said. He turned and ran to his father. The next moment they were off along the Shiloh road.

From the distance behind them came the woman's voice—a small sound, but quite clear, as if carried on wings—"You're a bad man, an evil man. You have sold your child to the devil."

His father walked faster than usual, throwing out his hands from time to time in jerky gestures and muttering to himself. The sun rose blindingly in front of them. Torquay blinked and then gave it stare for stare. The more he looked, the less he saw. Presently black balloons began coming out of the sun or out of his eyes, he couldn't tell which. They would rise from nowhere, arch, and then fall across the sky. He shut his eyes tightly, but he still saw the black balloons, springing up, falling, fading away without his being able to see where any of them went. He decided never to stare at the sun again.

His father continued to mutter. The sun grew hot; but as it rose it got out of the way. He opened his eyes and took stock of the world about him. On the right was a bit of snake fence, overhung by a tree laden with early apples. Attracted by their red cheeks, and still hungry, he pulled his father's hair, steering him to the side of the road. But he was not allowed to pick the fruit; instead, he was placed with his back to the tree on the top rail of the fence. Owing to a grass-filled gully which ran along beside it, he and his father, face to face, became of equal height.

In spite of the coveted apples, Torquay was fascinated. Up to that moment his father had been a familiar but indistinct blur, an ever-present background; now he was foreshortened, solidified. His face took on form and detail; it became as clearly defined as a map, something that could be remembered from day to day and from year to year. Torquay saw a high but corrugated forehead, bushy black eyebrows over blue eyes, closely set ears with hair wound around them, a nose like a hog-backed mountain; vivid red lips and a wiry curling beard which he remembered was rough to the touch. He saw all these things for the first time, and that clouds were passing over them, making them appear active. His father was angry.

"Never have nothing to do with a woman, Torque. Remember

17

what I've teached you; take them as they come, pay as you go. One here, one there, and tell the lot to go to hell. Women? Look now! Watch!"

Torquay regarded him with solemn eyes, very much interested. He watched him scuff windfalls out of the grass with his foot, pick out the largest, rub them bright on his sleeve and set them in a row on the rail.

"These is women, see? And this is how you find out what they be like inside."

He took up an apple and broke it in half; it was black at the core. He picked out another and it crushed in his hands, a mere shell around a mass of rotten pulp. So with a third and a fourth. He caught up another. Placing it on the rail, he struck it a tremendous downward blow with his fist. The apple was shattered into glittering bits of white clear flesh, its juices making a dark stain on the dry gray wood. The other apples bounced into the air and rolled off.

"There!" he cried, the blood rushing to his face.

"That was a good one, but it's too late. You never can tell till you've busted 'em, mashed 'em up into little pieces. You heard her, Torque, the woman back there. She called me a bad man, an evil man. She said I'd sold you to the devil. But never forget what I'm telling you. You don't have to mash a man to find out if he's rotten inside."

CHAPTER II

THEY traveled far that long morning. They passed through Hopetown and out along the Buckshutem road to a place where fifty men were taking out silica for the Damon Glassworks. Here was work closely allied to Strayton's traditions. It was the simplest form of all mining, and watching it made his lip curl in scorn; but it was mining. Loam had been stripped away to a depth of ten feet, exposing the banks of broken white sand. Smooth sand from the seashore or the desert, varnished hard by wind or water, would not melt; he knew enough for that. Glass sand, made up of tiny triangular crystals that melted at the sharp points first, had to be mined.

He stood for an hour watching the primitive operation, discovering flaws, clumsy waste and sheer laziness. His hands began to itch. He despised the job and the men who were handling it, but he could not tear himself away. Torquay grew drowsy; his head would bob forward and then come up with a violent jerk which almost sent him over backward. He was in agony, but he would not complain. He wished his father would start on and give him something to do to keep himself awake.

A man, the contractor, shouted up at Strayton from the bottom of the pit. He asked him if he would rather be a nurse than work. A moment later Torquay found himself seated on his father's coat, doubled into a cushion and laid on a flat stump at the edge of the excavation. Immediately he went to sleep, his hands folded in his lap, his shoulders hunched and his head fallen forward. When he awoke, the afternoon was almost gone. He sat erect, watching his father do the work of three men. When the time came to knock off, the contractor climbed up to the stump behind his father.

"Aren't you afraid, leaving him like that at the edge of the hole?"
"He won't fall."
"Why didn't you set him comfortable under a tree?"

"He don't like to be comfortable."

"Perhaps you're right, at that," said the contractor, staring at Torquay and answering some thought of his own. "Well, you've only been here half a day, but I won't deny you done two men's work. Here's a dollar."

Strayton took the money, but said nothing.

"Will you be back in the morning? I can give you a steady job at a dollar a day."

"Two dollars."

"I done wrong to treat you right. I ought to of handed you fifty cents, the regular price."

Strayton had put on his coat; he swung Torquay to his shoulder.

"Two dollars," he repeated, and started off.

"All right," called the contractor angrily. "Seven o'clock sharp."

In giving in on the matter of wages, the man thought he was doing himself a service; but within six months he was to sell out his contract with the Damon Glassworks to Thomas Strayton for a bonus of a thousand dollars. Within a year he was to discover that Thomas had bought an option on every known sand pit around Hopetown and on two or three others whose existence nobody else had guessed. Within five years he who had once employed what he took for a roving half-wit at two dollars a day was to apply for a job as foreman of a gang at work on the foundations of Thomas Strayton's Pine Tree Glassworks.

This rival of the Damon plant was born in such humble form that it aroused more ridicule than interest. Just as Thomas had wasted no money on borings to locate his silica beds, finding it much cheaper to look for ant burrows and then tie up unsuspecting owners of likely farms with a small payment in cash and a promise of royalties, just so he avoided all display in the location and building of his plant.

The spot he chose was a flat on the edge of the river, which he bought for a song, as it had long been known to be unstable land, little better than a bog. What the oldest inhabitants could not be expected to realize was that the recent draining of the meadows, ten miles away, had effected a mysterious transformation through minute and unsuspected channels. Not being dulled by tradition, Thomas had only to walk across his flats to know that they would bear much more weight than he would ever need to impose on them.

At some distance from the river there stood a single pine. It would long since have fallen had not its roots been buttressed against one of the mounds of oyster shells which form almost the only remaining relic of Indian settlements along the Atlantic Seaboard. This stalwart and solitary tree dominated the flats, the new enterprise and many years of Torquay's childhood. For him it marked a transition, a graduation from vagabondage to fixture. Sitting on the solid mound within its shade, he could look back from his ninth birthday on a finished chapter of the book of things happened and stored away.

He could face in half a dozen directions, shut his eyes and see every hamlet from Head of Greenwich to Mullica Hill or from the sources of the Maurice river to the mouth of Alloway Creek. He could follow each turn of many a road to its termination at the edge of a sand pit. He could remember hours and days of watching his father work; and then weeks and months of watching him make other men work.

There came the period when he would be left daily on the stoop of the nearest schoolhouse. Never would Thomas by any chance enter one of these isolated outposts of knowledge; for a woman, mostly a young girl, was sure to be in command. He would leave the boy at the door, and say over his shoulder as he turned away, "Walk in, Torque, and tell them who you are."

The first time it happened Torquay obeyed at once. He pushed the door open, passed through the entry and into the rectangular schoolroom. It was empty except for the teacher, bowed low over a table raised on a commanding platform. He stood staring at the rows of weird desks, at the blurred blackboards, ragged maps, and at crude copies of portions of them, pinned to the walls. There were many smells, one of which he knew—the musty odor worn clothes leave behind them. The smell of chalk was new; so was that of dried spit on ancient slates and the greasy emanations of thumbed and tattered books. Attracted by his silence, the teacher looked up, and then stared in surprise at Torquay, dressed at this time in a double-breasted reefer jacket and a peaked woolen cap.

"Whose boy are you?"

"Thomas Strayton's."

"Where does he live?"

"He don't live nowheres."

"You mean he doesn't live anywhere."

"That's what I said; he don't live nowheres. He's working over to the sand pit."

"Oh! In that case I'm afraid—"

Other children came in noisily to interrupt her. She assigned him a seat doubtfully and at the noon hour tried to keep him in, but he pretended not to hear and was presently surrounded in the yard by a swarm of demons shooting their darts at the outlandish jacket which made him look like a small barrel, at his dirty face, and most of all, at his woolen cap. One of the boys knocked it from his head and it became a football. He stood with his back to the schoolhouse wall and glared at his tormentors while he searched with his toe for a stone. He was so angry he could see no individual faces, only an encircling blur.

"Go to hell," he muttered.

The circle dissolved. Several of the children ran to tell the teacher what he had said, while others drew back and stood spellbound. Gradually one of the faces came out toward him until it stood alone. It belonged to a little girl smaller even than himself. She had yellow pigtails, staring eyes and a mouth that hung open for a moment before she said, "Oh! Oh! I know who you are! You said that to my mother!"

He realized his time at that school was up. He retrieved his cap and trudged off to find his father, while, from a window, the teacher watched him go with a feeling of relief. But there were to be other schools—a succession of them. Sometimes he was taken in as a matter of course, but more often every difficulty was put in his way. The thing that stood him in best stead was his capacity for waiting an incredible length of time. Refused admission, he would sit on the steps of a school for hours, even for days, until some passing farmer would descend to find out what was the trouble and perhaps give the teacher a piece of his mind.

The boy became a living example of the astonishing power of persistence. In appearance he was small and ineffectual; it was quite easy to dismiss him with the statement that he had come to the wrong school, or with a question as to why he did not remain in Hopetown. His only answer was to stay. Put out forcibly, he would sit on a step in plain view of the road through storm and sunshine, heat and cold, until regulations, boards of education and systems of taxation crumbled about him.

Teachers who held out longest against the pressure came nearest to a nervous breakdown. Even those who gave in most readily gained little through their good nature, for there was something peculiar about the way this waif of the country roads looked at all women and girls. It made them restless, sometimes to the point of panic. The older the woman, the surer was she to resent every moment of the child's presence. That he should be docile and attentive was only an added aggravation; it made resentment doubly ridiculous.

Torquay never bothered to explain he could not stay in Hopetown because he and his father seldom occupied the same room for long, and often camped in shacks near the sand pits. Despite his obstinacy in its pursuit, he did not care for learning except in the matter of reading. He entered one school after another because his father told him to, or because the weather was cold, or because he craved the excitement of swearing at ugly little girls and fighting with uglier little boys. More by propinquity than through industry, he picked up the rudiments of knowledge; but a long time was to pass before he could recognize in them the tools men use to pry loose the stones with which each builds his house of life.

Now he was sitting, immobile as the cap on a monument, on the oyster-shell mound in the shade of the lonely pine. He had just returned from a visit to the great brick schoolhouse in Hopetown, set far back from an iron fence across an expanse of packed clay. One look, and he had realized that a small boy could sit in front of it unnoticed till he grew old. He knew without being told that the tactics he had used against the isolated schoolhouses of the countryside would not avail him here. He could not prey on this huge building or its guardians; they would prey on him.

Over on the far verge of the flats was a wagon and a team of horses surrounded by many boys and a group of men, one of whom was his father, easily distinguishable by the breadth of his shoulders and his towering frame. The men were gesticulating, discussing, arguing. Once in a while there was a shout of laughter or a jeer. The man with the team stood up in the wagon and waved his arms, looking down and about him, and all the while talking excitedly. Torquay would have been interested could he have heard what he was saying:

"How do I know? I know because everybody knows. I tell you the horses would sink to their bellies, and the wagon, too, afore I got halfway across. What I say is, get a team of your own if you want to throw it away or pay to have it drug out. That's what I say."

"A good idea," said Thomas Strayton. "I'll buy your outfit. I'll give you five hundred if it sinks the way you say it will; but if it doesn't sink, you get only a hundred."

"It'll sink, all right," muttered the man; "but five hundred ain't enough."

"Six hundred," said Strayton; and, after a long pause, "seven hundred."

"That would be betting."

"It would be betting if you'll take a thousand or nothing, but I'm offering to buy at seven hundred if the horses flounder to their bellies or the wagon sinks to its hubs. If they don't, you sell for a hundred. One of us is a damn fool and it's worth the difference to find out which, ain't it?"

Torquay saw the circle of men draw in closer, looking up intently at the teamster, who turned his eyes slowly, scanning their faces. The man stood quite still for a long while with his head fallen forward, then threw it up, dropped the reins and jumped from the wagon. Strayton climbed into it and picked up the lines. The team started off; the wagon bounced as it careened down the bank to the level of the flats.

The horses came straight for the pine at an easy trot. They were white, with great dapples of gray, and bright red tassels hung from their headstalls. The sun made their skins flicker and the bosses on the heavy harness shine. Behind them streamed the men and boys, shouting and laughing as they were forced to break into a run. Some of them looked back over their shoulders at the teamster, who was following slowly with staggering footsteps.

The wagon came to a stop beside Torquay. His father climbed down, tossed him the reins to hold, drew out a roll of bills and waited for the teamster. He paid him a hundred dollars. The man scarcely looked at the money as he thrust it in his pocket. He went to the horses' heads and began to fondle them awkwardly, while they nosed at him and then butted him impatiently, evidently demanding their feed bags. The men who had run after the wagon began unloading picks, shovels and crowbars. The teamster drew near to Strayton.

"Who you going to let to drive 'em, Tom?"

"I don't know," said Strayton. He lifted his beard toward Torquay. "You'll have to ask Torque. It's Torque's team now."

Torquay stood up and looked at the horses with round eyes; then at the teamster, who stared back at him unsmilingly.

"What do you say, bub? Do I get to drive 'em?"

Torquay was embarrassed.

"What's your name?" he asked.

"Bill Teason. Everybody around here knows Bill Teason and his team."

"I guess he's all right," said Torquay looking questioningly at his father.

"Two dollars a day," said Strayton to the teamster; "three if you find their keep."

"Three, all found," agreed the man.

That was the beginning of money to Torquay. At the end of the week he was handed his pay with the rest of the men, the difference between three and five dollars a day. He became Bill's shadow for the entire summer. They hauled building materials, and when that job was done, went back to carting sand, sometimes from one bank and sometimes from another. The trip Torquay liked best was to the Jenkstall wash within sight of the great brick house at Babylon.

Here old man Jenkstall and his four sons had cleared a growth of blueberry scrub and a thin layer of soil from a lode of poor-quality sand. They had rigged up a rough sluice box with a trap at one end. Into it they would dump the sand just as it came from the bank, throw in buckets of water and then stir the mixture with hoes. The silica would settle and the lighter soil flow out through the trap. But it was not this familiar process that interested Torquay half so much as the nearness of the brick house, already on the way to ruin through neglect.

One day as the team was straining to pull out of a gully on its way home with a load, a group of young people carrying berry pails broke out of the bushes and crossed the sunken road at a run. The frightened horses sank back on their haunches and then reared. Bill swore. The group paused, but presently melted away—all save one small girl. She had been the last to dart under the noses of the horses. She stood on the bank to catch her breath, turned and stared at Torquay with widening eyes. As the horses calmed down, settled into their collars and drew away, he heard her calling loudly, "Oh, look! He's the one! He's the little boy that said that to mother!"

It was on that same day Torquay saw Jake Damon for the first time. Burk Damon, Jake's father and the head of the Damon Glassworks, had come over to the flats to verify some of the stories he had heard. Bill Teason, arriving with the load of Babylon sand, had to drive around the buggy and team Mr. Damon had left exactly in the wagon tracks as if he, too, could not persuade himself the bog he had known all his life had turned into fairly solid ground.

"What are you up to here, Tom?" he was saying as Torquay climbed down from the wagon, took a step toward Jake and then paused.

"It's going to be a glassworks, Mr. Damon," said Strayton. "Nothing much; only a five-pot furnace."

"Going to run the Damon factory out of business, eh?"

"You know how much chance I got of doing that."

"You haven't gone so far with the work you couldn't use it for something else, Tom. Let me give you a friendly word—lay off."

"Lay off what?"

"Building. Quit where you are and stick to your contract with us for as much sand as you can haul."

"That's it," said Strayton slowly, as if he weighed his words.

"I can bring in more sand than you can use."

"Perhaps you could," replied Mr. Damon. "Perhaps you could," he repeated meaningly; "but can you use all you haul?"

"You mean you wouldn't renew the contract when it's time has run," said Strayton. His eyes wandered to where Jake and Torquay had come so near together that they appeared to be studying the pores in each other's noses, and then came back. "Mr. Damon," he continued quietly, "contract or no contract, you'll buy sand from me as long, as—"

He was interrupted by the sound of a blow. The two men turned to see their sons rolling down the side of the mound locked in a single mass which seemed to have as many tentacles as a giant squid. They were fighting as only the young can fight, with unquestioning enthusiasm. If they did not use their teeth it was only because they did not think of it. They pummeled, scratched and kicked. While they rolled, the honors were equally divided; but when they struck level ground, Jake happened to be on top and stayed there.

"—as long as you live," completed Strayton without change of tone.

"What?" said Mr. Damon. "Oh!"

He was distracted beyond returning to their conversation. The rage of his son, and the sort of thing that rage was permitting itself to do, sent a chill down his spine. He knew that children are more brutal than any other breed of animal, but he had forgotten it. As he started down the knoll Strayton laid a heavy hand on his shoulder.

"Leave them be," he said. "Your boy's on top."

"What difference does that make?" cried Mr. Damon. "Do you suppose I'd do any different if he wasn't?"

He shook the hand off, but paused as he caught sight of the expression on his son's face. It was true that Jake was on top, but he was only wearing himself out. Torquay had retired in good order and was resting his forces in what was virtually an impregnable position. Holding the stout hem of his woolen cap with both hands, he had dragged it down to his neck so that his face, ears and mouth were shielded as effectually as the thick, tightly buttoned reefer protected the rest of his person. That he was by no means defeated was evidenced by a muffled string of oaths which so horrified Jake, even in the heat of battle, as to sap the remaining strength from his arm. He rose to his knees. Torquay bounced forward like a tumbleweed, and the next moment Jake was lying flat on his back, the wind knocked from his body by Torquay's lowered head used as a battering ram.

"Your boy isn't licked," said Strayton. "Wait till he gets his wind back; then let them take off their coats and finish it."

"No!" cried Mr. Damon.

While Torquay was struggling madly to tear off his cap, Mr. Damon ran to where Jake lay writhing, his knees doubled to his chin, picked him up and helped him to the buggy.

As he gathered up the reins he called, "I don't understand you, Tom. If I can help it my boy won't do that kind of fighting any more than I'll buy your sand."

"That's the point," answered Strayton, unmoved. "You can't help it."

"He said I looked like a pig in this coat," explained Torquay—"a fat little pig, he said."

CHAPTER III

It was a long way from that Homeric episode to the day when Thomas Strayton lit his fires and started the slow process of heating a new furnace; a longer time to the passing of a trial batch; and still a greater interval intervened before the primitive plant was to turn out the first lot of windowpane glass ever produced in Hopetown. But to Torquay, looking back through the reversed telescope of time, all these events seemed jammed into a single moment. As if touched by a magic wand, the boyhood of the Pine Tree Glassworks and his own became one, synchronized into an indivisible whole with a pear-shaped blob of molten glass for its symbol.

In memory he could see an entire process in a flash. The great ramshackle shed, spreading its wings over the furnace it had taken so many months to build, became a spontaneous foil. Against its shadows stood silhouetted the figures of men at work and dots of golden light. The red full moon of a ringhole. The pipe thrust in, twirled, and brought out with a golden ball on its lower end. The ball rolled on a marble slab, heated again, and then handed to the blower. Here began minutes of never-ending fascination, of movements apparently slow, and yet incredibly swift in their results.

The man would first blow lightly, drawing out the vitreous mass to the shape of a pear. Balancing his pipe in a vertical line, he would raise it swiftly, gathering the glass downward. Then came the move to the foot bench over the swing hole and immediately the swift rise of action. The workman's breath, aided by a motion like the swing of a pendulum, blowing harder and harder. The pear becomes a huge cylinder, swaying in a wider and wider arc. The workman changes his grip constantly, twirling the glass, holding it against too quick a flow. Sometimes to show off he whirls the whole mass in a vast circle, broadening steadily to the lengthening of the glass. He slows down; as by a miracle, there has been no crash, no disastrous thud.

29

He brings the oval tip to the heat of the furnace, softens it, pierces it. By a balancing movement the opening is increased to an even circle and its edges pared. The cylinder becomes firm and is laid in a rack. A thread of hot glass is wound around its closed extremity and touched with a cold iron rod. More magic; the end drops off. A red-hot iron is passed swiftly in a straight line from end to end within the open tube. A touch from a wetted finger and the cylinder divides along the straight line. It goes to the flattening oven, where under the manipulations of the flattener it lies down as if tired out, opening slowly into a sheet of glass. To Torquay, years of this operation, watched hundreds of thousands of times, could become a single rounded moment, shaped like a pear, and laid away.

There was a truce between Strayton and the Damon Glassworks because the latter were not interested in window glass; they made only bottles. But every time Burk Damon laid eyes on Thomas Strayton he flushed. Why couldn't he have told him he was going in for sheet glass? If he had, those words about the contract would never have passed. The Damon Glassworks still bought sand from Strayton; they even had begun to suspect they must buy from him or die. However, there was no longer any contract, but only because Strayton refused to sign.

"It's this way, Mr. Damon—why should I sign? I'm not looking to raise the price unless the costs goes up, but there's nothing more treacherous than sand. You never know when you're going to strike a whaleback or lose your bank in water. If I've tied myself up to deliver and can't, you've got me, and no good to neither of us. You'll get just as much sand the way things is now. I don't see no use for a contract."

The spring that brought Torquay's twelfth birthday saw the Cumberland Grays go off to war. His father, though foreign-born, had volunteered, and had been refused. The reasons given were that he was too old, and Torquay too young to be left alone, or that Strayton's absence would throw too many men out of work. But none of these was the real reason. Company F felt it could do without his presence. He was not liked, and there still lingered at that time the memory of his vagabondage, tainted by doubt as to his sanity and clouded by ignorance as to his origin.

Torquay, attracted by martial music, joined the throng of little boys who followed the Cumberland Grays to the point of embarkation at the lower wharf, because the tide was so low the steamboat could not come up into the town. There were flags and speeches, besides the band, and a present from the ladies of a Bible to each departing soldier. One man dropped his copy as he stumbled on the gangway; it fell into the water with a great fluttering of its leaves. Torquay slipped over the edge of the wharf, climbed down a ladder and caught the book before it sank; but when he came up, the steamboat was already casting off.

"Keep it, son. Guess I can borrow aplenty!"

Less than a year and a half later came the call for the nine months' men, but they did not go away by steamer, for the railroad had at last arrived. The Fairton troops left by the morning train and the Hopetown contingent by the afternoon train of the same September day.

There was an old house directly above the flats which had been severed from the rest of the town with the coming of the railroad. In summer it had been completely buried from view behind three towering tulip poplars and two wide sycamores. In the late autumn, with the falling of the leaves, it stepped out suddenly and looked almost as surprised as did Torquay when he first discovered it. His father bought this place and all the land that went with it, four acres jammed into a sharp point where the railway divided to form the Y which served as a turntable, for Hopetown was a terminal stop.

Father and son moved in exactly as they had moved into many a shack. Torquay could not remember ever having had the freedom of a whole house before. All his life he had been one of two things—a roomer or a camper. His father had purposely lost the sense of order; for nine years he had been fleeing from its memory. As a couple, they were too much alike in training and tastes to make anything but a mess of living. Thomas was willing to cook, so was his son; but at that point housework ceased. Each washed a plate in cold water when he needed it; pots and pans went uncleaned.

31

Odd pieces of furniture, all in a dilapidated state, had been left behind by the previous owners. Moth eaten carpets, a broken range and a cracked stove formed the skeleton of existence. A mildewed mirror and a heap of books in the attic, abandoned when the bottom had fallen out of a trunk, struck the only note of alleviation. To Torquay the house became a hell and, by contrasts, the works a paradise. There were boys younger than he employed in the glass-factory, but none stronger for his age or more assiduous. A day came when his father looked upon the unspeakable filth of their living quarters and revolted.

"You better stay home today, Torque, and clean up everything. Take Bill and your team into town and buy some things—anything you think we want. Throw away all them blankets. I'm going out to the Buckshutem sand wash."

Two hours later Strayton came back to the glassworks and noted with relief that Torquay was absent from his usual post as second-hander, but a moment later he caught a familiar outline against the glare of a ringhole. The boy had merely promoted himself to the job of gatherer. Stripped to the waist, the sweat trickling down his thin back, he was handling a man's size blowing iron with astonishing dexterity. He would plunge it into the pot, twirl it, lift a ball of glass and hand it to the blower beside him with an upward questioning glance. The blower was nodding automatically. The boy had caught the rhythm which makes no mistakes; but his upward glance had become part of the timing; he dared not leave it out. In those days, when pots had not yet surrendered to the continuous tank, there were intervals of loafing sandwiched in between batch and batch. Strayton waited until the batch was finished before he spoke.

"Did you do like I told you, Torque?"

"Do what?"

"Did you clean up the house?"

"No; I ain't no house cleaner," answered Torque. "I'm a glass gatherer now."

Strayton laid a quick hand on his son's shoulder, but he had not counted on how slippery it would be from sweat; it oozed from between his clamping fingers. Torquay ducked, snatched up his shirt and coat and ran. He crossed the flats, but not toward the house. Turning his back directly upon it, he made for the open country. He knew in his heart where he wished to go, but he did not go there directly. For three days he wandered in a vast circle on hidden byways, ate with farmers, woodcutters and fishermen, and slept wherever night found him. On the fourth day, setting out early with a deliberate intention, he traversed the Buckhorn road from end to end and came out before the great brick house at Babylon.

Even while he was still a long way off he knew that it was deserted. No smoke issued from its chimney, no chickens scratched in the yard, no cattle lowed. He drew near. The place was closed, all but one wooden shutter, hanging aslant on a single hinge and creaking to the wind. He scrambled up to look in the window. The room was the same in which he had eaten, only now it was empty. It had been swept clean, scrubbed as he had been scrubbed, and then abandoned. He trudged back to his father's glassworks.

"Hello, Torque. There's a new cap and coat come for you. The coat has brass buttons."

Clothes were the only thing that linked Strayton to his native Cornwall. No love of family would have driven him to letter writing, but the need of a stout tweed suit once a year and of garments equally durable for his son had kept communications open. The letter, posted every twelvemonth, was invariable except as regarded Torquay's age:

> "Ada, send me a suit when you get a chance. The boy is twelve years old. Draft inclosed. THOMAS."

"I'll buy the clothes from you," said Torquay, "but I come to get my team."

"Don't be foolish; I'll never lay hands on you again," grunted Strayton. Then he added shamefacedly, "There's a woman up at the house."

"A woman!" exclaimed Torquay, staring curiously at his father.

He turned and walked slowly to the house, which he found transformed. Several of the rooms had been fully furnished and all were as clean as mop and broom could make them. A high voice called out to know who had come in, and the next moment a colored woman appeared from the kitchen. Without being stout, she was full-bodied and seemed to forge toward him. Her sleeves were rolled above the elbows so that he noticed first her arms, muscular as a man's; then his eyes passed to her face. He knew at once she was no runaway slave, nor even from the South; she was from near by.

Not far from Hopetown there was a settlement of colored folk whose origin was already clouded in the obscurity of a long past. In spite of a missing link of three generations, its inhabitants claimed descent from the disowned kinswoman of the British founder of Salem. Though this dignitary was an untitled commoner, he had held his patent as Lord Protector of the Salem Tenth, which led them to believe further in a strain of noble blood. It was natural that they should transpose Fenwick, Lord Protector, into Lord Fenwick, and wear their dusky mantle of humility with an aggravating difference. As strong presumptive proof of their lineage, they could cite Fenwick's last will and testament, extant to this day.

Thus runs the passage:

> "Item, I do except against Elizabeth Adams of having arry ye leaste part of my estate, unless the Lord open her eyes to see her abominable transgression against Him, me and her good father, by giving her true repentance and forsaking yt Black yt hath been ye ruin of her; upon yt condition only I do will and require my executors to settle 500 acres of land upon her."

"Who are you?" asked the woman, pausing in her stride upon seeing a child.

"I'm Torquay Strayton, and I want my new cap and coat."

"Yes, Mr. Torquay." She measured him with grave eyes and then added unhurriedly, "They's in your room."

"My room?" questioned Torquay.

"I'll show you."

She led the way to a small room which had been fitted up for his convenience, and left him. To anyone else it would have seemed bare as a cell, but to Torquay it was the lap of luxury. There was a strip of carpet, two chairs and a large table, braced against the wall. On the table were all the books from the attic, stacked with their titles right side up, and a lamp. Beside the lamp lay the Bible he had rescued from the river, its covers curled back and its leaves indented with dried watermarks. There was a washstand, with a mirror, soap, and the only clean towels he remembered seeing. There was also a chest of drawers and a small bed, on which were laid his new clothes. The window faced northward and at the moment a train was pulling out.

The engine, belching sparks from its drum-shaped smokestack, looked like the small head of a very large dragon. Directly behind it came the tender, piled so high with cordwood that it completely obstructed the driver's view of what might happen behind him. To overcome this interruption there was a seat, with a top like a buggy's, perched at the rear end of the tender. Here sat the gigman, riding backward and holding a rope with which he passed on the signals of the conductor to the engineer. When Torquay first saw a train, he had wished he might some day be a gigman; but during the preceding winter an occupant of the exposed position had been frozen at this post, an event which had weakened ambition into hero worship. The train passed so close to the window that Torquay could see the operator's face quite distinctly. He was amazed to find it was someone he knew well enough to call by his first name, a common digger from the sand pits. It was Ed Waller!

"Hey, Ed! Ed!"

Confused by the clatter of the train, the man never thought to look up at the window. Thinking it was the engine driver who had called him, he became greatly excited and almost fell from his precarious perch in his efforts to meet an emergency for which his signal code made no provision; finally he pulled his rope violently. Far up the track Torquay saw the train come to a halt. The gigman and the engineer stood up and shouted at each other over the intervening wood pile; then they descended from their posts and engaged in an animated discussion face to face. The conductor joined them; passengers began to lean from the windows. At last the matter was settled or compromised; the train started on.

Torquay, feeling more amazed than guilty, watched it disappear into the distance; then he stripped, washed and dressed himself. The new reefer was of heavy blue cloth and had brass buttons on each of which was stamped a raised anchor. The cap was of the same shape as his old one, except that it was a size larger and had a broad white band worked in the wool. He stood before the mirror, passed his hands down the front of his jacket and stood quite still for a moment, startled, staring at himself in the glass. His fingers had felt something in the breast pocket. He took out a letter, folded very flat, and read the superscription: "To Master Torquay Strayton."

Sitting down at the desk, he spread the sheets before him and spelled out the words, one by one:

> FALMOUTH, 10th May, 1862.
> Dear Boy: I trust this may reach you, for you are now old enough to know reading and writing. I have asked many things of Thomas, but he answers not at all, only to write once every twelvemonth for a suit for himself and clothes for you. He never speaks of Maida, and though I have sent her presents and many a letter, no word have we had of her these nine years. I know something must be amiss. I am not well—I am going to die, and though I may not see your dear face, I would like to hear from yourself and from Maida, how you both are. Write to me. Send the letter to Mrs. Polperro, for I am married again, as you may not know unless Thomas has told you, 12 A Upper High Street, Falmouth.
> YOUR AUNT ADA.

He folded the letter along its original creases and packed it away in the worn leather wallet in which he kept his money. Many of the factories issued their own currency, redeemable only at the company stores; but his father always paid in cash, and as a result had his pick of the workmen available at a time when labor was necessarily scarce. Torquay did not need to count the contents of his purse; he knew he had ninety-four dollars. He gathered up his discarded clothes and went in search of the colored woman.

"What's your name?" he asked.

"Omega Lee, but family folks call me Mega."

"These things ought to be boiled and scrubbed," said Torquay, laying his bundle on a chair.

"Looks to me like they ought to be burnt, but you leave 'em there and I'll see what I can do."

Torquay turned toward the range and sniffed; seldom had he smelled so promising an odor.

"I'm hungry," he said.

"Supper is at six, and it's pushin' down five now. I guess you can wait that long."

That night Torquay said nothing about the letter. The next morning he went to the works, laid his new reefer carefully aside and took his place at the furnace. As his father stood watching him critically, a man approached to ask for work. Torquay saw out of the corner of his eye that it was Ed Waller, the gigman, frightened out of a job by a mysterious voice. He smiled, but did not interfere. His thoughts returned to the letter in his wallet; he thought about it all day, frowning as he tried to remember each word. Who was Maida?

He and his father ate their suppers in silence, as if sound would interfere with the eager tickling of their palates, awakened to an orgy of sensation through the art of Mega's cooking. She was different from most darkies in that she did more than one thing well. She was neither slovenly nor lazy; she got things done. No relatives haunted her kitchen. Twenty women had started to answer Strayton's call and turned back from a distant sight of the isolated house. Half a dozen more had thrown up their hands in horror upon looking through the door at the filth within; but it was the disorder that had attracted Mega.

She was ever present, and yet cloaked in a mantle of aloofness which could make her appear to be alone in a room while other people were about. Torquay, remembering his tricks with many a teacher, caught her eye and tried to stare her out of countenance. She met his insolent look with a gaze as unmoved and impenetrable as a brick wall. He decided that darkies were not women in his father's unforgettable demonstration of the term, perhaps because the blackness was on the outside. Thinking of women reminded him of the letter.

"Father—"

Mega had cleared the table and Strayton was just pushing back his chair preparatory to rising. He stopped and looked at Torquay.

"Well?"

Torquay's lips went suddenly dry; he wet them with the tip of his tongue and tried to look away, but his father's face fascinated him. It was shaggier than ever; his brows hung above his cavernous blue eyes like penthouses, and his matted beard had spread until only his nose and two round spots on his cheek bones stood clear of the growth.

"Well?" he repeated.

"Did you ever have a woman?" asked Torquay faintly.

"Many a one," replied his father, frowning.

"I mean for yours—your own."

"No man ever has a woman for his own—only while he thinks it. They come and they go, and putting out a hand won't hold 'em. Like the Bible says, 'more bitter than death the woman, whose heart is snares and nets.'"

"Does the Bible tell about women?"

Torquay was interested; he almost forgot the question he had set out to ask. But his father did not heed him; he seemed to be staring through the wall of the room with such effort that tiny drops of sweat were gathering on his wrinkled forehead.

"'Counting one by one, to find the account,'" he continued, "'one man among a thousand have I found; but a woman among all those have I not found.'"

"Does it say that?" persisted Torquay.

38

" 'God hath made man upright; but they have sought out many inventions.' That's what it says. You and me invents things outside, but women invents them inside theirselves."

There was a long pause.

"Who was Maida?" whispered Torquay.

A gleam of fright gave way to a blaze of fury in his father's eyes; the spots on his cheek bones turned lurid, like opening one of the furnace doors at night. He leaned forward and struck Torquay across the mouth with the back of his hand. His roughened knuckles were like files; they tore the child's lip so that blood spurted out and began to trickle down his chin.

"That's my answer," he bellowed, "and it will always be my answer to that name!"

Mega came to the door, looked in and went away again. Torquay's lower lip trembled with minute muscular vibrations. The trickling made his chin itch. He wiped it with the back of his hand, stared at the blood with genuine surprise, and then cleaned his fingers on the tablecloth. The red blood showed only pink on the white cloth. He arose, picked up his cap and started toward the hallway.

"Torque," called his father, "come back!"

Torquay went out through the front door, closing it quietly behind him.

"Torque," cried his father, raising his voice, but not moving from his chair, "did you hear me?"

CHAPTER IV

D RAWN by a half-formed intention to go away on the train, Torquay stumbled through the dark to the railway station. It was closed and locked, but near by was an unfinished shed which offered all the protection he needed. With the coming of daylight, he changed his mind about the train because it would pass so close to the house. He wandered down to the river, and when the steamboat pulled out for Philadelphia, via Salem and other points on the Delaware, he was on board. The deck hands knew him, and some hours passed before they discovered he was unaccompanied by his father. They held a consultation and decided the only thing to do was to carry him for the round trip. But they counted without Torquay. Upon arrival at Philadelphia, while the entire crew was occupied with the gangways, he slid down a hawser and disappeared in the maze of the water front. In due course his escape was reported with misgivings and from a safe distance to his father.

"Never trouble yourselves," called Thomas, apparently unmoved; "the lad will come back when he gets ready, just like he went away."

They talked of the hardness of Thomas Strayton, how he would not lift a finger to get back his boy, and the talk grew stronger weeks later when rumors drifted down river of a youngster who appeared to have established an abode on the top of an abandoned snubbing post of the city piers, where he could watch from close quarters the maneuvers of an occasional ocean steamer and the activities on board the many sailing vessels, notably the famous Falmouth packets, still full of pride, unaware that their days were numbered. When the rumors dressed him in a blue reefer coat with brass buttons and added word of his amazing readiness in blasphemous retort, there could be no doubt as to identity, and yet Tom made no move. People said he was a hard man—the hard father of a harder son.

Those were troubled times, and a boy adrift was no unusual matter. What made Torquay so noticeable as to figure in the news of the day was neither his circumstances nor his strange appearance, but his immobility. A pose is one thing; endurance is quite another. The fact that he could keep still for hours, sometimes from sunrise to sunset, without flinching, was enough to awaken respect among men who made their living in the taking and giving of hard knocks.

They could detect a pose quicker than the next man and needed no one to tell them the difference between a lap dog and a bull terrier. Where he slept, what he ate, why he waited, were questions he declined to answer; but they discovered he could become voluble under playful abuse. Asking no favor of man or weather, minding his own business and directing others to mind theirs, it was inevitable that he should become a person—something as definite as the post he sat upon and against which one might stub a toe.

To the mind's eye, Torquay at this time appears as a forlorn figure of a small boy against an overpowering background of warehouses, wharves, masts and cargoes, enlivened only by toiling and cursing men; but he saw himself in no such pitiful light. It is true that houses, trees, bridges, hills and streams loom much larger to children than to their elders; but in spite of the atmosphere of exaggeration in which they live, children are much less terrorized by realities than are grown-ups. Also, anything that remains fixed long enough for a boy to grow into a man becomes surprisingly smaller. When he grasps the relative proportion of the objects around him, he is middle-aged; when he perceives accurately the size of all things, he is dead. For no other reason than this, youth and illusion are one; and by the same token Torquay, at fourteen, quite aside from his exceptional upbringing, had a valor unknown to grown man. He had no fear of the next step, because he gave no thought to the step after the next.

He looked on the ships as he had looked on many a country schoolhouse. Without thinking out a definite plan, he knew he was laying siege against these vessels and that he had a distinct preference as to which should finally admit him. He had no doubt whatever that success would eventually crown his efforts, because many tentative advances had already been made by crews in liquor toward persuading him to come aboard. He refused these invitations with such vigor that more than one lot abandoned half-formed intentions of kidnapping him for a night or a voyage, and gradually he took on the qualities of a prize—something worth winning in open competition. A day came when the gray-haired Yankee boson of a Falmouth packet, accompanied by his captain, stopped beside him.

"Well, bub, it's too bad you ain't fifteen years old this day."

"Why?"

"'Cause our cabin boy has run away."

"I'm fifteen," said Torquay, straightening, after a calculating pause. "Been fifteen a long while."

The boson spit into the water twice before he turned shrewd eyes on Torquay and continued, "Your dad was a Plymouth man, see? He enlisted himself and got shot. The last thing he says to you before he goes away with the troops was to go back to his folks in Plymouth, see?"

"I thought you was Falmouth," said Torquay, settling back on his post.

"We're Falmouth-built, but they ordered us to Plymouth, worse luck."

"How far from Plymouth to Falmouth?"

"A matter of forty knots by sea and sixty miles by land."

"All right," said Torquay, after another pause, "I'll sign for Plymouth."

At the commissioner's office the boson took it upon himself to tell the harrowing details of the boy's predicament—a tale so amazingly near the truth that Torquay listened stolidly, convinced that his history must be generally known.

"Make your mark here, if you want to go," ordered the commissioner finally, pointing with a grubby finger. Torquay was not to be hurried; his eyes followed up the column and he shook his head.

"That says for a year. The captain don't want me for a year; he wants to take me back to my father's folks in Plymouth, like he said."

"You're right," said the commissioner, and scrawled the word "voyage" in its proper blank; whereupon Torquay signed his name in round schoolboy letters.

The boson stared, and the captain, scratching his head, muttered as the three left the office, "Where'd the lad get that name? You been teaching him that too?"

Torquay was horribly seasick for three days; but once out of the nightmare of the first illness of his life, he fitted himself into his duties like a hand into a loose glove, and found them mere play. Accustomed as he was to men and hard work, there was little chance to gibe at him. No one could tire him out in industry or even shame him in an exchange of oaths. No language could make him shudder, no tale could make him pale, and the equal placidity with which he took his allotment of the grog or accepted some hair-raising yarn, told for effect, soon brought the talk down to its normal level. As a consequence, he was received into the brotherhood of the foc'sle as completely as if he were one of its fixtures, and through a single remark was all but enthroned. The men were comparing the pitfalls of the port of London against the bawdy dangers of the rest of the combined world.

"Women is black inside," murmured Torquay sleepily. "You never can tell till you've busted 'em, mashed 'em up into little pieces."

Sailors have other childish qualities than the superstitions with which they are popularly stamped. They mix mysticism with filth, allegiance with treachery and shrewdness with the most stupid credulity. Out of these contradictions they weld a uniform attitude toward just one thing—the mascot of their choice. In this case it was Torquay. They pampered, taught, teased and abused him collectively; but any special privilege exercised by an individual brought down the avalanche of the majority against a minority of one. The more Torquay perceived the pedestal on which he was being placed, likening it to the position of teacher's pet, the more did he despise sailors; but he kept his low opinion to himself.

An exception was the white-headed sail-maker and rope splicer. Here was a man who by a miscarriage of justice ranked lower than

Chips, the carpenter, and yet surpassed him by far as an artificer. Anyone could learn to hammer, plane and join; but only an ancient of the seven seas could cut a huge sail to pattern by eye or bend the severed ends of a hawser to a splice with the aid of nothing but his two hands and a marlinespike, or turn from such Herculean labors to fit a great shirt from the slop chest to a small boy, or make that same youngster a pair of board-like trousers out of the remnants of a poop-deck awning.

There were times when Torquay tired of listening to the obscene stories of the watch below, or even to those yarns which pictured the glory of Falmouth as against the presumption of Plymouth, or the older tales of the costly lawlessness of Fowey and the haunted cavern of Polperro. So that was the name of a place as well as of the husband of his Aunt Ada. The thought of her set him to wondering and he would make his way far into the bows, settle himself on a heaped coil of rope and stare at the limitless uneven sea. How far did it go? How many days or weeks or months to the shore? He knew better than to ask questions; the way to get the truth, and not chaff, was to listen to words as they fell. He hated the sea with a vindictive hatred; it had made him ill. The shadow of the sailmaker fell across his crouched figure.

"I wouldn't be for staring at the water, lad. It has a way to draw people into the sea."

In spite of the warning, he was in the bows when the crow's nest called the first landfall. He struggled to his feet and stood rigidly erect until the pillared escarpment of Land's End loomed above the broken water. He was there again when a long tack brought the ship past the Crane Rocks of the Lizard and carried her head on for Plymouth Sound.

"You got folks at Plymouth?" asked the old sailmaker from the side of his mouth.

Torquay shook his head. "Falmouth."

"Falmouth, eh? Well, I wouldn't wait at Plymouth to get paid off if I was you."

"Why not?" demanded Torquay belligerently.

"Hush now! There's them that thinks you're the luck of the ship and a fair voyage. They'd gladly buy the grog that would keep you drunk till anchor's weighed again. Stick by me when we gets ashore." And again, when Torquay was helping him stow away his stores in the peak: "Your best road for walking will be by way of Liskeard and Truro, but it would do no harm did you cross first to Kingsand to put the Sound between them and you."

"Which way is Polperro?"

"Ah, Polperro!" The old man straightened and smiled absently. "Kingsand and Coresand, Whitesand Bay, and then the two Looes, East and West. It's after that you come on Polperro, halfway to Fowey."

Torquay was not to be done out of his pay, but he clung to his old friend as the crew left the office and started around the belly of Southeast Street with their minds fixed on the taverns of the Barbican. They drank at the Old Ship, the Tar and Bucket and the Mayflower, then they doubled back to the Seven Stars and turned noisy over their liquor. They nagged Torquay to hear him swear, and when he did not show off before strangers to their taste, tried to ply him with grog.

It was a warmish evening, and the old sailmaker, leaning back, managed to lose his cap out of an open casement. He leaned forward, stared intently, threw the dregs of his glass in Torquay's face and cried hoarsely, "There's liquor for ye; now go get my cap."

Torquay scrambled down from the bench, dived under the table and came out by the door. He slipped through it and sat crouched against the wall beside the cap. Presently the sailmaker came out, took him by the hand and hurried him around the corner into the Barbican Parade, where many small boats were warped to the quay.

"Who's for Kingsand?" he asked of a group of fishermen, and a voice answered from one of the boats, "I am, if you look sharp."

"There you are, lad," said the sailmaker, lifting Torquay up and dropping him into the boat. "He'll put you across for tuppence, won't you, mate?"

By paying a penny extra, Torquay was permitted to sleep in the boat. He awoke to a rare May morning—how rare he little knew. A blue haze hung over the sea, but the rounded hills were of a vivid living green that sparkled as the sun came up over them. They were crowned with trees, feathering in the late spring into clouds of foliage so light they looked as if they might float away. He walked up toward them and stopped to stare at a grove of larches with pale hanging plumes.

A vivid patch of golden gorse made his eyes grow round, and a feeling came over him that he had waked in another world, infinitely divided from the brawls of drunken sailors. Here was not the semblance of gold, but the metal itself, heaped by the roadside. He laid a hand on a tempting mass of bloom and snatched it back, sharply pricked by the spines on guard beneath.

He walked westward unhurriedly, sometimes within sight of the sea, sometimes led inland by the narrow high-hedged roads. To him the hedgerows were walls, because upon investigation he found they were built of stone, filled in with earth, capped with sods and then permitted to grow masses of hawthorn for a crown and gardens on their steep sides. He would not have believed they had not been planted and carefully tended. Here and there the banks were enameled with bloom. Topped with the gold of the gorse or the star-like flowering thorn, they walled him in between confusing masses of color.

Mauve wild hyacinths vied with the snowy tufts of garlic and the pink of the wild parsley; bluebells and violets added to the shadows; pennyroyal paved outcrops of the stone with burnished copper, and filmy mists of tiny daisies seemed about to rise and flutter. But triumphant over all were the nestling patches of primroses. They were of the palest, gentlest yellow he had ever seen, like sunlight fallen in the grass and too lazy or too shy to move.

He was dazed and mooning. Sometimes he half put out his hand to steady himself with a grip in shaggy hair, as if he were back in his babyhood riding the roads on his father's high shoulder. A two-wheeled cart, rounding a corner, almost ran him down from behind, and at a shout, he dug his heels into the bank and lay back to let it pass. The driver glanced at him and then drew up.

"Which way, lad?"

"I'm going to Polperro," said Torquay.

"Climb up; I'll give you a lift."

After he had got used to seeing over the hedges, Torquay asked, "Do you know of any people called Polperro?"

"Well, no. It's not what you'd call a proper family name. There was a gentleman come through here from England says its right meaning is the Dog Stream, and it's from the Spanish Armada, like Raphael and Barcelona and some more names around here. Smugglers too. They'd come over with a pair of kegs from Spain and stay for a pair of blue eyes, so I'm told."

"Are there any smugglers now?" asked Torquay.

"No, indeed. Only fishermen and the like. Here you are. Take the lane there and turn right when you come to the cross. Mind you don't miss yourself or you'll be going back to Looe."

Torquay thanked the man, hurried down the lane and came to a full stop at the first turn. The village lay beneath him. It looked as if some force had spilled huge blocks of granite down the narrow gorge of the Pol, only the blocks had windows and chimneys and sunken roofs of untrimmed slabs of slate. So steep was the way that he had to brace himself for fear he would slip and slide through the village into the sea. He bargained for food and explained about his Aunt Ada as he asked his question of a gray-haired fisherman in charge of the great kettles where nets were being cooked in tar. The old man paused in his work and looked him over smilingly.

"There's no people of that name; but many a lad has gone out from here and called himself this or that of Polperro. Sooner or later folks would be bound to call such a one Jack of Polperro, say, and in the end Jack Polperro. It could happen that way, for this place is mortal old."

Yes; it was old. From where he sat Torquay could see the mark of centuries on every house, the deep dishing of steps cut in the living rock, stone crop making a garden of many a roof and chickweed in full flower turning a black wall into a breath-taking bridal veil. He dodged through the narrow lanes and clambered up the old road to Fowey. For miles he was walled in by hedgerows which showed him only themselves, the sky and a bit of the twisting way. Never had he felt quite so alone in a lonely world. When darkness fell he slipped through a gate, curled up in the grass and slept. He awoke to broad day and a terrible din. At first it seemed he must be attacked by roaring lions, but presently he saw it was only a half circle of curious sheep, baaing threateningly with surprisingly deep-toned voices. He knew little about the potentialities of sheep, and since they cut off all other avenues of escape, he jumped up and turned, determined to scramble over the wall behind him. But when he moved they scampered away.

While the morning was still young he came out on the sheer escarpment where the Fowey meets the sea. Under his left hand was the gray ocean; under his right the grayer village of Polruan tumbled down the hill to spread itself out on the lip of the bay. Across the narrow water, the full-grown town of Fowey rose and dipped and rose again against the rounded, green-clad cliffs. He sat down in a cup of the turf and stretched out his legs. Broken thoughts were running in his mind. This fairy world into which he had dropped from sailors' brawls was as solid and enduring as any other. Wherever he wandered, he would surely come back to this spot some day, to find it as surely unchanged.

CHAPTER V

It took five years less a few months for Torquay's premonition that he would surely return to the cliff over against Fowey to fulfill itself, and in all that time he had never been more than a full day's walk from the spot where, without knowing it, he had said good-by to boyhood. When, nineteen years old, he climbed the precipitous street which divided the village of Polruan in two like the leaves of a half-opened book, he drove the heels of his hobnailed boots into the slippery clay, stopped and stood for a long time with head bent. It was then that the feeling came over him, vague and yet insistent, that he was not going back to a remembered moment, but on a visit to the boy he had been.

He found the cup in the turf, and it was as it had been; only he himself was changed. His thighs had filled out until they were too big for the hole; so he moved aside and looked at it. He saw Torquay, the boy, sitting there. He followed him down the hill, into a fishing smack bound for Falmouth, and watched him searching the streets for his Aunt Ada's house until he found it without having asked a question. He saw him getting the news that she was dead and buried, and explaining himself to John Polperro, her widower, a man with the cavernous eyes of a born fanatic. Then thought skipped over months of disillusionment and the approaching specter of penury to the night when he had asked, "Who was Maida, sir?"

The light in John Polperro's eyes had turned to a red glow and he snapped his knuckles one after the other with a gesture that seemed somehow symbolic of torture. For some reason he could not have defined, the boy had delayed asking the question he had come so far to put; now he wished he had waited not months but years, holding to the rule that only the answers life gives of its own free will are worth the having. The old man waved Alfred, a son by his first marriage, out of the room before he spoke.

49

"So you don't know who Maida was, eh? Her name was death; the wages of sin is death. I didn't tell her sister Ada, though many's the time I lay awake thinking I ought to; but I can tell you."

He cracked his knuckles more rapidly and glared at the boy as if he saw in him a channel of expiation.

"Never mind," that small Torquay had said in a dry-lipped whisper, but John Polperro went on as if he did not wish to hear.

"Maida left wedlock and your father for another man, and then that other man left her. She came back with enough shame on her to keep away from Ada and this house, but she ended up in the Rag at St. Austell, following the wages of sin. She's dead, and you can fall on your knees and thank God for the mercy of that!"

"The Rag at—"

Even in that cruel naked statement there were impenetrable shadows to a boy of fifteen, but he asked no more questions. He bent all his efforts to wresting enough money out of fairyland to go back to his father; but the smiling land was like the gorse—tender bloom above, sharp spines beneath. He heard Alfred mutter that there was work to be had in the clay pits, and that he was going. He watched and followed him; they walked all day and came upon the village of Roche in the twilight.

Just outside it were the high rocks capped by a cathedral arch, older than the written records of history, older even than legend. Untroubled by the mystery which has brought white nights to countless antiquarians, Torquay and Alfred climbed to what once had been a belfry tower, curled up within its meager protection and slept. In the early morning they cut across the slope through the wet bracken to the top of Hensbarrow Hill and Captain Nicholas Williams. There were no foremen at the clay pits, nor are there to this day, but only captains—a title before which even owners' boards are wont to bow their heads.

Cap'n Neck was short with them; he said he had nothing to offer and ordered them off the works. Alfred turned away docilely, with slumped shoulders and empty face; but Torquay stood his ground, his eyes staring unbelievingly at the vast shallow pit. He waved one hand awkwardly and stammered, "I know all about that."

"So you know all about chiny clay!" exclaimed Cap'n Neck with mock respect.

"Yes," said Torquay. "Stripping the overburden, washing out the loam, letting the sand settle—it's all the same as my father's sand washes."

"And who was your father, might I ask?"

"Thomas Strayton."

"Who?"

"Thomas Strayton."

Cap'n Neck called to Alfred, several years older than Torquay, for confirmation:

"Is the lad speaking the truth?"

"Yes; it's the truth. His father was Thomas Strayton that married Maida Rashfell and went away to America."

"Lad," said the captain, turning to Torquay, "your father and his father before him worked just over the brow of the hill yonder in the Old Beam when it was a proper bal."

"A bal?"

"Yes; a mine. In the days when they were pumping out chiny clay and letting it go to waste because they thought there wasn't anything but tin in the world that could be sold for money."

He gave them work; Alfred at a shilling and thruppence a day because he was all but a man, and Torquay at ninepence, rising to two shillings at the end of four years. Four years on Hensbarrow Hill! Four years of running errands to St. Austell, of carrying picks and dubbers to the smith to be sharpened, of making tea at all hours, of warming taty pasties in the ovens above the drying furnace and running with them to the men waiting in the dark and noisome cuddy. Years of hurrying, blinded by the sleep in his eyes, to take charge of his favorite engineman's two wheels and a donkey, and leading the donkey out in the gray night to tether him on the downs. Four years on Hensbarrow Hill, staring away across the moors to St. Austell's Bay and the rare gleam of the open sea.

Men and boys in billycock hats and their cuddy-house rags, women in sunbonnets and bulging skirts, worked from seven in the morning until half past nine, when they were given twenty minutes for creb; then came denner at noon, and work again until four, when all left off for their labors out of core—tilling the gardens that kept them alive with potatoes, leeks, and the annual pig; building hedgerows wherewith to reclaim the downs; tending to all the chores of orderly though miserable households, and preparing for Sunday chapel—the one social event of the week.

Pay day was the second Saturday after the end of the month, so that a newcomer sometimes worked six weeks before getting a penny, and even then the company kept two weeks of his pay in hand. The owners would drive out in style for the settling of the monthly accounts and sit down to an invariable dinner of fried steak, potatoes, tea and ale. There was cake or bread; if the office cat would eat the bit thrown to her it was cake. Then came hours of waiting in line as the tally in shillings and pennies was doled out to the lesser folk, and gold to the enginemen, the aristocrats of the working fraternity, whose work never ceased, night or day. They were paid by the month, Sundays and holidays included.

Torquay missed no chance to establish himself in their good graces, for he had no money to spare for lodgings and the engine room was a warm refuge on a cold night. It was a strange room, almost as strange as the one-cylinder, single-action engine, with a box full of rocks on the end of a long beam as a compensator. There were two rough benches, on the longer of which the man in charge, having set the engine to pumping, would snatch a nap, leaving the other to Torquay.

The alarm clock was of a piece with all else. It consisted in a wire, several hundred feet long, with a weight tied to the end in the room and placed on a table. From this weight, upon which the engineman never failed to lay a heavy hammer, the wire ran upward over a pulley, then through a hole pierced in the wall, and down to a float in the bottom of the clay pit. As the water was pumped out, the float would lower, the wire would tauten and the weight rise, until finally the hammer would fall to the floor with a tremendous clatter, giving warning that the engine would go in fork if not

52

promptly stopped. How many times Torquay had leaped to his feet at the bang of the hammer and stood trembling for a moment, wondering where he was!

Alfred Polperro married himself into food and shelter, but Torquay clung to his nomad ways and his hard-earned pennies, thinking always of how he would go home as soon as ever he could save a sum as big as that with which he had started out from Hopetown. Tom Jago, the youngest of the enginemen, trained from childhood at the foundry in Charlestown, became his model and goal. If only he could be an engineman at three pounds a month, how swiftly he would save! He had the strength and the knowledge already, but Cap'n Neck still laughed at his aspiration.

One day Tom Jago stared at him as if he looked at a stranger. Torquay had grown up; he had the broad shoulders, hollow belly and strong thighs of a man, and there was a glow in the somberness of his dark eyes which whispered of banked fires. He was ripe for women, wine and a roaring fight at the shoulder of a pal.

"Let's you and me go to St. Austell together come Saturday."

Torquay could hardly believe his ears, but he nodded his head automatically in acceptance. Tom was for taking the coach that would carry them in for sixpence apiece, but not Torquay. To him a tanner was still as big as when it had represented two-thirds of a day's work; he would spend it willingly enough, but never to save his legs. Together they footed the miles into town, arriving at the Ship and Halter with a mighty thirst.

Even before the first drink, Torquay's throat swelled to memory and his eyes assumed the dogged stare of Jack ashore and heading for the gutter by the fastest route, for the place was teeming with deep-sea sailors up from the port of Charlestown. Husky voices reverberated from the low ceiling in ribald jokes, curses and yarns as old as the granite pillars, split square by the ancient method of feathers and tares—stories that live on forever, measured not by familiar content but by the skill of the telling. Tom, watching his companion, was filled with wonder at his boldness and with admiration for the way he took his liquor and held it down.

53

"Lad," he said, "you only growed up yesterday; where did you learn the drinking? You've had vower to my dhree, and you're fresh as a saffrony cake."

"That's nothing," muttered Torquay darkly. "You'd ought to hear me swear."

"What about women now? D'you know about them?"

Torquay frowned.

"Women is black inside," he recited. "You never can tell till you've busted 'em, mashed 'em up into little pieces."

"That's so," said Tom slowly, staring harder than ever. "Come along with me and let me see you mash one."

"To hell with 'em," said Torquay, swaying his head from side to side. "Not me."

"Just down the Rag once, and back again. There's girls there, Torque, young and old, thin and fat, dark, favored and light as beer—on the outside. Let's you and me—"

Something started running backward in Torquay's brain, like the turning of the leaves in a book, and stopped. He could see old John Polperro's words as if they were printed on an open page: "She ended up in the Rag at St. Austell."

"All right," he said, staring blankly and stumbling to his feet, "I'll go."

An hour later he raged back into the crowded room of the Ship and Halter with Tom, wide-eyed and gasping, at his heels. He stood up on a form by the wall, his head and shoulders against the ceiling, and bellowed, "All you graybacks, hear me swear!" His eyes were as red as garnets, and looking out through them, he saw the world in flames. The next instant he had launched himself at the circle of startled faces before him, his fists crashing out to a sudden echo of groans, cries and curses. Bedlam and chaos; then grunts, blows, a shivering tinkle and darkness. Above it all, Tom's voice, barking hoarsely in rapid repetition, "This way, lad; here's the door. This way, lad!"

He had never gone back to Hensbarrow Hill. Here he was, staring at a hollow in the turf and wondering dumbly how the thread of life could be cut with shears and yet go on. His eyes were still streaked with blood. Today the sea was not gray, nor was the tumbling village of Polruan, or the waving line of the houses of Fowey. They were all tinged as if seen through a red veil—the torn veil of the Rag at St. Austell where Maida Rashfell had gone out of life through a cesspool.

He looked at his legs and tried to think how it would feel if they, too, were cut off. Thongs were tied about them just above the calf, navvy fashion, to give his knees freer action; now he took them off, stood up and gazed at the ships anchored in the harbor. Money or no money, he would go home. He threw away his billycock hat, stuffed his smock inside his corduroy trousers, tightened his belt and started down the hill.

Three weeks later, from the waist of the *Saracen Prince*, he was trying to make out Salem and Penn's Grove through the murk of a rainy morning. He had gone away as cabin boy on a windjammer and come back as stoker on a steamer.

CHAPTER VI

THE train from Camden to Hopetown, even though it had suffered several changes, among them the discarding of gig and gigman, carried him back in more senses than one. While still on shipboard he had been linked to the strange land of his sojourn, gentle to look at, hard to the touch; but now, quite suddenly, a vast curtain of sea and fog seemed to descend between him and the five years of his absence. It did not wipe them out; it set them aside. Just as a pear-shaped blob of molten glass stood for his own childhood and that of the Pine Tree Glassworks, so did granite colored houses against the rounded cliffs of Cornwall merge into a single door, locked upon a finished chapter of the past.

When one a wakes from a dream, one steps back to where that dream began. It was so with Torquay; he was a child again. He heard himself shout "Ed! Ed!" and watched the amazing confusion resulting from his cry. He saw a look fixed like a straight bar between two people; at one end, himself; at the other, Mega, the dark woman. Looking upon her inscrutable face, his mouth watered with anticipation of delectable food. Lastly he saw himself in the glassworks, half naked in the glow of the ringhole, or standing in file, waiting for his weekly pay and the hire of his team—a huge sum!

He sank deeper into memory until he became merged with the throbbing dry-lipped moment that stood like a black period at the very end of his hours in the lonely house above the flats. Now he was sitting across the table from his father, whispering the fatal question. Utterly absorbed, drugged with recollection, he felt his chin itch as on that night. He touched his lip with his fingers and looked at them. He was amazed to find them dry; he could not go on with the picture because there was no blood to wipe off and no tablecloth to wipe it on. That lack waked him to the present and to the fact that he was now fully grown and afraid of no man's work.

The thought of the wages he had had from his father, with never a word as to what he should do with the money, made him wince. What a waste the five years of absence had been! It shamed him to think he was going back a pauper. If the newborn Pine Tree plant could pay so generously, what of the great Hetney works which already had endured through three generations? He made up his mind as the train rolled into Glassboro to try there first for a job.

Within an hour he had wormed his way into the holy of holies of the huge shed which sheltered the furnaces. Immediately he was at home, and yet not at home. The methods of the men with the molten glass were practically unchanged, but his eye quickly grasped innovations in other things. Coal as a fuel had been substituted for wood, and the pots which had necessitated alternate spells of furious work and wasteful loafing had given way to the continuous tank. At one end of the tank was the dog house, where the batch was shoveled in; at the other was the ringhole, where it was taken out, melted, without a single interruption from Monday morning to Friday night.

The blowing of bottles differed very little from the turning out of the hollow cylinders intended for sheet glass. He had never made a bottle, but he had often been in the Damon Glassworks, and now he noticed two slight improvements over the ancient practice. In the old days the finishing touch had been to shear the neck while the base of the bottle was still glued to the end of the pontil. Now the bottle was held in a snap while a molded band was added to the neck, and a smooth hollow base had taken the place of the scar caused by the breaking away of the pontil. His hands itched as he watched; the years fell away. What these men were doing, he had done and could do again. He filled his lungs with the burnt air; it was as though he had been drowned for a long while and had now come up where he could breathe.

A foreman approached and stood beside him for a moment before he asked, "Who are you, and what do you want?"

"Torquay Strayton. I don't want anything."

"Turnkey Strayton, eh?"

"Not Turnkey—Torquay."

"Any kin to Thomas at Hopetown?" continued the foreman, his eyes narrowing.

"He's my father, but I haven't seen him for five years."

"What are you?"

It was the question Torquay had been waiting for.

"Glass blower," he answered promptly.

"The hell you are!"

"It's easy enough to find out. Give me a blowing iron and I'll show you."

He displaced one of the men at the furnace. At a wink from the foreman, the gatherer gave the rod an extra twirl.

"Go to hell," said Torquay, pushing him aside. "What do you think I am?"

His lips curved to a smile of scorn. The gatherer had purposely bungled his job and by so doing had given him a chance to start with what he knew best of all. He dripped some of the glass from the iron, rolled the mass deftly on the marver to harden it, thrust it through the ringhole for an added layer, shaped it with a preliminary breath through the blowing iron, and then cast a look at the gatherer.

"Now I hands it to me from you," he sneered.

His hour of watching stood him in good stead; his movements were only imitation, but imitation tuned accurately by a master craftsman to whom molten glass was friend as well as slave. Twirling the mass, he let it lop, looking for impurities on the thinned side, and with his pincers snatched a bit of scum from its incandescent depths. Then he gathered it, expanded it with a breath, set it in the mold, blew it to shape, kicked the release and passed the blowing iron with the bottle attached to the wetter-off.

"I guess you won't learn nothing here that will hurt us much," said the foreman. "You can start with the night shift."

In those days bottles were used almost exclusively for only two things—patent medicines and hard liquor. The medicine flasks took on weird shapes, but none that amused Torquay as much as the quart-size whisky bottles made in the shape of a log cabin, and first put on the market to further the presidential campaign of William

Henry Harrison. The neck stood for a chimney; on the face were molded three windows and a door, and on the steep roof and side were stamped the words, "E. C. Booz's Old Cabin Whisky." So well had the brand been established that the bottles were still being turned out to meet the frequent declaration, "I'll take some Booz."

He was fascinated by the variety of other molds as well; they gave an individuality to glass which windowpanes could never attain. He remembered his father had once hinted at going in for bottles and wondered if the change had yet been made.

The foreman who had given him a job had taken a fancy to him and he was assured of steady work and a rising wage; but without thinking things out, he knew that sooner or later he would go back to the Pine Tree plant. Meanwhile he hung around in off hours, watching the preparation of the batch without seeming to watch, chatting with the test crew, and frequently entering the mold room, where he was occasionally permitted to lend a hand.

But he always drifted back to where the rough stuff was being mixed. The men all liked him, and gradually forgot that he was Thomas Strayton's son. Even if they had remembered it, they would have told him the proportions just the same, for two centuries had passed since certain youths of Strasburg had found it necessary to hide on the roofs of the glassworks of Murano, staking their lives against discovery, in order to steal the secrets by which Venice had held her long monopoly in fancy mirrors. Now every detail of the composition of glass was public property, everything was known that was worth knowing save the undiscovered formula which would make it unbreakable.

"What are you snoopin' around for, Torque?" said the works manager. "Ask me and I'll tell you."

"There's nothing I don't want to know."

"That sounds like a tall order, but in this business it ain't so big as you might think. Glass is seven-tenths silica; you know that much. You mix the sand with soda and lime for window and plate glass; add oxide of lead for crystal; swap your oxide of lead for oxide of tin and you get enamel. When it comes to bottles, it is oxide of iron that does the trick. The cleaner your sand, the better the mix; and the slower the annealing leer, the stronger the glass. It won't stand to be hurried; remember that. When a bottle crushes in your hand, sort of blows up, the glass was cooled outside first and inside last."

"What would make it so it would bend?"

"Bend!" exclaimed the manager with a wide stare.

"Ye-ah. What would make it so you could hit it with a hammer and it wouldn't break?"

"Heat, you fool! Two thousand degrees of heat, and nothin' else!"

Torquay was unabashed; he scuffed his toe into a heap of cullet.

"Some day they'll make it so it won't break."

"Don't get me wrong," said the manager with gentle irony. "I ain't looking to stop anyone from turning their hand to a miracle. But folks has been making glass just like we do for four thousand years or more. Half the world could even forget how to make it any way at all for a thousand years. Then they learned all over again, but nothing that somebody hadn't known before. Think that out."

CHAPTER VII

IN the old days, from the first of June to the last day of August, the glasshouses used to shut down. But the continuous tank had done away with that. A few days later Torquay was on the train again, bound for Hopetown with a full purse. He overheard two fellow passengers talking, but paid no attention to what they were saying until suddenly he realized that the conversation revolved around his father and Mr. Damon.

"The way it ended," one was saying, "Burk laced him with the whip, and Tom laid hold on the buggy wheel and ripped it off. It fell to pieces, with the spokes rattling to the ground, and the horses took fright and run across the flats. Burk slid out, but he wouldn't leave go the lines, and that's how his face come to get all cut up on the dried sedge. Tom never put hands on him."

When the train slowed up for the opening of the switch, Torquay dropped off and started toward the house, hut a glance at the works brought him to a full stop. The pine tree and the oyster-shell mound were still recognizable, but the old shed had shrunk so that it seemed impossible its roof could ever have bridged the spaces where men whirled huge cylinders of glass at full arms' length. The shed was dwarfed partly by the years that stood between him and his childhood, and partly by the ramshackle additions which made it look like a hub in a wheel.

It was mid September. The tulip poplars around the house were in black-green leaf and the leprous white scalings on the sycamores shone in the shadows like silver plaques. Sunlight drenched the flats, throwing into dark relief the tumbled mass of sheds and smokestacks clustered around the pine. The submerged river appeared as a narrow gleam, thin as a knife edge, the dividing line between ugliness and beauty. On this side, rutted, stubbled mud; on the other, drooping willows, standing like showers of green water at the edge of the lawns which sloped upward to the back of the Damon house. The house itself was out of sight, masked by century-old trees. Far to the right appeared the cap of a high brick chimney, cut off by a rounded knoll and hanging against the sky as if to mark the hidden location of the Damon Glassworks.

Torquay struck across the flats through an oven of heat. He knew what the plant must be like on such a day, but at least the low eaves promised shade. He passed beneath them and wandered here and there, gradually linking the new to the old. Nobody paid any attention to him. Every man and boy in the place was hollow-eyed and intent only on individual automatic movements. He did not see his father, nor did he ask for him, for already he was absorbed in the discovery that bottles of a most commonplace shape were being blown of molten glass drawn from a continuous tank. He watched the men for a few moments. Presently a blower staggered to one side and leaned against a pillar while he swept the sweat from his face and hair. Torquay stripped to the waist, stepped forward and took the man's iron.

"It's all right, Ed. Go take a rest."

The man stared at him. His face twitched in the impulse to show amazement, but its muscles were too tired. It was fully a minute before his lips murmured, "Hello, Torque"; and by that time Torquay had taken his place at the ringhole. He caught the rhythm so quickly that the blower's helpers were scarcely aware of a break. Once his swaying limbs had seized the pace, time ceased. He could think of anything he liked; he could plan, and even dream. Half an hour later, two hours later—he could not have told which—he was aware of the presence of his father, standing by as he had stood years ago, waiting this time for the whistle which would blow for the six-o'clock shift.

Although a new vigor crept into his blood, Torquay did not turn his head nor change the tempo of his motion. For a moment he stood outside himself, so that it seemed he could look on his own broadened shoulders—all muscle, bone and weight—flexing under the steadily descending glistening film of sweat. He could see how the bare flesh stopped at the waist below the bridging arch of his strong ribs, pinched in by his tightly drawn belt. He could see and feel the pillars of his legs, half straddled, holding him firmly in a pose of defiance within the glare of the ringhole.

"By God," he was thinking, "he'll never hit me again! Let him look—look! He'll never hit me again!"

The whistle blew. He and his father were walking side by side and in silence across the flats. They came into the wide-flung shade of the first sycamore.

"Well, Torque," said his father, straining awkwardly to cloak admiration with a thin veil of humor, "I guess I won't be knocking of you around no more."

"I guess you won't," said Torquay. "I guess I can say what I damn please from now on. I guess I can ask about her that was my mother, Maida, or anyone—"

He reeled from a jolting half blow to his throat that changed speech into a squawk. He whirled. He was facing his father's bloodshot eyes and driving his fist at his father's hairy face. The blood was pounding in his veins, singing a song that lifted, higher and higher. Now they would have it out, here under the tree. Never again! He'd show him! He couldn't hit him any more! Nobody could hit Torquay Strayton! His fingers caught and closed in his father's beard. That was it—hold him with one hand and hit him with the other. Pull, swing and hit!

His wrist was seized in the hot clamp of a merciless grip. He struck with his free fist, and that, too, was caught and held with the downward twist of a giant thumb. He was imprisoned. For an instant he stared into his father's face and was amazed to find it calm—as calm as a huge comber of the sea. Then something happened to his feet. The earth swirled from under them. He was in the air, the weight of his solid body came to nothing. He was a child again—no, a cylinder of glass, whirling in a wide circle at the end of a blowing iron. What if his father's hold should slip? Crash! He struck the ground and bounced like a ball. His head clicked sharply against the bole of the sycamore. The huge comber had broken and he was drowned.

When he came to, the sun was just setting and he was alone with a splitting pain. He put his fingers automatically to his lower lip and then looked at them. They were dry. He passed his hand slowly over his head and stopped it with a wince against a great egg-shaped bump. He raised himself and sat on the ground, with his back to the tree, for a long time. Presently the light came back into his eyes and his lips began slowly to curve into a smile. He had known strong men all his days, but none the equal of his father. Like a cylinder of glass, whirling in mid-air at the end of a blowing iron, and then—crash!

He got up and went into the house. His father was already seated at the table, but Mega was only now bringing in the supper. She stopped in her stride as she saw the stranger—a great boy with black hair, matted and curled with sweat; dark eyes, alive with fire; swarthy cheeks as smooth as the skin of an olive, but glowing beneath with the red of health and youth. A smudge of black hung on his upper lip and a lighter growth shadowed the oval of his chin. For a moment she stood frowning, then her brows cleared as she regained her habitual poise.

"Good evening, Master Torquay. I'll bring your supper directly."

As she went out to the kitchen, Torquay took his place at the table—the same place where he had been sitting when childhood had come to a sudden end.

"I guess I was wrong," he said pleasantly.

His father nodded.

"It never hurts nobody to think they can lick twice their weight and size, no matter how wrong they are," he said after a pause. "Trying's the only way you'll ever find out when you're right."

There was another pause while Mega brought in extra plates and food. Torquay caught her eyes upon him as she stood back from the table, and hungry as he was, he forgot to eat. She appeared not to have aged a day; everything was the same about her. Her sleeves were rolled up to the elbows over arms as muscular as a man's. She still wore the same old threadbare cloak of humility over pride of lineage, and the mantle of aloofness still hung like a veil before her eyes. He stared at her, determined to pierce it now or never, adding

64

all the weight of knowledge to the blind insolence of his youth. A moment later he knew he had been beaten again; he dropped his eyes to his plate and began to eat.

"You're a clean bottle blower, Torque, and a fast one. Where did you learn it?"

"I'll tell you if you'll tell me where you got that calabash mold. Don't you know those bottles ain't being made any more?"

"Yes, I know. That's why I could buy the set down at Salem so cheap."

"If they didn't pay you for carrying them away, they weren't cheap."

Thomas waited a long time before answering. His hands, feet and even his head were built heavy; but for upward of fifteen years he had trained his tongue. Looking at his boy, he almost forgot what he wanted to say. Fires were burning inside him that had been banked for many a day—the fires of a concentrated affection. He could slave for his glassworks as no man under the lash had ever pulled at a galley oar; but if there was such a thing as love in the world, he could place it nowhere save on this bear cub of a boy whom he had half killed for a welcome home.

"I know there ain't much of a market for those bottles, and what there is, is dying fast. But I ain't been making them to sell; I been making 'em to learn how."

"Your glass is cleaner than up at the Hetney works," said Torquay quickly, "and they think they make the cleanest glass in West Jersey."

His father nodded again, half in reply to Torquay's words, half in acknowledgment of the information as to where he had acquired his skill.

"Yes," he said, "our glass is clean, and that ain't all. Nothing we've got has cost us a cent. What I mean, Torque, is this: Everything we have—this house here, and the flats and the works and the sand washes—has paid for itself. I mean there isn't anything we couldn't sell for more than I give for it. Even those bottles you think so lightly of, they come inside the line too. Every one on 'em sells for more than it costs to make it."

Torquay's eyes began to glow. They were not fixed on his father, but were staring through the walls toward the works. The coolness of the house at night, the food, and now his tacit inclusion in the ownership of hard-earned possessions, gave him such a feeling of home-coming as no superficial welcome could have induced. In a moment his father had become more than a huge man of strength; vaguely he seemed to have widened out into a broad hearth with ingle seats, where they could sit and talk. Grouped around them like blobs of unworked glass were the patched-up works, the primitive sand washes, the rotting house and the ugly flats, all waiting for the blowers' breath and hand.

"Never mind," said Torquay presently. "Whenever you're ready, bring me a sample bottle and I'll make the mold to fit it. We won't ever have to buy no more secondhand molds."

There followed another comfortable silence, and then his father said, "Burk Damon hit me with a whip the other day."

"I know. I heard two men talking on the train."

"What did they say?"

"They told how you ripped the wheel off his buggy and when he slid out, the sedge stalks cut up his face without your touching him."

"His son, Jake, the boy you had the fight with, is married. It was foolish for him to marry so young."

"Why?"

"Because the Damon Glassworks is built on sand, and we own the sand."

Nothing startling in the way of sudden revolution followed this evening's talk. All the movements of the glassworker are slow; only their results are swift. Torquay went back to his station at the ringhole, choosing the morning shift, from four o'clock to midday. After a long rest at the lunch hour, he would return to the works on his own hook and disappear into a small shed which he had chosen to be the mold room. He acquired a bench and all the necessary tools and set about designing a bottle which should take the place of the old-fashioned trade shape they were then using. Into the wet sand, after many attempts, he traced a fair representation of the tree which in after years was to be known the country over as the emblem of the Pine Tree Glassworks.

Little as he or his father realized it at the time, the first bottle cast in the new mold marked the turning point between manufacturing for a small margin above cost and manufacturing for revenue. The new form did not sell any better than the old, but it drew and held the attention of every buyer who happened upon it. Up to the time of the Civil War, bottles had been largely restricted to two shapes—the flattened oval flask and the calabash, all made of amber or green shades of glass of poor clarity, and most of them sheared at the neck and scarred at the bottom. Into Torquay's bottle went what he had learned at the Hetney plant, added to all his father had worked out for himself through years of experiment in turning out windowpanes without a bubble. The result was a straight-sided transparent container with smoothly molded neck and a pushed-up bottom. What the buyers thought who saw it was that whoever made that bottle could make any other.

Samples began to come in with requests for improvement and estimates on steady shipments. Thomas Strayton was pleased but not stampeded. During years of close contact he had come to know almost as much about the marketing methods of the Damon Glass-works as Burk Damon himself. He knew, among other things, that a variety of customers was of no advantage to a manufacturer. He had formed a shrewd opinion of his own that diversity rather than vain-glory had been at the root of William Henry Stiegel's crash almost a century before. Baron Stiegel, they had called him, because of his three cannons, fired to announce his passage from one of his glassworks to another. When Thomas Strayton heard the story it made him spit. He was glad Stiegel had died a pauper.

Things had indeed changed. Better far a few accounts with those who used largely of a single model than many with those who used little or who split their orders into so much of this and so much of that. Every change of molds would stand for a dead loss of time, to say nothing of the greater gaps in profit caused by making up batches to suit individual requirements in color.

Torquay chafed under the restraint; he could not understand the workings of his father's mind, and Thomas Strayton had never been the kind to explain himself easily in words, for the greatest dreamers are those who hide their dreams even from themselves. A silence fell between them as request after request was ignored. Even when the boy had been to the trouble to turn out a mold on the chance that, once it was done, his father could not refuse an out-and-out order, Thomas stood fast against the rage of his son and the pressure of the bewildered prospective purchaser.

"You don't want to do it?"

"No."

"Why not?"

A shrug.

"Name a price, man. You can do that, can't you?"

"I'll name a price for ten thousand gross when you can give the order and back it with cash."

CHAPTER VIII

THAT answer might have meant a lot to Torquay had it not sounded as outrageous to his ears as it did to those of the buyer. He abandoned the mold room in a sulk and went back to the automatic labor of the blowing iron, where weeks spread into months so smoothly that a year divided itself into two equal parts—winter and summer.

He welcomed interruptions which once would have galled him and smiled on the parties that occasionally came to the works, perhaps after having exhausted the mysteries of the Damon plant. As for the children of the locality, including himself in what seemed now a far-off day, there was scarcely one of them who had not some friend among the blowers willing to steal a moment to make those two great prizes, glass balls, and flip-flaps.

The balls were merely spheres, as iridescent, thin and fragile as a soap bubble, something to be borne with many tremors on the palm of an outstretched hand in the hope, which was generally vain, that it might be carried home intact. The flip-flaps were still more to be desired. They consisted of a hollow stem attached to a globe of glass so thin that its bottom could be made to flip in and out by just the right quantity of breath, producing a lugubrious sound. Torquay descended so far as sometimes to waste a moment in the making of these toys. But a day came when his father called him aside, handed him a sample bottle, and asked him to design a mold.

"Somebody that wants ten thousand gross?" asked Torquay.

"No," said Thomas; "not yet."

Then Torquay looked at the bottle.

"Why, that's Damon glass!"

"Yes; it's Damon glass right enough. They crowded him out on an order. They don't know he's going to need three times as much in a month as he ever bought in a year."

69

It was the entering wedge. Inside six months the flames of competition which had been smoldering in unseen depths ever since Burk Damon had paid his first visit to the oyster-shell mound were to flare high in the sky, open to anybody's view, between the lone pine tree and the great chimney stack of the Damon Glassworks. To look at Strayton's ramshackle sheds, and then to cross the river, climb the knoll and gaze down on the imposing Damon plant, was to jeer at the thought that such a David could make mock of so established a Goliath; but there were two men who knew the truth.

For years Thomas Strayton had possessed the sling which could have laid Burk Damon low and for years he had withheld his hand. He had not spared his enemy through any impulse of generosity or even of fair play but through a shrewdness colossal in its patience. The selling of sand was a profitable business and Damon his best customer. It would not have paid him any sooner to raise his prices or cut down deliveries, for had he forced his rival to the wall he would have imperiled the very foundations of his own enterprise. But now things were different. The railways had made it possible to reach two or three other factories and his own works were prepared to use an increased amount of sand.

The pits he owned became a great forceps wherewith he might squeeze one customer at a time out of the Damon following and yet let the Damon works live on a profitable though steadily declining basis. That they could so live only by buying such sand as Strayton was willing to supply was gall and wormwood to Burk Damon, but there was no way out. He had to keep going. Just as long as he could get enough sand to meet his orders without going into bankruptcy, he had to run his works even though he knew he was walking the path of a slow death with torture.

He began to spend money lavishly on borings on every bit of unencumbered land that showed the slightest traces of silica. He supplied the funds for more than one farmer to attack Strayton's titles in the courts. He bribed another to sell him rights which had already been disposed of, set his own gangs to work, and took out sand in the face of injunctions and a suit for damages. That was his

70

greatest coup, for Strayton could recover only the market price of the sand added to the costs of the action. At last, he discovered a sandbank of excellent quality and promptly committed the great error of his life. He broke openly and finally with Thomas Strayton.

The aristocratic portion of the community applauded, seeing only his present victory, and never scenting ultimate defeat. For three years it had watched the battle rage with steadily ascending interest. The Damons stood for everything that was best and most cultured in Hopetown, while Strayton was worse than an upstart. He had come from nowhere, carrying a child who must have had the most temporary of mothers. He was an Ishmaelite, a scoffer and a slave driver. His whole establishment was a blot on the landscape, and he was credited with living with a colored woman popularly supposed to be possessed of the evil eye and certainly as vicious a creature as the local housewives had ever attempted in vain to subdue.

To gather all the implications of this picture one should catch at least a glimpse of the background against which it was projected. Well over two hundred years before, the Hooker Company had come to New England, and some of its members, finding the climate too rigorous, had scattered. Many migrated to what is now known as Southern New Jersey and founded the ancient hamlet of Deerfield Street. A far smaller and wiser number had settled in Hopetown, destined in the course of time to become a city. This parent stock was still in the ascendancy when the shadow of Thomas Strayton first fell across Burk Damon's path, and never did hierarchy reign with a heavier hand.

Its men were as stalwart a combination of virtues and vices as ever graced an urban setting. They not only founded churches but went to them with the regularity of the calendar—and paid their midwives with twelve bushels of corn to every gallon of rum. They built lovely homes and met for games of hazard in places of far less attraction. They counted it a sin to eat hot food or even to take a walk on Sunday but swore like troopers and drank like the sands of the desert during the rest of the week. Greatest of all their feats, they fooled their wives through generations into thinking they led immaculate lives.

Incidentally, they established schools of such excellence that at certain seasons the steamboats from Philadelphia and the stagecoaches that plied down the Burlington Pike or dragged their way up the Babylon Road from Salem, were laden with young ladies bearing introductions which would admit them to the first families and give them a chance to partake of the exceptional schooling.

Even after the Civil War, and coincident with Torquay's return, there was such a cleavage between those who considered themselves to the manner born and lesser folk that shopkeepers, menials and laborers were as subservient as the bootlicking counter jumpers of the Old World and bowed blindly to the domineering ways of their self-constituted betters. It was easy to be a pariah in such a community, and as a matter of fact, the pariahs were rapidly becoming an overwhelming majority, with Thomas Strayton as their uncrowned king.

As a consequence, it was scarcely strange that Torquay should have grown to be twenty-three without ever suspecting he was an outcast. He knew that the well-dressed sightseers who came to his father's works were as one to a hundred who visited the Damon plant; but he thought it only natural because the Pine Tree Glassworks were altogether such a scurvy-looking affair. Also, it so chanced he had lived his whole life within the element that met him on equal terms; and if on his rare visits to the shopping district of the town, he noticed at all the beruffled and hoity-toity misses or the more severe ladies of the elect, it was merely to reflect that they were nothing but women and uniformly black inside.

Only twice during the years since his return had he come face to face with the younger Damon. On the first of these occasions he had said, "Hello, Jake," and received a level stare for his pains. On the second, in Striker's drug and cigar store, which the war had democratized into a general meeting place, he had spit in such a way as to force Jake to move his foot very suddenly. Torquay did not connect these skirmishes with social complications. He had spoken to Jake in a friendly manner and Jake had preferred to perpetuate their boyhood quarrel. When he spat at Jake's foot, he was only serving notice that the challenge was accepted. There were loafers who might have enlightened him as to his relative position in the regard of the dominant public, but fortunately Torquay had little time for loitering or loiterers.

Root, branch and tendril, he was absorbed in the Pine Tree plant. So genuine was his devotion to the manipulation of glass that it set him definitely apart from those who make things only for money and gave him the stamp as well as the unconscious dignity of the artisan. And yet his nature had no room for even a touch of the aesthetic. He cared for thoroughness, not for beauty, and valued an ounce of utility against a pound of art for art's sake. Inside him was a dream that he might someday discover the formula for unbreakable glass. This inner vision was his heel of Achilles, his one soft spot, but it was buried in his own soul and protected under a surface as tight and hard as the bark on a young hickory. For his age, he was exceptionally cool, level-headed and farseeing. His father never hesitated to give him free rein in any trade; but when Torquay protested bitterly against the cheap patchwork of the sheds which were going up to take care of the constantly increasing flow of orders, Thomas stepped out for a moment from the shadow of his habitual silence.

"Why, Torque, we ain't going to be here always."

"What do you mean? We've been here always already."

"What I mean," explained his father darkly, "is that it's better to have money in the bank than in bricks and mortar you can't move. Never you mind about these sheds. They'll serve out their turn and more."

The discovery of a sand wash by the Damons had brought about more than a lull in the war between the two glassworks; it had severed them completely. No longer did Strayton's wagons converge on the bridge from three directions, cross it and wind around the hill to deposit their sand in the bins beneath the distant chimney stack. Instead they stopped at the railway station, or came on to heap their loads on the Pine Tree pile, or even stayed at home, releasing their crews for more urgent duties at the works. With the Damon people limited to the sand they could mine themselves, and forced to stint their clients, Strayton stood on velvet. For every dollar he was losing from the stoppage of his old trade, five would come in as long as his restricted equipment could take care of the customers he chose to accept.

To all outward appearance, there was peace in Hopetown, but in reality it was the tense quiet of a death struggle. Men laughed, joked and went about their affairs as usual only because they could not make themselves believe that the one industrial giant and pride of the town was tottering to a crash. There were a few who knew, and who had gone to the verge of straining their own financial backs in order to save Damon. They had even gone so far as to attempt to dicker with Strayton's skilled and unskilled labor, and there they had come up against a force so new in their experience that it had no name.

Strayton's workmen did not love him; they even suspected that his triumph would mean harder conditions in many ways for themselves; and yet they stuck to him and to one another like leeches. They made more than a mock of the efforts to dislodge them. Far from yielding, they worked as never before in their lives. Victory for the long-despised Pine Tree Glassworks hung on stretching its ramshackle resources to far beyond their normal capacity, and they bent their backs to do it. Gatherer, blower, wetter-off and taker-in not only smelled out the crux of the struggle, but for some obscure reason each promptly adopted the battle as his own, and when men forget the love of pay and work for the love of fighting, God help the big battalions.

To Torquay, swaying rhythmically hour after hour in the glare of the ringhole, the days seemed to flow into the molten glass of the continuous tanks with the evenness of a tideless river. One year swallowed another, for the monotony of idleness is a sloth while the monotony of action is swift as the hunting leopard. His muscles, settling into the strength of full-blown manhood, never faltered; but there were times when his mind toyed with revolt. While he was standing with feet anchored, the days were flowing away. Where were they going? How far behind were they leaving him? If he should run around to the dog house and dive into the other end of the tank, he could be blown into bottles and shipped away by train; but he would never catch up with even the most laggard of these passing days!

Turning from fancy, he looked up and saw a vision of another sort. Two children were standing entranced, staring at his naked torso and his heaving ribs. One was a girl of five with fluffed-out skirts and a blue sash; the other was a boy a year or two younger in velvet pants and a white shirt waist. There was something familiar to Torquay in his eyes and in the formation of his chin. Between the children was a nursemaid, holding a hand of each. Torquay glanced up at her. He forgot the plastic glass at the end of his blowing iron. It flopped to one side, then downward, gathered weight, and presently shot to the floor with a wet thud instantly followed by the tiny cracklings of burning dust. The children cried out with delight and jumped up and down. His own crew gaped at him, amazed, while a neighboring blower, casting a look over his shoulder, laughed derisively.

"Oh, go to hell," retorted Torquay to the jeering laugh.

The nursemaid had started to lead the children away; now she turned swiftly and stood transfixed, staring at him intently. She had pale yellow hair done in small braids and wound about her head in such a manner as to show beneath the rim of her bonnet. Her eyes were deep blue, and just now absurdly round and wide, two dark pits in the vacant pallor of her face. It was a queer face to look at; not ugly, but pinched and small, as if childhood had been too suddenly snatched away, leaving some of itself behind. Her mouth hung half open, then suddenly closed with a click of even teeth. She swallowed nervously, and Torquay could see the ripple pass down her white throat like a falling shadow. Her lips moved as if they were about to speak, but he forestalled her.

"Yes," he said, with an impudent grin, "that's what I said to your mother."

Her face flushed red for an instant and then broke into a shower of smiles, only to clear and settle down to gravity before she murmured rapidly, "I thought it was you, and then I thought it wasn't; but when you said that, of course I knew."

"Ask him for a flip-flap, Janie," cried the little girl in a loud whisper, and her brother added his demand, "Make him give me a flip-flap, Janie."

Torquay, looking boldly at Janie, paid no attention to the children; but she dared not ignore them.

"It was they made me come here," she explained. "They're tired of their gran'-daddy's works and I guess his place is tired of them. Could you make them a flip-flap? If you don't they'll yell."

Torquay continued his bold stare until her face flamed again as red as the ringhole; then he said shortly, "Let 'em yell their heads off."

There was an instant of incredulous silence before two shrill shrieks pierced the air.

"I want a flip-flap!"

"Me, too!"

Janie's face grew as old as her years, and thoroughly efficient. She stooped swiftly, gathered one child under each arm and carried them, squalling and kicking, out of the shed and away. Torquay turned back to his work, his jaws set, his brows gathered in a frown. There were ribald cries of "Who's the lady, Torque? Who's the mother of your kids?" He paid no heed except to curse his helpers into swifter action, striving to regain the automatic rhythm that would let him think at his ease.

CHAPTER IX

S OMEHOW, in a moment, the days had stopped streaming past
him. Instead, they were banking up, flowing backward with a rush
to the sources of time.

The great brick house at Babylon rose before his eyes, not deserted as he had last seen it, but with a woman looking out from the
kitchen door, children gathered about her, and this same Janie clinging
to her skirts. He could hear the woman's voice, floating on the still
morning air: "You're a bad man—an evil man. You have sold your
child to the devil."

There followed the memory of his father and the apples, quite
suddenly, as if his father had found the apples while still in sight of
the house. He saw him break one in half, black at the core; crush
another, a bright red shell around a mass of rotten pulp; smash still
another on the top rail of the fence with his fist, but that one had
broken into glittering bits of clear white flesh. He could see even
now the dark stain its juices had made on the dry gray wood.

"You never can tell till you've busted 'em, mashed 'em up into
little pieces."

Before he knew it, the whistle was blowing for the midday shift.
After his dinner he tried to sleep and then to read, but in vain. A fever
was in his blood. The printed words would not stay on the page. The
more he looked at them, the more they ran off to reappear on the
gummy pages of the primers and readers of a dozen musty country
schools. He saw whole sentences he had long since forgotten, and
heard over and over again a cry just out of the reach of recollection.
He strained his ears to catch its phrases, but only when he abandoned
the effort did they come to him quite suddenly. He could hear them
now, and even see them:

"Oh! Oh! I know who you are! You said that to my mother!"

He got up from the bed, where he had been lying on his back, staring at the ceiling, and paced up and down the small room. Presently he went idly to the open window and looked out. He drew himself quickly to one side and stood listening intently. His father and Burk Damon were walking about under the poplars behind the house. He could not quite make out what they were saying; but he had seen a queer slump to Mr. Damon's shoulders and had caught a note in his voice that trembled between desperation and anger, as if he were barely controlling his temper, guiding it along a knife-edge ridge, destruction on either side.

Then, quite sharply: "I tell you it's robbery! It's been highway robbery from the start!"

"If that was so," rumbled his father, "you could take it to the courts. Much luck you've had of 'em! It's not been robbery. It's been work and common sense; that's what it's been. You owned a sand wash forty years ago and ran it down to water. Did that teach you to go out and buy? No; it didn't. You were too lazy; you turned the wrong way and took to contracting. And when you struck a rotten little bank along two years ago you were so dumb blind you thought it was going to last forever. No; I should say I don't want a partnership. Torque is all the partner I need. If you can find any fool big enough to buy without seeing me first, go to it. If you can't, take my price or leave it."

"Mr. Strayton"—that name rang strangely in Torquay's ears; he had scarcely ever heard it before—"Mr. Strayton, I've got a wife and a son and two grandchildren———"

"Yes, you've got all that," interrupted Thomas quickly, "and book learning and fancy blood and the respect of the town and shut-in pews and friends that spit inside their brains when they see the likes of Torque and me and my workmen walk by. You've got all that, and what have we got? I'll tell you. We've got the dirty end of every stick but one, and its name is the Pine Tree Glassworks."

"Tom—Mr. Strayton———"

"I'm through with talking."

The voices passed out of hearing. Torquay waited, but they did not come back. He leaned out of the window, looked around,

and then crossed to the other side of the house. He saw his father
and Mr. Damon already far down the railway track, walking toward
the town. That evening he ate his supper alone, sat around for a
while and then went down to the works. He passed from one shed
to another, staring around, and thinking back to the day when his
father had said, "Never you mind about these sheds; they'll serve
out their turn, and more.". He went into the mold room and looked
at an uncompleted bit of work but was too restless to set his hand
to finishing it. The blowing iron was the thing. He took off his coat
and spelled one of the men at the ring-hole. He caught the rhythm
and held it for an hour; then a strange thing happened. The rhythm
fitted itself to a song:

"I thought it was you, and then I thought it wasn't; but when
you said that, of course I knew."

He left the iron standing upright from a mold, picked up his
coat, stepped out under the starlit sky, stood for a moment and then
started for the house. When he was scarcely halfway across the flats,
something in the pit of blackness beneath the sycamores caught his
eye. It was like a huge white moth. It fluttered toward the house as
if drawn by the light shining from the dining-room window, and
then fluttered back again, to sink with folded wings beside the tree
trunk against which he had all but cracked his skull on the day he
had thought himself a match for his father's strength.

He quickened his pace until he came near to the tree; then slowed
down and approached cautiously. The white object had not moved
again, and it was so slumped into itself that it had no distinguishable
form. He drew closer still, and stopped; he had made out a woman's
flimsy summer dress. It was Janie, with her head hidden in her arms
and her thin back shaking to dry sobs. His hands grew clammy and
sweat sprang out on his forehead, but before he had time to name
the fear that was in him he had called out sharply, "What are you
doing here, and what are you crying about?"

She sprang to her feet and started to run; but he caught her arm
and whirled her around.

"Let me go!"

"No; I'll not let you go. What are you crying about?"

"I'm—I'm not crying."

"You were. I heard you."

"I didn't know about them hating your father."

"What do you mean?" He shook her. "What are you talking about?"

"Oh, please, please don't shake me! I'll—I'll tell you everything. That's what I came for."

He let go her arm and stood beside her while she dried her eyes on a loose bit of her sleeve.

"Those were Jake Damon's children I had with me down at your works. They squalled all the way home because you wouldn't make them flip-flaps. They told where we'd been and about me talking to you. That's when I began to know something was the matter, because everybody shut up, even the children, and looked at me so funny. When Mr. Jake came in and heard about us coming down here, he turned as white as paper and said any nursemaid that was on speaking terms with Torque Strayton wasn't fit to wash dishes, let alone, children. Are you Torquay Strayton?"

"Yes. And who are you?"

"I'm Janie Tilwell. I started to tell them I'd known you since you were a little boy, ever since you came into our kitchen at Babylon to get washed and fed, and how we'd been to school together—only for one day, but we'd been to school together—and then I couldn't."

"Why not?"

"Because I remembered about mother and how she said your father was a bad man, an evil man, and had sold his child to the devil."

"She lied. I guess my father's as good a man as they make and a damn sight better than any blackhearted woman."

"Oh!"

Janie drew back and turned her head as if planning vaguely to escape.

"Aw, go on," said Torquay. "I didn't mean nothing, only you leave my father alone."

"I guess that's right. You wouldn't be good for much if you didn't stick up for your own father."

"What did they do to you?"

"Mr. Jake pushed me out of the door, and when I tried to run back to get my things, he slammed it shut and locked it."

"Why didn't you go home and tell your folks?"

"It's a long way for me to go home."

"Further than Babylon?"

"Oh, yes; much, much further. My father had the Babylon farm on shares; he never owned it, and he never took any good out of it, not even enough to feed and clothe us. They've all gone away, somewhere I've never been. They left me behind because I had the promise of a place at the Damons'."

Torquay's eyes had grown so accustomed to the dark that he could see her face quite clearly. He remembered how that morning it had broken into a shower of smiles, and he thought now that it could surely never do that again, it looked so drawn into a tight knot. They were standing close together as they talked. All nervousness fell from them, leaving behind a faintly palpitating sense of content. It was natural that they should stand thus, close together.

She looked up at him from deep down in a sudden well of peace and her eyes filled to the thought that his face was the most beautiful she had ever seen. Not soft beauty like the pink that goes with babies, but the beauty of a rock with dark shadows lying on it. It was hard and frightened her; if it should come alive, there was nothing it might not have of her. Abruptly, amazingly, the peace within her became turmoil. Now she knew she must run, no matter where. She drew a deep breath and took a step backward, but Torquay's hands shot out and caught her wrists. They were so thin that by tightening his fingers he could have broken them.

"Well," he asked quietly, "why did you come here?"

The level tone of his voice reassured her, even though she thought she could feel the blood beating quickly in his hands; but perhaps that was only her own racing pulse. She hesitated for a moment just the same before she whispered, "Because if you'd only made the flip-flaps it would never have happened. The children knew well enough they were doing wrong to go to your works, but I didn't. If they'd got what they wanted, they'd never have opened their mouths."

"I see. So, it was me lost you your job."

"Oh, no, no. Don't say it like that! I just had to tell someone. I was frightened. I didn't know where to go or what to do. I didn't know anybody in this place, only out in the country, and it was already dark. Even coming here, I was afraid. I would never have called you out. If you hadn't come, I would have lain under the tree until morning and then I'd have gone away."

His brows drew into a knot and his eyes began to smolder as if the slow fires inside him were about to burst into flame. Unconsciously he tightened his hold on her wrists.

"Let me go!" she whispered, panic-stricken, struggling to free her hands.

He released her so suddenly that freedom stunned her, and she stood looking at him stupidly, too dazed to run.

"You got no call to be afraid of me," he sneered.

"Don't be angry," she begged. She came close to him and laid her hand hesitatingly on his arm. "You see, I'm not afraid, only please don't hold me."

"Come with me," he said, shaking off her hand and starting toward the house.

She followed slowly, but stopped at the foot of the steps.

"Where are you going? What do you want me to do?"

He turned and looked down at her.

"I'm going to give you a room to sleep. In the morning, leave it to me to get your things and any pay that's coming to you."

"Oh, Torque, I don't dare! My knees are beating against each other so I can hardly walk."

"All right then, go to hell."

He started on and threw open the door.

"Torque!" she gasped. "Please!"

He waited for her and they entered the house together. A beam of light struck into the hall from the dining room, and at its other end he could see his father's broad back, bent over the table. He started up the stairs noisily.

"Is that you, Torque?"

"Yes," he called back.

"Come here. I got something to tell you."

"In a minute," he answered, keeping on. Janie followed him as silent as a shadow. He glanced over his shoulder and asked loudly, "What are you keeping so quiet for?"

"What's that?" called his father. "I didn't hear it. You come here."

Janie sank against the wall, one hand at her breast, and looked up pleadingly at Torquay. Her eyes had grown enormous; lighting up her face and giving it an unexpected beauty. Her full lips were parted and trembled with tiny vibrations as if they were terrified lest they utter a cry. He shrugged his shoulders and walked on.

It was an old house. At the top of the first flight of stairs there was a platform, leading off on the right to his father's room. Beyond the platform there were four steep steps and a door which opened on a narrow hall, with his own bedroom just within it. He went in, lit the lamp and opened the window at the top. When he turned he saw Janie had followed and was standing in the narrow hall, watching him. He took the key from the bedroom door and handed it to her.

"Go in," he said, "and lock the door after you."

"All right," she whispered.

"I'll wait here till I hear you lock it, and mind you don't open it before morning."

"Why?" she stammered. She was trembling violently; tears welled over her eyelids and splashed down her cheeks. "Torque, if it was just you, I wouldn't be afraid—really I wouldn't."

He pushed her into the room, closed the door and listened until he heard the key turn; then he went down to his father. Thomas was standing by the table, staring toward the hall.

"Who were you talking to? Who's that you've got up in your room?"

"The Damon's nursemaid."

Clouds swept across Thomas Strayton's face. His bushy eyebrows twitched as if someone were pulling the individual hairs. Sparks seemed to snap in his deep-set eyes and his beard moved forward in a mass with the thrust of his lower jaw. Then his whole aspect changed, crumbling into a vacuous expression under the impact of the colossal coolness of his son.

"Your face looks funny," said Torquay, moving toward the table. "What was it you wanted to tell me?"

Thomas put up his hand and pushed the mat of tangled hair from his forehead.

"Oh, nothing much," he said with a short laugh, "coming after your bit of news. I've bought the Damon Glassworks—that's all."

CHAPTER X

TORQUAY felt sorry for his father. He wished he had not over-heard his talk with Mr. Damon and that he could have received with spontaneous astonishment the news that the despised Pine Tree Glassworks had performed the miracle of swallowing something much bigger than itself. Had things happened that way, the glow of his interest might have melted the sudden barrier which had arisen between them through the incident of Janie's arrival and drawn them into mutual understanding. But it was not in his nature to pretend surprise when he felt none, no matter what the advantage.

"I was by the window when you were talking to Mr. Damon," he said as he arranged four chairs in a row, took off the tablecloth and rolled it into a ball for a pillow. "I heard enough to guess he'd have to sell."

"What are you doing?" asked his father.

"Fixing myself a place to sleep," he answered.

"Here?" sneered Thomas. He stood watching Torquay for a moment and then sat down by the corner of the table where he could finger the ledger he had been pouring over when Torquay had seen him from the hallway.

"They've still got a few accounts worth saving," he continued, "but there are a lot more they lost that somehow we didn't get. I'm out for anything now, Torque, small or big. The way this country's moving, you can't tell from one day to another what's going to jump from nothing into a big order."

"That's right," agreed Torquay. "I remember you wouldn't run a batch for Jim Farless, even after I'd made the mold, and look where he is now."

"There's a time to chest your cards," continued his father, "and a time to lay them out. I've been thinking you and me haven't been spending enough money on ourselves, I mean."

"I can't eat more'n I've been eating," said Torquay, "nor wear two suits at a time."

"That needn't stop us from owning half a dozen suites apiece, and a buggy or two, and good horses, with a man to look after them, and perhaps someone to help Mega with the house."

"To help Mega!" repeated Torquay blankly.

It seemed to him the limit of absurdity that Mega should either need or accept help. A silence fell between them. His father appeared to be annoyed, or perhaps only nervous. Did the boy think he could keep the girl with no excuse at all? He ruffled the pages of the ledger, and then arose to walk about the room with short, unnatural steps.

He turned and asked abruptly, "How did you come to bring her here?"

"I didn't," said Torquay. "She come of herself. The first part of it was this morning, when she brought Jake Damon's kids to the works. The second part was when Jake found out what she'd done and threw her out."

"It was a poor day for her to pick to bring any of the Damons to the Pine Tree Glassworks, but where did you come in on it? That's what I'd like to know?"

"She said the kids would never have told where they'd been if I'd made a couple of flip-flaps when they asked for 'em."

Thomas laughed nastily.

"So that was enough for her to hang herself around your neck, eh?"

"No," said Torquay, frowning. "She didn't say anything about it, but perhaps she remembers you owe her father money."

"I owe no man money!" flared Thomas.

"You do. You owe fifty cents for the food we had from the folks in the brick house at Babylon."

It was fully a minute before his father could remember. That far-off day did not stand at the beginning of conscious time to him as it did to Torquay, and yet it was not quite without its red mark.

"Ah!" he exclaimed. "It was the day I showed you about women with the apples. Rotten. Black inside. That's what they are. You got a

Bible in your room because I seen it laying there. Read it. 'Counting one by one, to find out the account . . . one man among a thousand have I found; but a woman among all those have I not found.' That's what it says. Bah!" He took a fifty-cent piece from his pocket with a ten-dollar note and placed them on the cover of the ledger. "There you are. Give that to the girl when you see her—two shillings and interest and tell her where to go."

He stamped out of the room and up the stairs. Torquay got up to blow out the light, and then lay down once more; but he could not sleep. The chairs made a comfortable enough bed, but every time he closed his eyes, they snapped wide open again without his knowing why or when they did it. He could keep them closed only by force, and that tired his eyelids and made his head ache. He arose and sat with his hands thrust in his pockets, staring at nothing. His father was awake too. He could hear him pacing up and down in his room just above. There was a board which creaked regularly, showing that he was walking in the same place each time.

Torquay got to thinking of Janie. He could see everything in his room—the washstand with its ewer and basin, and a fresh towel every day. That was Mega! The cheap rug; the braced table with its load of books; the well-thumbed Bible—strange book to the unguided mind—with its leaves still indented from the wetting they had suffered so many years ago—or was it yesterday? His mind crept around to the bed. He could see Janie lying there, her yellow hair spread out and her face as white as the pillow. If he should split her open with an ax, perhaps she would be black inside—as black as her blue eyes had looked in the dark under the sycamore.

He got up, slipped out quietly and walked around the house. The light was still burning in his room. So she, too, was awake. Perhaps she was sitting on the edge of the bed, just staring as he had been staring. He wanted to call to her, but a lump rose in his throat, squeezing his voice to nothing, and he was afraid to force it for fear of the kind of sound that might come out. If she should come to the window, he would wave to her. He stood still a long time, but the square of light remained a blank. Finally, he went into the house again, closing the door noiselessly behind him. He looked up and saw a light at the top of the stairs. It was his father, standing with his back to him, and holding a candle in one hand. He was dressed only in a short nightgown which showed the figure of a colossus with straddled legs, but his other hand was gripping the jamb of the door that led to the narrow hall as if to keep him from tottering.

Torquay felt a violent tremor, as if he had stepped into charged air. He remembered that to his father, should he look around, he was invisible at the bottom of a black pit. He crouched as if to spring, but changed his mind, drew erect, stood with his back to the front door, his hands spread out against it, and waited and listened. When his father spoke, even though it was in a low voice, he could hear quite clearly, so intense was the silence.

"You there—come out. I know you're awake because I can see the light under the door."

A long pause, and then Janie's voice: "Is it you, Torque?"

"No; it isn't Torque. Torque's asleep. I'm his father, and I want a word with you."

Again, a pause, and then Torquay heard the turning of a key; Janie stepped out from his room fully dressed.

"Oh!" she cried at seeing Thomas in his nightshirt. She shrank back as if to reenter the room, then changed her mind and advanced boldly. "Let me go."

"Listen, lass."

"I want to hear nothing." Her voice rose and half broke. "I'm going; isn't that enough?"

"Hush now! Torque will hear you!"

"What if he does?"

She raised both hands as if to strike Thomas on the chest. He receded until he stood at the top of the main flight of stairs, and she followed him to the platform.

"In there," he whispered hoarsely, nodding his head toward his bedroom.

"No!"

She stooped and tried to dash under the hand in which the candle was upheld. It fell with a clatter and in the darkness Torquay heard the sounds of a struggle and a sob. He went up the stairs so swiftly that he was unconscious of touching the steps. His eyes had measured the distance to his father's ankles and his hands found them unerringly. A surge of strength came into his shoulders and arms; he lifted the feet higher and higher until he could force them over the banisters, then he let them go. As Thomas slid downward he seized spindle and rail, and would have stopped his fall had not the balustrade been old and brittle. It bowed outward, then shivered into a hundred fragments. There was a dull, heavy crash that shook the house.

Torquay felt around blindly for Janie and presently a gasping sob guided him to her. She was crouched on the top step, with her hands and body flattened so tightly against the wall that he could scarcely force his arm around her. He picked her up. Feeling his way with his shoulder, he walked carefully down the stairs and opened the door. A sooty, gray dawn was in the sky, and a billowing blanket of white mist, lying over the flats, caught the light and threw it back, clarified. Janie looked up and a glow of wonder filled her eyes as she recognized his face. Her limbs relaxed and she sank against him with a sigh.

Torquay was amazed at the roundness and the warmth of her body. Up to that moment he had thought of her, if at all, as something cold, fragile and angular. Suddenly he wished he might free his hands to wipe the dripping sweat from his hair, for though she was as light as a feather, she weighed in his arms more heavily than his father's bulk had strained his wrists. And yet he never thought to put her down until she spoke.

"It's you, Torque."

"Yes; it's me."

He stopped to set her on her feet, but she still clung to him, her hands holding to his coat and her body pressed against him.

"I love you, Torque; indeed I do. I love you with all my heart."

"You'd do anything for me, wouldn't you?" he asked coolly.

"Yes; anything."

"Anything at all?"

"For you, Torque, anything."

"I knew it," he muttered.

"What's that?"

"Nothing."

He guided her to the foot of the sycamore and they sat down close together with their backs against its trunk. He held her hand; in spite of looking so thin, it was warm and round like her body. He threw it away from him and she let it lie as it fell. He felt her shrinking into herself as if she were withering. It was too much for him; he took her in his arms and kissed her.

"What was it you said, Torque?"

"When?"

"Just a minute ago."

"Never mind what I said. Are you afraid of my father?"

"Yes; terribly."

"We'll get married in the morning. That will fix him."

"But it's morning now," she stammered, "and I'm shivering with the cold."

"So it is," he said, rising. "You come with me."

He led her over to the glassworks, where his shift was just going on, sat her on a box near the furnace and took his place at the ringhole. One couldn't get married at four in the morning, so there was no sense in losing the working time. Presently a blower glanced at Janie and dared a remark. Torquay twisted his iron free of glass and turned on him with such a ripping gush of curses as she had never heard. The blasphemous words did not offend her ears; instead they started the blood leaping in her veins and made her bosom swell. The blower turned white, glanced at the iron dangling in Torquay's hand and then forced a smile.

"All right, Torque," he interrupted. "You've said enough for me to know I was dead wrong."

Although she had not slept, Janie did not tire of watching Torquay. The ripple of his muscles, the steady flow of all his movements;

above all, the red glare from the furnace, made him appear in her eyes a dark young god forging his own thunderbolts of fire. At eight o'clock he knocked off, and by ten Janie Tilwell had become Mrs. Torquay Strayton. Instead of going back to the works, he crossed the bridge and started up the hill.

"Where are we going, Torque?"

"To get your things."

The Damon place stood well back from the main street of the town on the brow of Lion Hill. At the entrance to the driveway were pillars of Jersey red stone surmounted by two huge balls of devitrified glass. They were freaks of the scum in an underheated furnace and were of an aquamarine color, shading into white. Directly behind the pillars, and almost burying them, rose two thickets of evergreens beyond which the road curved between closely cropped lawns, marked by three century-old shade trees, to the shallow steps of the house, and then around it. The house itself was built of that lost quality of brick which turns to a deeper and deeper red with the passing of the years. Although Torquay had often visited the Damon works in his childhood, he had never before approached the house.

"Not that door," whispered Janie, as he started up the front steps. "Let's go round."

He paid no attention to her, lifted the heavy knocker and let it fall. It was Mr. Burk Damon himself who opened the door.

"What do you want?" he asked, staring at Torquay out of haggard eyes.

"I want Janie's things, and her pay."

"Janie? Who's Janie?"

"Her trunk is on the back porch," called Jake's voice, "with her money in an envelope tied to the handle." Then his face appeared over his father's shoulder. "You! What are you doing here? Get off the place."

"I'm here to get my wife's things," said Torquay, "and if you weren't too white-livered to step out here I'd make you carry them down to the gate."

Jake Damon leaped forward, but his father threw his weight against him and slammed the door. Torquay stood looking at it for a moment, while Janie called, "Oh, Torque, please come! If you don't I'll get the things myself."

Finally he walked around the house with her and shouldered the trunk as if it were empty. It was a quaint receptacle even in those days, with a rounded top and studded arabesques of brass-headed tacks. He hated to carry it through the town and past Striker's, but there was no other way without swimming the river. As they passed through the main street they met not only the tittering crinolined girls of the Misses Kinkheads' school but a carriage, driving close to the curb. The two Damon children were in it, and they jumped up and shouted, "Janie! Janie!" Their mother said sharply, "Be quiet, Gwen! Hush, Robert! That's not Janie. You never saw that girl." And the children began to cry.

"I'll remember it," muttered Torquay between set lips.

"Gwen is nasty, but Robert isn't a bad boy," said Janie, pausing and half turning. "Look! He's really crying for me!"

"Come on," said Torquay roughly.

When they got to the house he set down the trunk in the wrecked hallway and they went in together, to find Thomas half reclining on the chairs Torquay had arranged for a bed. Pillows were at his back, and one great leg was outstretched to the floor. Mega was standing over him, and as she turned to face them her true spirit was unveiled for an instant in a glance like the naked blade of a knife; but Thomas' eyes were serene, almost mocking.

"So, you've come back with a double load of baggage," he said sneeringly—" the trunk and her."

"She's no baggage," said Torquay. "She's my wife."

"Your wife!" bellowed Thomas, struggling in vain to rise.

"Yes, my wife," said Torquay. "If you don't like it say so, and we'll get out."

His father's whole manner changed.

"Torque," he groaned, staring blankly at Janie, "didn't I tell you they're all rotten black inside? Wasn't I going to show you, if you'd

92

only given me a little more time? What the hell did you marry her for?"

"So you wouldn't have to show me," said Torquay; "so I could do the finding out for myself."

"And you will!" cried Thomas. "She'll put horns on your head. She'll leave you for another man when you're least thinking of it."

"Oh," gasped Janie, "how can you say that?"

"Don't listen to her," continued Thomas. "You've done for yourself. She'll fool you, and she'll leave you."

"No, she won't," said Torquay; "not with you and Mega watching her, and me waiting to break her neck. She won't never leave me."

"Torque!" cried Janie, gasping and unheeded. "Of course I won't! I'll never leave you, never!"

"She'll leave you as sure as the sun rises in the east," rumbled Thomas; "as sure as it takes two matches to light a pipe, as sure as the best glass will break against a stone."

Word went out that Thomas Strayton had dislocated his hip and had fought against having a doctor for three days. According to the tale, he had got roaring drunk over buying the Damon Glassworks and had crashed through the railing of the stairway of his own house. At any rate, he was laid up for six weeks, and when at last he appeared he was a changed man; but not altogether in the way one might have expected. It is true he dragged one leg and could walk only with the help of a heavy cane, but these were the least of his alterations.

His shaggy beard was trimmed. He still wore heavy tweed suits, but they were most carefully made to order by a tailor brought all the way from Philadelphia to take his measure. He had sent for a variety of hats and had chosen a hard-felt model, high in the crown and flat on top a style he was never to abandon. There was an excellent custom cobbler in Hopetown and from him he ordered an array of square-toed congress boots, surely the most comfortable footwear ever devised by man, with instructions that they be delivered one pair every six months until the day of his death.

"Or mine, Tom," growled the cobbler.

"Well, anyway, live or die, you can never come over me with a list of all the orders booked ahead of mine."

In that speech there was a touch of the shrewdness which had made Thomas Strayton the man he was; for this same cobbler had kept many a Damon waiting weeks on his pleasure or sloth, but Thomas had spiked his guns at the outset. In addition to matters of mere apparel, he had imported the smartest buggy and the fastest pair of road horses yet seen in Hopetown, which even in that day was saying a great deal, as there was scarcely a farmer in the county who was not as good a judge of horseflesh as of his home-cured pork.

Needless to say, this sudden departure from a stoic mode of life aroused violent comment and some awe. Especially at Striker's drug store, the central pit of the whirlpool of local news, did speculation rise to proportions which threatened to choke an outlet never before utilized to capacity. Was Tom Strayton mad or sane, rich or poor? There were backers for each of the alternatives; there were old-timers who whispered hoarsely of a towering half-wit roaming the roads with a baby on his shoulder, and there were younger men who figured for hours with stubby pencils on possible tonnages of sand at varying prices and declared he must be living and dealing on borrowed money. Even the bankers, who carefully avoided Striker's, puckered their brows and would have liked to know if his record stood as clean on their rivals' books as on their own.

One benefit certainly accrued from all this gossip: The more was curiosity aroused by so picturesque an outward change in a figure which had up to that time been lost in the grimiest background of the town, the more was attention deflected from the mighty yet cruel stroke by which the Damon Glassworks had been brought low, and from Torquay's suspiciously hasty marriage to the Damon's nursemaid. These two events were cataclysmic, one to the life of the community and the other to the structure of a household, and yet they could be all but lost to view in the spectacle of new clothes and a shining buggy and pair.

CHAPTER XI

IN the process of the amalgamation of the two glassworks, Torquay was made a full partner, his father reserving a preponderance of only the one share which would give him the last say in any dispute as to policy. Torquay had no means of realizing how unusual was this procedure. Questions of generosity had never entered into the relations between himself and his father. The very simplicity of the tie which bound them to each other was enough to make them stand out like a monument amid the family and commercial bickering's of their neighbors, and yet they themselves perceived no phenomenon. They seldom talked; they never dissected motives; they simply were as they were for reasons too profoundly established for their own comprehension.

First among these was the rough-hewn wisdom which seems so often to reside in men of large yet well-proportioned frames. Thomas Strayton, with his huge hard body and sledge like fist, might crush or crash, but never pinch. All the gestures of his limbs and mind, however crude, assumed the whole element of space. Just as he could turn on women only to hate them totally, so he could not descend to picayune parings in his dealings with his son. He might throw him over his shoulder at the risk of cracking his skull wide open on the butt of a tree, but he could not tweak him with tweezers or attempt to govern his movements by the childish art of the marionette. Much less could he hold resentment at the turning of the tables which had left him with a dragging leg.

He had his reward in Torquay himself. Half orphaned, cut off from friendships which ordinarily come as a matter of course to people who live for any length of time in one place, and further isolated by the social conditions existing at that period in Hopetown, Torquay had acquired a habit of mind almost as direct as a woodman's ax. Life to him, as to his father, was simply something embedded in the growth of the Pine Tree Glassworks so intimately that there was no room for sentimentalities to squeeze in, either between him and his father, or between them and the sturdy offspring of their handiwork.

Under such conditions, where was the call for gratitude, or even for the open expression of mutual affection? Put to the question whether there was any love between him and his father, Torquay's tongue would have been tied, although he might have hit out instinctively with his fist. He could not have answered even to himself, for he had not the capacity in mental expression to sound the depths of a communion which had its roots fixed in a lifetime of silence.

With the purchase of the Damon interests, he became the general works manager of the combined plants, while his father devoted all his time to the overhead branch of the enterprise. Suddenly Thomas Strayton loomed out as a figure to be counted with in circles which had been to the moment unconscious of his existence; they perceived that he was more than a shrewd dealer, more even than a financier, when the term was still new in the land. He was an indomitable force, rambling ponderously toward an indistinct goal, and it behooved all who were in his way either to get out or travel with him. Cast aside by the wash of his passage, Burk Damon found himself stranded beyond the reach of any helping hand. His spirit broke; he sickened and died.

If the Pine Tree Glassworks symbolized an oak sprung from an acorn, the Damon factory might have been likened to an offshoot from the parent tree of the fine old homestead which stood on the crest of Lion Hill. To some it seemed that the limb had become greater than the trunk, but generations of unbroken tenancy gave the house a dignity which could never be overshadowed by mere bulk. The house faced south and was divided from a pretentious gardener's dwelling of later date by a high row of cedars, matted together, as they had originally been intended for a hedge. Just to the west of this latter house, and still on the Damon property, a road gave access to the works. They were situated on a stretch of leveled ground bordering the river, which, at the time they were founded, had been the only channel of transportation. Needless to say, Thomas Strayton had not failed to buy the right of way to this back road, and the flash of his brightly painted buggy as it passed back and forth four times a day was a frequent reminder of fallen glory to the occupants of the homestead.

For a time, Torquay also used the road, generally accompanying one of the slower vehicles engaged in transferring such materials as could be utilized at the new plant; but soon he procured the right to throw an arched footbridge across the river. He rushed the work on it because, for some reason he could not quite define, he disliked passing so close to the Damon house. It had a way of drawing his eyes against his will, and of distracting his mind from the one thing that mattered to him—the faultless equipment of the remodeled workshop which was his individual responsibility.

Just before the bridge was to be opened an incident occurred that made him regret it had not been finished a day sooner. Jake Damon came out in front of the gardener's house, hatless and with his face flushed from drinking, shook his raised fist and uttered a thick-tongued stream of injuries. Torquay jumped down from the wagon on which he was riding, motioned to the driver to go on, and then stood uncertainly, listening to the almost indistinguishable words. Jake was only two or three years his senior, but at the moment he looked like an old man.

"I don't want to hit you, Jake," said Torquay. "You're drunk."

"What do you mean by calling me Jake?" roared Damon, infuriated, as he rushed forward.

Torquay did not bother to parry his blows. He placed his open hand against Jake's stomach, took a grip on his clothes, lifted him half off the ground and sent him hurtling backward into the cedars as if he were putting a shot. The branches opened to receive the reeling weight; there was a crackling crash, and then they closed again. Jake had fallen in the center of the thicket, with one foot caught higher than his head and his arms hopelessly entangled. He lay there helpless, spluttering with inarticulate rage, while Torquay turned away with a smile as rare as the occasion curling his lips. As he started to go,

Jake's two children came running from the house and their shrill cries and laughter when they found their father playing a quite new game, apparently for their benefit, followed Torquay down the road. It had been no fight, he was thinking, but its sting would last longer than that of any blow.

Up to that day he had had a vague liking for Jake Damon, unexpressed even to himself, which under other circumstances might have grown into friendship, or at least into good-humored rivalry. Jake stood for so many things beside the unforgettable moment of their first childhood encounter. He was the symbol of the old order in Hopetown, the visualization of all that side of life which to Torquay had remained behind a barrier no less real because it was translucent. If it had been a tangible wall Torquay might have tried to break it down. As it was, he had been content to stay on his side, respecting himself and Jake as the outstanding exponents of two brands of pride. But there had been something about the feel of Jake's stomach and his collapse into the cedars which was fundamentally revolting to Torquay. He did not know it, but already his dream of finding the formula for unbreakable glass was setting its mold on his character. He was on the road to applying one test to all things, animate or inanimate: What was unyielding was good; what was soft or fragile was despicable.

Having obtained permission for a footbridge across the river, it required but slight pressure of Thomas Strayton's growing power to procure authorization for a superstructure carrying a conveyor. Immediately thereafter, strongly built sheds, totally unlike the slope-roofed ramshackle makeshifts of the original Pine Tree plant, began going up on the flats which had been bought for a song and were now the most valuable acreage in the vicinity of Hopetown. The railway woke up to its error as well, and offered ten times the price at which it had been bought for the property surrounding the house in which the Straytons still lived.

"What about it, Torque?" asked Thomas. "It'll make them throw in our siding just the way we want it in double-quick order."

"We'd have to move," said Torquay, frowning.

"Pick out anything you like and I'll buy it." Torquay looked up, started to say something, and then changed his mind.

"I say don't sell yet." He paused and frowned again. "I'm not ready to tell you where I'd like to move."

"All right; we'll let them wait. I'll get the siding anyway."

Not all the original Pine Tree plant was destroyed. Torquay kept for himself one shed adjoining the mold room, mounted in it a small continuous tank of modern design and equipped it with a slow-annealing leer and the implements necessary for such tests as he wished to make from time to time. He met all the expenses out of his own pocket, thus gradually acquiring a proprietary right to the entire premises which his father accepted in his usual wordless manner. Here Torquay spent such hours as he could steal from the routine of managing the main works. He would recruit a makeshift crew from the men and boys off duty, always glad of the chance to earn some extra pay, and sometimes worked half the night through.

His father dropped in once a while, generally to talk over some matter of business. He was one of those rare individuals who can be observant without curiosity, and his presence was as natural as the rising of the sun. He had a right to be there; that went without saying; but he assumed no right to trespass inside Torquay's mind. That also went without saying. What Torquay was doing and which way he was headed were his own affair, but by no means of no interest to his father.

Months went by before he said out of a clear sky, "Keep at it, Torque. You know you'll never find it, and then again perhaps you will."

Torquay nodded his head. Without asking a question, his father had deciphered his consuming ambition. Any other man might have grown loquacious, or at least suggested that since the main plant was bound to benefit occasionally by indirection from the experiments, the entire undertaking was chargeable against their joint profit-and-loss account. But Thomas Strayton needed no pilot fish to guide him away from such a needless collision. There was enough of his own boy in him to value rightly the importance to Torquay of an atmosphere of independence. He knew how such an offer, with its emphasis on insignificant details, could bring a chill to the heart of a hidden aspiration. It was this same instinct which had led him to declare so cabalistically his discovery of Torquay's dream, for Janie was crouched on a box nearby, and undoubtedly listening.

She stood out against the drab background of the house, of Mega, of the lurid workshop and of the two men, like a white moth against a black wall; and yet she remained to all intents as invisible as the will-o'-the-wisp upon whose capture Torquay had centered his being. There are personalities which become evident immediately, such as those of the group of three among whom she had been cast; there are others so elusive that they are never seen in the present, but only in retrospect. She was like that. Nobody saw her; nobody would ever see her until she was dead; she could not even see herself.

Everything she had been taught to believe, or had gathered from the little bushes of knowledge within her reach, had turned into withered leaves in that moment when Thomas Strayton had stared at her blankly while he launched his prophecy of her faithlessness, and when Torquay had given his answer, "Not with you and Mega watching her, and me waiting to break her neck." Immediately those words, devoid of love as they were of trust, had become the key-note of her existence. They left her too dazed to struggle, and yet strangely resolute. She was fragile in body and mind, and as lost as a fluff of thistledown on the wind; but in an instant all her frailties were crystallized into a single determination. She would never leave Torquay; nobody and nothing should ever drive her from his side.

She had not had long to wait to put her decision to the test. Nobody called her on the morning after her marriage; she awoke alone in Torquay's room to the sound of a stifled cry. It was her own voice, choked in her throat. She lay in the bed with her teeth chattering, her eyes suddenly wide open and stinging. She fastened them on each bit of furniture, striving to soothe herself with trying to make friends of the chairs, the washstand, the rug, the table. She counted the books on the shelves, the figures in the paper on the wall; she even tried to count the motes in a narrow shaft of sunlight which slanted through one corner of the east window. Finally, she got up and stood for a long time in the center of the floor, with tears pouring down her cheeks silently but so fast that they soaked through her cheap cotton nightdress. The feel of the wet cloth against her breast was startling; it woke her again; but this time into calm realization of where she was and what she must do.

When she came downstairs, she found the living rooms empty and the cleared table looking as neat as if no one had eaten. She realized that Torquay must have gone to his work as usual, come back for breakfast and left again with his father. She was dizzy; her head felt as if it might float off her shoulders; but even if she had connected her faintness with hunger, she would not have dared to call Mega and ask for food. She crossed the floor, sat down on a straight chair by the window, with her hands folded in her lap, and looked out at the warm sunlight. How much better it would be if people could dry up like leaves, be blown down by the wind and toasted by the sun, instead of being buried! Her youth found something to laugh at in the thought, and her lips were twisted into a smile when Mega came into the room, stood by the door and waited ominously for an order. But Janie did not speak; she only turned her face, wiped clean of its smile, and offered it in a sort of surrender to the attack of the colored woman's eyes.

"You'll have to get up earlier if you want breakfast in this house," said Mega, speaking with a deliberation that amounted to insolence.

"I know," stammered Janie, trying to keep her teeth from chattering. "Mother was always angry if we were late for meals. But I don't want anything to eat; I'm sure I can wait."

"Perhaps Mr. Torquay expects you to do the cooking and the washing and the sweeping for nothing, since he married you."

Janie's relaxed body slowly straightened to a thought of hope, and a betraying gleam lit her eyes. If she could work, her fingers to the bone, she would be happy.

"I can do anything he asks me to do," she said quickly. "I'm much stronger than I look."

Mega had read her mind accurately, and immediately changed her manner.

"I guess Mr. Strayton will have something to say as to that," she said rapidly, almost running her words together. "I'll ask him if he wants me to leave."

"You needn't ask him," said Janie, returning to her attitude of surrender. "There's no reason for you to go if you don't want to. You heard what they said yesterday, and you know I'm only something Mr. Torquay brought in with my trunk."

"Well," continued Mega, still speaking with a rapidity which made her a different woman from her usual taciturn self, "if you lift a finger to touch any of my work, I'll go without asking and leave it to Mr. Strayton to fetch me back."

She disappeared but returned presently with a breakfast prepared with all the art of her expert hand. She set it on the table, and without saying a word went out again, closing the door behind her. Janie hesitated, but she could not long resist the food. She ate it to the last morsel, left the table and wandered about the house, at a loss what to do. Her dizziness was quite gone and her returning strength demanded an outlet. Finally, she went up to the room which had been Torquay's and was now hers also in the most intimate sense known to woman. Her lips set in a straight line; here at least, come what might, Mega should not enter. She put everything in order, took some unfinished sewing from her trunk, locked the door and went down to sit by one of the front windows where she could look out across the flats.

Mega went about her work as if the house were empty and in due course climbed the stairs, still without a balustrade, to the second story. Janie heard her go into Thomas Strayton's room and come out after the passage of considerable time; but she listened in vain to hear her try the locked door. She could feel her standing for a moment at the entrance to the narrow hall, divining what another woman would do, and finally accepting the situation without troubling to put out her hand to make sure she had guessed aright. Only thus could she avoid the appearance of acquiescence, leaving it to Janie to wonder whether the room would have been attended even if the door had been left wide open.

Weeks passed, and then months. By spring the work of combining the two plants was finished and Torquay settled to a new routine. From her post at the front window Janie could watch the nearer end of the bridge. Immediately to the south of it came the obstruction of the long line of new sheds, but between them and the pine tree beside the oyster-shell mound there was an open stretch along which ran the path to Torquay's private workshop. When she recognized his swinging figure on this path she would drop her work and run bareheaded across the flats to sit as she had sat through the morning before their marriage on a box set within the warmth of the furnace, and yet out of the way. The first time she came he dropped what he was doing and hurried to her.

"Well, what's happened?"

"Nothing, Torque; nothing at all. Only it's so lonely at the house, I want to sit here and watch you, just like that day. Please let me."

She talked breathlessly, like a child begging for a favor. It gave him a strange feeling to see her standing there and to remember that she was his wife, although sometimes she seemed only half grown up. Her frailty did not appeal to him; on the contrary, it lessened her value in his eyes. She was something so weak that it was actually out of range of a blow.

"Want me to make you a flip-flap?" he asked derisively. She did not answer, but the color rose to her pale cheeks and her lips trembled. "Oh, all right," he continued. "Sure, you can sit around; but you'll soon get over that feeling lonely."

"I'm never lonely when I can see you," said Janie fervently.

In the house as well as in the workshop she learned the secret of immobility, which consists in the power to live within a dream. She could sit for hours with her sewing, or a book fallen in her lap and dream of a changed world. Something would surely happen if only she could wait patiently. Mega might fall dead; she did not wish her to suffer, but she hoped she might die suddenly. She could see herself taking charge of the house, doing all the work so smoothly that Torquay and his father would scarcely know the difference. In that dream her hands would grow moist and her fingers open and shut to the thought of an eggbeater, or a broom, or a knot tied knowingly in apron strings, secure, yet easily undone.

Of course there was the dream of children, nebulous but so profound it was more like a trance than a dream. When it seized her, her own body was transported into realms of the intangible where cries, laughter and faces lived behind floating veils, always threatening to emerge, and sometimes succeeding for a breathless instant. To see a face, and not have time to name it; to tremble at a gurgle, and not feed it; to hear a cry just beyond the reach of hearing; to feel the curl of fingers and toes, and find emptiness against her breast, was not unhappiness. It was a game as old as the human heart, a devourer of untold idle hours, a state of breathing coma that could make four years seem like an unbroken day. She would wake from it to hear Torquay and his father talking about her as if she were not in the room.

Thomas Strayton was sixty-six years old, and his rebellious hair had turned to a gray streaked with steel, while his heavy eyebrows and beard had retained a darker color. He sat in a hideous morris chair, recent acquisition, with his bad leg stretched out interminably into the shadows near the floor and looking as if it scarcely belonged to him. His shirt, made of the finest linen, was pulled open at the throat, displaying a chest almost as matted as his beard. In one hand he held a pipe lightly; the other infolded the curved extremity of the arm of the chair with a suggestion of somnolent power. It seemed to say that the whole house might creak at the stirring of his weight.

Torquay was sitting at the table, his head bowed over technical books and papers spread under the lamp. He was frowning, rumpling his hair, and only occasionally answering his father. Even in the midst of her dreams, Janie's eyes seldom left him. To her he was an anchor, always hidden in impenetrable depths, to which she was held by a chain welded out of her determination to give the lie to Thomas Strayton's prophecy of disloyalty. Far from galling her, this bond was her salvation-something on which she could concentrate all the energies of her waking hours. But she was so occupied with confounding Thomas that sometimes she almost lost sight of the fact that what really held her to Torquay was love in its simplest, most unquestioning form.

"To look at her," Thomas Strayton was saying, "you'd say she was as true as a dog, always following you, always running her eyes after you as if she couldn't bear to let you go. But she'll leave you just the same."

"She can't go so far or so fast but what I can catch up with her," muttered Torquay.

"You can't catch up with a woman," continued Thomas. "I'll tell you why. A woman can travel for weeks and months without moving her body. That's the way they're made. She can leave her body fussing around the house, and all the time she's traveling, getting a start on you before you know she's gone."

"You don't understand," murmured Janie, almost inaudibly.

"That's what they always say," went on Thomas imperturbably; "and it's true. We may understand 'em yesterday, but never today or tomorrow, because they jump in their minds like fleas. She's here, she's there, then she'll be nowhere, and you won't even know which way to look for her. That's the way it will be."

"That's not what I mean," said Janie, twining her fingers and knotting her brows. Her voice fell to a whisper. "I—I love Torque."

"Did you hear that, Torque?" rumbled his father. "She loves you, and I wouldn't wonder but what that's true too. They can love a man steady, until they lay eyes on somebody else."

"I haven't noticed anybody hanging around for her to look at," commented Torquay absently.

"Talk about a dog being faithful," continued Thomas. "He's faithful all right, but never to a bone. Give him a new bone and off he goes, head and tail up, prancing as if he was proud of himself. Women chews on us like we were bones until we lose our flavor. That's the way it will be with her."

"Oh, how can you say that?" cried Janie, echoing the words she had spoken four years before. She was thinking, did four years count for nothing? But she could express the thought only in her tone.

CHAPTER XII

TORQUAY picked up a thick letter from among the papers before him and passed it to his father. "Read that."

Thomas put on his steel-rimmed glasses, hunched himself forward and studied the long letter carefully. For a moment Janie continued intent, then she sank back as she realized they had turned to a matter of business as casually as they had just been discussing herself. Thomas smiled ironically as he returned the letter to Torquay.

"Thinks he's got it all figured out perfect, don't he? You ought to get him down from New York and rub him up against a furnace—a hot one."

"I don't know why it is," said Torquay, frowning, "but there's always a lie in the truest book. This letter, too. He hasn't made a single mistake, and yet you and me knows he's all wrong. I guess the only way to make him quit writing would be to have him down, like you say."

Changes had come upon the house in so offhand a manner that they were as imperceptible as the hourly growth of a tree. Neither Torquay nor his father was mean; what they wanted they bought or ordered others to buy. A bed was a bed, a carpet a carpet, and a table a table, subject only to dimensions; anybody could pick them out. These additions, when they arrived, were not placed according to any strict plan. They were merely left around in locations of momentary convenience. It was as if the two Straytons had either never quite shaken off their nomad habits or looked upon the house in which they had dwelt for fifteen years as a temporary makeshift.

Almost as casually Torquay had one day directed that a large, deserted room at the front of the house be fitted up for himself and Janie. When the work was finished, they had abandoned their old, cramped quarters just as they stood, except that she had moved the books herself, one by one, and then by armfuls. Torquay's little bedroom was thus left fully equipped and was easily made ready to receive the writer of the letter when he arrived some weeks later. He was a young man, Henry Malcolm by name, of slight build and ardent near-sighted eyes.

A careful selection among thousands could not have hit upon a guest more adaptable to the ways of the strange household. He scarcely heard Torquay's half defiant "This is what we have" as he showed him to his room. He did not even bother to answer, but stooped over, opened the larger of his two bags and took out numerous packages of chemicals, examining each before he set it down on the floor. When the bag was quite empty, he put all the parcels back in again and looked up at Torquay with a smile.

"There you are," he said. "I'm ready whenever you are. Nothing is broken or spilled."

"I'm not surprised, the way they're packed and tied and labeled," remarked Torquay.

"When shall we go over to the works?" Torquay smiled, feeling suddenly at his ease.

"Oh, I guess they won't burn down while we have a bite to eat."

At table, Mr. Malcolm was equally matter of fact; he talked knowingly and ate blindly. Janie, shy at first, watched him finally with growing wonder, and almost laughed aloud when twice in succession he put an empty fork in his mouth. Little things like that did not bother Mr. Malcolm; he was merely thinking of something else. He was such a thorough enthusiast that he failed to notice the elder Strayton's almost unbroken silence, accompanied by a look which actually came near to pity. Its only effect was to make him address himself more and more exclusively to Torquay. But sometimes he would seem to feel Janie's limitations and, out of a courtesy as simple as his manner to the men was direct, he would try to avoid technicalities.

"What I say is, if you start right and just keep on adding up the things you know, you simply can't fail to come out the way you're headed. Certain elements have certain properties. That's static, isn't it?

107

In conjunction, they have certain other properties, subject to known laws, and that's mathematical. If you add this and make allowances for that, finally you're bound to get into amalgams, aren't you? And that's where we're going to find what we want, now isn't it?"

"You've got to melt your batch," murmured Torquay.

"Yes, of course," said Mr. Malcolm, half absently. "Oh, yes. But I believe you said we'd get to that immediately after supper."

When it came time for them to go Torquay questioned his father with a nod.

"No," said Thomas . . . "Reckon I'll stay here and keep my eye on Janie."

She had already half risen from her seat to accompany Torquay, but at his father's words she sat down again and stayed quite still for half an hour. Mega came in, cleared the table and went out. Thomas lit his pipe, moved into the morris chair, took off his collar and started to unbutton his shirt. Janie could scarcely remember when she had been left alone with him before. Feeling his ironical gaze fixed on her, she kept her eyes down and tried in vain to lose herself in a dream. Then she picked up a book from the table and read steadily for more than an hour. It was an advanced volume on certain aspects of chemistry, of which she understood no single sentence. Finally, she arose abruptly and made straight for the front door.

"Where are you going?" called Thomas.

She did not answer except to slam the door behind her as she ran down the steps. As soon as she got clear of the trees, she could see the illumination beneath the shed across the flats, red and low like the gleam of a glowworm in the grass. She hurried toward it, entered almost unnoticed and took her usual place on the up-ended box. It was Mr. Malcolm who first paid any attention to her.

"As I was saying just before you came in, Mrs. Strayton," he said, with a quick inclusive gesture, "all this is new to me. I've been tied to theories and a laboratory; but this is real. It's practical, that's the word practical."

Janie could count on the fingers of one hand the occasions on which she had been addressed as Mrs. Strayton. It gave her a delicious tremor of importance and made her regard the young stranger very gravely in an effort to appear adequately dignified. He was rather nice-looking, she thought; not handsome and strong like Torquay, but clean and wiry, and very much alive for all his absent-minded lapses. He seemed more nervous than he had been at suppertime, with much more reason than she was capable of measuring.

For five years he had been slaving over an idea without ever having had a chance to put it to a complete test. So many things had been in the way. He had no means to put up a plant of his own, and not enough influence to persuade a whole glassworks to stop its process for the benefit of his experiments. Besides, he was not such a fool as to trust everyone. In Torquay's private equipment, and in Torquay himself, he had found what seemed to him a miraculous combination of the elements which go to make up a perfect opportunity. While Torquay had been neither talkative nor actively encouraging, he had been recklessly generous.

Malcolm had found at his disposal heaps of soda, lime and silica-glass sand so pure that one could spread it thin on the hand without finding a single discordant speck. In addition, there was a pile of cullet which he was permitted to discard, even though its composition showed no conflict with the formula he was to employ. Finally there was the furnace itself, drained clean before his eyes, and heated to a temperature well above two thousand degrees Fahrenheit. Immediately upon entering the glasshouse and finding everything to his most exacting satisfaction, he had supervised the weighing of all ingredients, adding his chemicals with his own hands, and watched the mixing of the resulting batch. When it had been shoveled through the dog hole into the tank, he had turned to Torquay with a triumphant smile.

"We've done all we can do, haven't we? I can't tell you how grateful I am, Mr. Strayton. Nothing to do now but wait."

The scene was one which Janie, the least interested person present, was never to forget. The shed had a wide-flung, peaked roof, sloping first sharply and then with almost an upward flare to low-hanging eaves—so low that even she was forced to stoop to enter. Directly beneath the peak, a high region where struts, cross braces and rafters lost themselves in shadow, stood the furnace and tank. The two combined formed an oblong structure of imposing size, built of fire brick and carrying an oval roof of the same material. It was so old that it undulated, and in one spot showed a marked depression, called the cap, near which were stacked against a pillar several sheets of zinc. She knew what they were for, because she had once seen them used. If the cap should break men would throw the sheets across the gap to keep the released flames from leaping up and setting the whole superstructure ablaze.

There were no protected corners in the glasshouse, which was cut into a web by unmarked paths and beaten areas, each one of which was immutably dedicated to a certain operation. The spot where she sat seemed exposed, but in reality it was a safe oasis in the midst of intricate operations. From her box she looked straight at the ringhole, the center of interest, and upward at the glowing flares. All about her were scattered the posts of the stokers, the gatherers, the blowers, the carriers-in and the finishers; while to her right stretched the long low line of the annealing oven. Here and there burned a great oil flare, turning the shadows into a dusky radiance which brightened at intervals.

Against this Vulcan background, littered with ladles, blowing irons; skimmers, molds and the marver, moved men stripped to the waist, while others stood around with their coats hung loosely over their shoulders, waiting for the completion of the fritting process. Directly in line with the furnace, Torquay sat on the edge of the marver, his face practically invisible to Janie, even though he wore no hat. Malcolm was too nervous to stick to one spot; he took short turns as he talked, but occasionally stopped to lean against a mold brace on Janie's right. Because he was the only one who said anything, her eyes were naturally fixed on him most of the time; and in spite of his attempts at a casual manner, she could see that he was under a terrific strain. Where everything else seemed tinged with the lurid glow, his thin face stood out unnaturally white. He addressed her quite frequently, and every time he called her Mrs. Strayton she felt an added thrill. Out of sheer gratitude she began to hope that he might not be disappointed in whatever it was that seemed to matter so very much to him.

"Yes; a flexible glass," he told her finally in his pleasantly modulated tones. "A malleable glass, Mrs. Strayton; that's what we're after, and that's what we're going to get."

"Not so much of the 'Mrs. Strayton,' please."

It was Torquay's voice, not raised, but as carefully directed as a blow. Janie heard it with horrible clarity, and so did Malcolm, but no one else. Malcolm's face assumed an expression which under other circumstances would have been ludicrous. Its white expanse opened at the mouth and stayed open while he turned astounded eyes on Janie and then on Torquay. Finally he managed to stammer unbelievingly, "What did you say?"

"I said, not so much of the 'Mrs. Strayton,'" repeated Torquay as distinctly as before. "She don't know what you're talking about, and doesn't want to know."

"Yes; quite so," said Malcolm, regaining his self-control. "I never thought of that. Of course not, but I'm so interested——"

He did not bother to finish the sentence; his lips closed, and from that moment he kept his eyes directed steadily at the ringhole.

Not so with Janie; she did not know where to turn her eyes. For a moment she had been embarrassed and frightened, but now she was neither. She only knew that an event of amazing importance to herself had at last come to pass. Her blood tingled in her veins. Her skin came to life, rippling with minute tremors. Her cheeks grew hot and cold with the surging of her pulse. Torquay loved her. Never before had he told her so, but she knew it now, for his voice had betrayed him. How long had he been watching her, his face hidden in shadow, before he had given way to his outrageous disclosure? What had made him speak like that? She herself had done it merely by looking at a stranger with the sympathy any woman might have felt in her place. Her heart gave a sudden bound and then grew still. She raised her eyes deliberately and fastened them on Malcolm's averted face.

A preternatural stillness pervaded the glasshouse, as if it had fallen under the spell of the immobility of Torquay, Mr. Malcolm and Janie. They were like molded figures cast in bronze, with hot fires still at work within each of their quiescent bodies. Malcolm believed himself to be at the threshold of a victory which would mark an industrial epoch. Janie stood, as on a mountain, looking into the land of her hope; while Torquay struggled with a demon suddenly sprung into life from the slumbering ashes of his father's implacable forebodings. He knew his eyes had gone bloodshot, because Janie's face, turned toward Malcolm, and even her white dress, had taken on the selfsame tinge of red which had bathed the sea, the houses and the cliffs of Cornwall.

Moment by moment, the quiet was becoming surcharged with an uncontrollable current that would laugh at retorts and pyrometers; but the lazy voice of the master shearer forestalled disaster.

"Guess the frit's done, Torque—much as it's ever going to git done."

Malcolm sprang forward as though a spring had been released and stood staring into the incandescent glare of the ringhole. Torquay arose without haste, picked up a blowing iron and handed it to him. But Malcolm did not know what to do with it and gave it back with a pleading smile.

"Please, Mr. Strayton——"

Torquay plunged the iron into the molten glass, twirled and lifted it; then twirled it again. He knew by the feel what had happened, but he kept on automatically and soon brought out a parison big enough to make a carboy. It did not look like melted gold, as it should have done, nor did it flow at the turn of his wrist like strained honey. It was full of knobs and impurities which shot sparks into the air, leaving behind them tiny spines as brittle as icicles. Presently the whole load on the end of the blowing iron lost its glow and became a nondescript, unyielding, discolored mass.

"My God," groaned Malcolm, "what has happened?"

Janie gave an involuntary little cry of commiseration: "Oh! I'm so sorry!"

"Happened!" cried Torquay, enraged at the sound of her voice. He slung the refuse, blower and all, on the cullet heap. "Fire, you poor fool! Your mathematics would have been fine if your chemicals hadn't gone up in smoke two hours ago. You'd better get over to the house and go to bed."

Malcolm needed no urging; he stumbled out of the shed as if the wine of exhilaration he had been drinking so freely had suddenly gone to his head and left him half drunk. Torquay gave rapid orders to the crew which they obeyed almost before the words were out of his mouth, for they all realized the danger that threatened. Should the frit, too heavy to stir, cease to boil, it would harden, and if that happened the whole tank would have to be pulled down. The stokers redoubled their efforts, sending the furnace heat up to three thousand degrees. The blowers took turns ladling at the ringhole while one of the gatherers hurried to open the trap which would permit the molten glass to flow away.

"Watch the cap, there!"

The stokers ceased their work. One of them climbed to the runway and stood by, with a sheet of zinc tilted forward. Janie arose and stood hesitating whether she ought to go or stay. Without turning his head, Torquay saw her.

"Sit down," he ordered.

In half an hour the danger was passed; in ten minutes more, what needed doing was done and the fires were banked. The men picked up their coats and left in a body. Torquay stood quite still until they had gone, and then went out toward the house. For a moment Janie remained where she was, thinking she would force him to call her, but the sudden solitude frightened her. She arose, crossed the shed and stepped out into the darkness of the flats. It was a clear night, spangled with billions of stars, but at first she could see nothing.

"Torque!" she called softly. "Torque!"

He rose before her out of the darkness as though a tuft of the black grass had suddenly grown into a tree. His hands came forward and gripped her shoulders. As the pupils of her eyes dilated to the starlight, his face became minutely visible and she could see the

113

twitching of his eyebrows, his bloodshot eyes, and even how his damp hair was plastered in ringlets on his forehead.

"The first man to come within reach of your eyes, and you never took them off him, did you?"

She did not answer, because she was too happy to speak. All the blood in her body seemed to have come alive for the first time in her life. Veins never before used swelled with a swift flood, racing to join in the mad dance of her senses. He shook her, and still she would not speak. His hands crept slowly along her shoulders toward her throat as he continued hoarsely, "The blackness is in you. I knew it when you said you'd do anything for me, and me not married to you. I know it again now. You're black inside your white body, but nobody ain't ever going to see it, only me."

She could feel his hands forming around her throat like a fork. She lifted her face to his eyes so that the starlight struck full upon it and smiled. Then her knees melted. She sank straight downward, her arms, laced about his body. His hands opened suddenly at the passing touch of her lips. For an instant he stood trembling, then he stooped, picked her up bodily and started for the house. Malcolm had been too distraught to think to close the door. It stood wide open, but was only faintly illumined by the indirect light from the dining room where Thomas Strayton must still be sitting.

"Is that you, Torque?"

Torquay growled an indistinct answer as he kicked the door shut with his foot. Halfway up the stairs Janie stirred in his arms. She had not been unconscious at any moment, even when she had sunk to his feet; but she had kept very still, afraid that the least movement might bring an end to ecstasy. To be held so by the man you loved, to be execrated, to be crushed by arms unconscious of their own strength, was somehow happiness. Joy was like that; it could spring out of such ugly things as cruelty and rage, and in an instant it could drop an iridescent veil between now and years of waiting, between herself today and what she had been on countless yesterdays.

This was a new body, softer, warmer and more pliable than any she had before possessed. She pressed it against Torquay and felt him quiver and shrink even while his arms tautened until they cut into her flesh. She lifted her hands and dared to feel his shoulders. They were like iron, and yet they flickered under the light touch of her fingers as she had seen the withers of a horse flicker under the annoyance of a fly. As he passed into their room she drew herself up and kissed his mouth. Instantly he dropped her feet to the floor and hurled her from him.

"Go to hell!" he roared.

She flung out her arms in an effort to save herself, tripped and reeled backward, but the bed caught her. She fell on it full length and lay there quietly, smiling at the ceiling and listening to Torquay as he shut the door with a crash, locked it and took out the key. "Go to hell!" That was what he had screamed at her mother how many years ago—twenty-five years ago! It was what he had shouted at a circle of tormenting children. It was not a phrase; it was part of himself, part of her childhood and his. It was what had first made him live in her memory so that her unconscious thoughts had grown up around him as a vine may grow up with a tree.

An instant later, a maddened Torquay dwarfed her previous conception of possession into child's play. She caught her breath with a gasp. Her senses threatened to leave her, but she clung to them through sheer determination to miss no drop of the nectar of utter immolation. She was not frightened. She had passed beyond fear into that exaltation where pain and joy become fused, indistinguishable. The thought that Torquay loved her became a blinding illumination, a deafening commotion, and an overwhelming fulfillment.

When she was permitted to come down in the morning, Mr. Malcolm had gone with his two bags, one of them as empty as his heart. But he had left something behind besides his futile chemicals. His innocent and absent-minded presence changed the whole atmosphere of the house. Torquay could knot his brows, Mega could shoot her enigmatic glances and Thomas Strayton mutter his prophecies at their pleasure, for all these things had lost their power to strike a shadow across Janie's face. Against their combined assault she presented a smile as unreadable to the older Strayton as it was maddening to his son. Up to the unforgettable moment in the glasshouse when Torquay had betrayed himself, she had lived in a world apart, barred by a great gate not of her own making. She smiled because Malcolm had given her the key to that gate. She could open and close it at will. She could even admit a partner into those silent mysteries which had once spelled only escape, and now spelled joy.

For weeks Torquay lived in a torment, as blind as to what was the matter with himself as he was to the true nature of his wife. He tended to the supervision of the main plant by fits and starts, doing work in an hour that would ordinarily have consumed a day. To his subordinates, it was as though he were constantly on the eve of a journey or were just returned from a long absence. They had to have everything ready for his consideration at a moment's notice, and a stammering tongue was apt to have to wait twenty-four hours to get in its say. He made frequent trips to the house, pretending even to himself he had forgotten something of importance, and he was relatively happy only during such hours as he spent in his private workshop, with Janie—though a different Janie—sitting nearby on her accustomed box.

The winter, however, brought him peace. In spite of all the seasons which had come and gone since the autumn when first he had felt surprise and seen it in the face of the old house above the flats, he could still stare in amazement at its nakedness, once it shook itself clear of its raiment of summer leaves. It stepped forth, came near, and was easy to watch. Then he had hated its bleakness; but now he welcomed its stark revealment as in their turn he was to welcome the snow, for they seemed to bring with them an assurance of privacy, a sense of embattled seclusion. What a blessing, he thought dumbly, if the obscuring leaves should never sprout again; how wonderful to be perpetually snow-bound and secure! He was even glad that Janie had to incase herself in heavy clothes, for he had grown afraid of the constant evidence of her body. Who but he had a right to know of its suppleness and hidden curves, and who but he had greater need to forget them?

CHAPTER XIII

A S the months slipped by, Torquay resumed gradually the habits of a regular routine, so that the summers, when then came, were robbed of their terror. The Pine Tree Glassworks were growing by leaps and bounds, and demanded more and more of his attention in proportion as his father grew older. Already there was no better-known brand in glass than the simple outline of the lonely tree beside the oyster-shell mound and the very name of Damon was forgotten in that steadily widening world which lived by and for the glass container in every shape, form and quantity—particularly quantity. The Strayton quality went without saying; it was above criticism, and no little part of its excellence was the by-product of Torquay's unceasing research.

As for his consuming ambition to discover a formula for unbreak-able glass, it was as far from realization as on that day when he had first voiced it to the foreman of the Hetney Glassworks and been called a fool for his pains in almost the same words he himself had used years later to Malcolm in the moment of his abysmal failure. Even so, Torquay never wavered in his quest. What is more, it had become such an integral part of his life, it is possible success would have been disastrous to what peace of mind he had attained, so narrow was the pedestal on which circumstances had forced him to rear his entire existence.

There was never a time when he was without a list of combina-tions to be tested out in the trial tank at the abandoned glasshouse; but not satisfied with actual experimentation he had painstakingly acquired a complete collection of all the works extant on the man-ufacture of glass. They seemed amazingly few until he absorbed the fact that here was an industry whose origin was lost in the shadow of prehistoric times, which had certainly continued for twice the lifetime of Christianity, and in all that vast period had developed no basic modification. Where was the room for books? What was there to say which had not been summed up by the pictures of Theban glassmakers at work, painted on the tombs of Beni-Hassan more than two thousand years before Christ?

There had been discoveries and rediscoveries, such as the process of blowing false pearls, resuscitated by Miotti after an interim of centuries. There had been endless variations in color and design, carried to an apex never to be surpassed by the glassworkers of Murano. And, of course, there had been a constant increase in the diversity of uses and applications. In the seventeenth century Louis de Nehou's discovery of a method for founding glass had enabled France to wrest from Venice her long primacy in the manufacture of mirrors. As late as 1824, Robinet had invented his famous pump which did away with the man-power limitation in the size of blown cylinders. Strangely enough, as far as the Pine Tree Glassworks were concerned, not even such developments as these could compare in importance with the advent thirty-three years later of the screw top for glass jars!

But Torquay had no interest whatever in the fantasies of glass-making. He would not have crossed the street to see the flamboyant mirror of Marie de Medici, nor paused half an hour to watch Emile Pilon perform the miracle of blowing a series of artificial eyes, each indistinguishable from the other. He even sneered at the myth that the glassworkers of the sixteenth century acquired patents of nobility automatically, for he had traced its origin to the decrees which permitted impoverished noblemen to trade their daughters, forests, silica and soda for glassware, and sell it without losing caste.

Baron Stiegel came into his mind—William Henry Stiegel of Mannheim, Pennsylvania. The myth had got Stiegel. It was the bug behind his cannons and his ruin. It had led him to imprisonment for debt and the miserable death of a pauper at Charming Forge. That he had turned out every form of glass known to his time, including certain pieces of transcendent beauty, meant little to Torquay. What interested him, aside from the successful operation of the Pine Tree establishment, had nothing whatever to do with airy fancies or mechanical improvements; he was occupied with only one thing.

Composition—the introduction of a basic element which would transform the known nature of glass itself without damaging its transparency—was his sole goal, and he kept his eyes fixed on it with bulldog tenacity. His stubbornness in the face of years of discouragement was alone enough to mark him as a big man; indeed, it was the one factor which saved him from being small. Robbed of education and destitute of every softening social contact, he was like a pruned tree with all its vigor directed to productive ends. Without his ambition, he would have been merely an outstanding exponent of the freshly minted phrase, "captain of industry." But with it, he was much more—something as unreadable and menacing as a black cloud waiting for a stroke of lightning. No one trifled with Torquay—not even his aging father. To argue with him was like trying to come to terms with a sledge hammer.

Under different conditions such a disposition would have invited disaster; but as far as business was concerned everything at that period was in his favor. The demand for the product of the plant continued to grow faster than its capacity could be increased and wage disputes were practically nonexistent. In fact, the Straytons had at one time brought consternation to rival manufacturers in neighboring towns by voluntarily raising their entire scale of pay, ostensibly in celebration of the opening of a new glasshouse. This action had been variously interpreted, but no one had hit upon the simplest of all explanations, summed up by Torquay to his father in the following words:

"We might as well have a call on the best men on the job, and plently of 'em."

To work under the sign of the Pine Tree was to be the cream of a guild, and carried at the same time a still subtler distinction. Torquay and his father were something more than proprietors; they were knitted into the toil they required of everyone under them. Did someone groan at an overload of labor? In answer, there was the derision of the old man's record, the legend and the memory of the days when he did three men's work and asked for more. Did a cry go up against child labor, employed in ever increasing numbers? There was scarcely a grown man on the pay roll who had not watched the birth of Torquay's mighty muscles at that selfsame toil and who could not recall at will the picture of him promoting himself to the post of gatherer at the age of fourteen.

Here in a nutshell was the explanation as to why the flotsam of the working fraternity had fought for a Strayton against a Damon. The Damons marked the passing of the American industrial aristocracy founded by Caspar Wistar in 1739 when he had built the first successful glassworks of the Colonies. A century and a half had seen Wistarberg change its name to Allowaystown and later to Alloway. Not ten years before Torquay had visited the spot only twenty miles away where a crumbling log house beneath a splendid sycamore marked the site of Wistar's once triumphant enterprise.

What had happened was a revolution actually more profound than the breaking away of the colonies from their mother country—a movement so knitted into the fibers of a new national entity that it had changed the natures of men while they slept, for who will dare say that either the Straytons or their workmen knew what they were about?

The fact remains that in 1750 Wistar was turning out not only window glass; lamp chimneys and many kinds of bottles but was making exquisite bowls, dishes, pitchers and canisters; mustard and sweetmeat containers, preserve jars and a vast variety of other objects, many of them excelling in two-color work. A century later a terrific blight fell upon beauty throughout the United States. It wiped out the artisan and substituted the piece-worker. It destroyed taste to such an extent that virtually every house built in the following fifty years remains to this day as an eyesore and a witness to the astonishing reach of the pestilence. It introduced quantity production, factory-made window sashes and democracy. It booted the laborer several rungs up the social ladder at the price of reducing his handiwork to the dead level of a commodity.

But when all is said, what consolidated the position of the Straytons and softened the brutality of Torquay's disposition was a fundamental truth too often lost to view, and consisting in the fact that every enterprise, however vast, stays human as long as its government remains in hands which have mixed real sweat with the sweat of their help, and no longer. The other side of the shield was that Torquay at forty years old was as embedded in his ways as the core of granite in a hill, and his father at seventy-nine already carried that suggestion of arrested age which gives grandeur to a ruin. He was a burned-out furnace; a mere shell, but a mighty shell which, put to the ear, still reverberated with the roar of unforgotten fires.

Looking back over the years that had intervened since the moment of torment when he had wished winter might never pass, Torquay's ascent to power would have represented the steady progress of a steam roller had it not been for certain violent interruptions which at long intervals had all but shaken the fabric of his inner life to pieces. The first of these explosions occurred two years to a day after Malcolm's visit. Janie was sitting by the window of their room looking out, her face washed white by a shaft of moonlight; Torquay was in bed, trying to go to sleep, but kept awake by her immobility. He told himself that if she would only move or make a sound he could fall asleep. But she did not move, unless the slow forming of a smile could be called a motion.

"What are you doing?" he asked at last. "Why don't you come to bed?"

"I was thinking of Mr. Malcolm and wondering if you've never heard from him."

It was as if a bomb had burst the silence asunder. Hours later, long after she was sound asleep at his side, he was still awake, trembling over what had happened and what had come near to happening. Running headlong against unexpected daring in her spirit, he had forgotten for a terrible instant the frailty of her body in comparison with his own strength. He could feel the blood mounting through his neck to his cheeks in an access of shame, and then retreating to leave him cold, held in the grip of unadulterated fear. He who all his life had been afraid of no man knew what it was to feel terror of an unseen enemy within himself.

121

And yet a few months was enough to calm him to the point of letting her make a long journey alone to see her mother. It had never entered her head to attempt to bring any of her family into her married life, so forbidding from the start had been the atmosphere of the Strayton caravansery. But she had written laconic letters from time to time, hiding more than they revealed, and now came word that her mother was ill and wished to see her. She was gone for four weeks and when she came back she was dressed in mourning. Torquay questioned her only with a glance and she said her mother had died. She did not try to talk about it; she seemed to know she had returned to a world where her mother had never lived, where even to herself her distant people had grown to be unreal. Torquay was glad of her black clothes and the grief they represented. They seemed to hold her in shadow and to lend her a soothing personality. But no sooner had he got accustomed to them than she tore their comfort to shreds, and that in the presence of his father. As on the night of the discussion of Malcolm's cursed letter, they were sitting silently about the lamp when Janie spoke. It was seldom she said anything unprovoked and the men's ears were instantly alert at the sound of her voice.

"I saw a man looked so much like Mr. Malcolm while I was away I spoke to him."

Torquay was struck dumb, but his father's deep eyes gleamed and he licked his lips.

"Spoke to him, eh?"

"Yes," said Janie, staring at nothing in particular. "Was it Mr. Malcolm?"

"No; he said his name was Robbins, but he wished it was Malcolm."

"Ha!" laughed Thomas shortly.

"Spoke to a man she didn't even know! There's only one thing to do, Torque. Take off one of her legs or she'll sure run away."

Torquay flung his pen down so violently that ink splattered from it and a little drop fell on the back of Janie's hand. She stared at it and so did he; never had ink seemed so black or hand so white.

"I'll have to go up and wash that off," she said rising.

He almost cried out after her, "Fool, don't go upstairs!" But instead he arose and started to follow her. With one hand on the newel post, he wrenched himself around, plunged through the front door and ran along the flats toward the upper reaches of the river. He stumbled for miles in the darkness, taking pleasure in feeling the branches lash across his face. The smart took him out of himself and finally calmed him by carrying him back to the beginning of memory when he had ridden the roads on his father's shoulder.

Ever since he had started watching her, Janie had been less sure to run across to his private workshop whenever she saw his figure stepping off the bridge and then striding along the path to the oyster-shell mound. But there came a day when she wished she had not sat still at her window. Her eyes stared at something they had never before seen on that path-a well-dressed woman, picking her way carefully as if every mud puddle were a bottomless pit, and leading a child. It was too far away to recognize more than that she was no workman's wife. As she disappeared into the glasshouse, Janie arose swiftly and stood trembling, one hand holding to the back of the chair and the other raised to her throat.

She was frightened at the suddenness with which her sense of well-being had turned into a distress that threatened to suffocate her. She started toward the door, thinking she would run across the flats as fast as her legs could carry her; but stopped and turned, flushing with the thought of the shame which would overcome her at breaking in on Torquay and the stranger. She sat down again, her hands locked together, and remembered that in all the years of their marriage he had never looked at another woman. Suddenly she realized that what she was now feeling he must have felt with much more reason every time she had made deliberate allusion to Mr. Malcolm. She had been wicked; she had tormented him to feed her own emotions. It would serve her right— She began to cry, but she would have been comforted could she have seen the surprise in Torquay's face as he greeted Mrs. Jake Damon.

She was a woman of about his own age, thin and angular in appearance and gesture, but with a spirited face and of excellent carriage. Rumor had it that her wit had once been as sharp as her elbows, but years of battling with a drunken husband and crumbling fortunes had long since blunted her tongue and brought a twitching affection to her mouth which forced her to limited and deliberate speech.

"I went to see your father on a matter of business and he referred me to you."

Torquay led her into the mold room where he had fitted up one corner with a desk and two chairs. Although they had doubtless passed each other many times on the streets since that day when he had been carrying Janie's trunk on his shoulder, and she had cried out to her children, "That's not Janie; you never saw that girl!" he could not remember consciously to have seen her. Now she was so changed as to seem another woman and he found it quite impossible to resurrect the rage he had then felt. He motioned her to a chair and seated her child, a boy of four, on a box at her side.

"What can I do for you?" he asked.

"That's the classical opening, isn't it?" she said slowly, as if forcing herself to feel at ease. "Well, I'm going to surprise you; I'm going to tell you at once what you can do for me. You can buy the Damon house on Lion Hill."

It was beyond Torquay's power to avoid betraying how well she had succeeded in startling him. An involuntary smile lit up his heavy face for an instant, making it almost boyish, and then a frown as suddenly clouded his brows.

"You have surprised me," he said quietly. "How much do you want for it?"

"There's a mortgage of five thousand. I want eight thousand over and above the mortgage, and excluding the gardener's house."

He thought for some time before he spoke again.

"Excluding the gardener's house?"

"Yes; we must have some place to live." His frown deepened and she went on. "It's quite large enough, now that Gwen is married and Robert at college. He'll hardly want to come back here."

That she could speak thus familiarly of her children had a strange effect on Torquay. She might have said "My daughter and my son," but she had not, perhaps even to her own surprise. It was as though her instinct had recognized not only a situation in which she was perforce a suppliant but a common ground where two minds of unusual directness had chanced to meet.

"I shouldn't think Jake would stand for it," said Torquay presently, thinking aloud.

"Jake has nothing to do with the arrangement," continued Mrs. Damon with a sudden twitching of the corners of her mouth that forced her to pause. "His father lived long enough to leave the property completely in my hands."

There was a long silence before she went on in so easy a manner that she did not seem to be presenting an argument:

"The gardener's house stands on a triangle of land by itself, cut off from the main house by the cedars. I should wish to own the cedars. You would scarcely know we were your neighbors."

A sardonic curve came to Torquay's lips at those words and he flashed a look at her as if he had caught her in a slip, but her eyes met his unwaveringly. She had inferred that no money could buy him past those cedars and she did not retract.

"Thirteen thousand dollars is a lot of, money in this town," he said finally.

"The land alone would soon be worth that, if I could wait," she answered; "but you and I are probably the only ones who realize it. It's something else that's bothering you."

"What do you mean?" he asked, frankly startled.

"I mean you're not worrying about the price."

He laid his hands on the desk before him in a gesture which seemed to suggest both strength and surrender. She knew at once that whatever he might say would be as final as doomsday.

"You're right," he said. "If you will move out with nothing but your distinctly personal effects and leave the house as it stands, I will give you twenty thousand dollars in cash, over and above the mortgage."

"So that's it," she said quickly, wincing in her turn from the blow, and then settling back to think, her thin hands locked on her knees. The child on the box grew restless, climbed down and went to her.

"I want to go now," he declared.

She brushed him aside. "Don't Ralph; don't bother mother."

He left her, stared at Torquay speculatively for a moment, and then approached him boldly. Strangely enough, though a late comer and born under conditions which are supposed seriously to handicap offspring, he was in every regard the finest of the three Damon children. It was as though the banked fires of motherhood, overcoming every weaker factor, had molded an image of Eloise Damon's individual aspiration rather than the chance product of a partnership. Ralph was sturdy, straightforward, good to look at—the embodiment of his mother's spirit and the darling of her heart.

He laid his hand on Torquay's rock-like knee and looked up expectantly; but Torquay did not meet his glance, nor did the knee show any signs of life. Ralph started on a tour of the mold room. He found a crank and turned it; nothing exciting happened. He came on a clay die left to set in a box and dragged it toward him. It fell with a crash from the workbench, narrowly missing his toes, and the clay scattered over the floor in fragments. He looked around with a gasp, his mouth wide open, ready to bawl his grief if grief were necessary; but neither the big man at the desk nor his mother had moved.

Her brows were drawn so closely together that only a deep line separated them. She was going over in her mind, one by one, all the treasures which generations of Damons had gathered about them and that now Torquay, the son of Thomas Strayton—heaven save the mark!—proposed to take over wholesale. Then she began to think of all the things she had always hated, of accumulations of years on end of gifts, of bundles of rubbish awaiting in the huge attic the era of the rummage sale. As she thought on these her frown gradually smoothed out and was replaced by a very small but indubitably wicked smile.

"You have bought the Damon place," she said, rising. "What do you consider distinctly personal effects?"

"I leave that entirely to your sense of honor," replied Torquay promptly.

She nodded—"Because you know it would coincide with your own."

On those words she went out, dragging the now reluctant Ralph with her and without bothering to make formal apology for the damage he had done. A direct woman, thought Torquay, a woman almost too thin to hold a black core. You couldn't break open a strip of rawhide, or even smash it. He had a strange feeling that he had been talking not only to a man but to his equal. She had not offered to shake hands on their bargain, and yet there had been no pointed omission, no awkward jar, for her parting words had contained all the implications of a handclasp. He was still Torquay Strayton, the upstart; and she still Eloise Damon, the essence of a passing age. But she could recognize a point of coincidence with a casualness which amounted almost to the acknowledgment of a bond.

The purchase of the Damon Glassworks seventeen years before by Thomas Strayton had been sudden enough in all conscience; but the clamor it had aroused was a mere chirp in comparison with the clacking of tongues which broke forth when it became known that between the rising and the setting of one day's sun, what was left of the Damon family had moved into their gardener's cottage and the entire Strayton establishment into the imposing mansion on Lion Hill.

The lawyers who attended to the details of the transaction had kept their mouths barred even against the temptation of the conjugal ear, and the peculiar terms had made a mock of the old saying that three movings equal a fire. Just as the Damons left behind them all the trappings of a tenure of generations, so did the Straytons abandon, lock, stock, and barrel, the fixtures and miserable sticks of furniture which for so long had cluttered the house overlooking the flats. Up to the moment of their desertion, the haphazard arrangement of these crude household effects had seemed unreasonable; but now it assumed a deep meaning. It seemed as if years of disorder had been pointing with a rigid finger at this day and hour.

Mega arrived ahead, with Jim Balden, Thomas' coachman, and the trunks. She accepted the change with sardonic silence, tinged to the verge of betrayal with joy upon beholding the glories of the new kitchen. But Janie had not been able to repress a cry as the buggy into which she, Torquay and his father were crowded turned in at the familiar gate she had never passed since the day of her marriage. Struck too deeply with the humor of the situation to weaken its flavor with words, Torquay had merely told her to pack all her things for a journey. Of course she guessed they were moving, and even that they were abandoning everything except their clothes, but nothing had been said which might arouse a suspicion that she was going back as a nominal mistress to the house she had left in disgrace as a nursemaid.

On the evening of the day Eloise Damon had made her call, Thomas Strayton had raised one bushy eyebrow to Torquay across the table and Torquay had nodded his head; not a word was said. The old man had not bothered to ask the price of the purchase then or later. Money had never held any absorbing interest for him and lately it had become such a nuisance to trouble with it that Torquay wrote all the checks and kept his father supplied with cash as perfunctorily as an indulgent uncle might keep his nephew in funds.

Though neither of them ever hinted at it, the truth was that Thomas Strayton had become a figurehead and was rapidly approaching the point where a pipe and a bench in the sun would represent all that money could buy. One thing alone bothered him—he wanted to live long enough to see his prophecy fulfilled in regard to Janie. If he prayed at all it was to ask that she might prove faithless before he died.

He must, however, have felt some deep emotion when Torquay stopped the horses at the front door of the Damon house. Under that portico Burk Damon had come out early one morning in answer to the summons of a complete stranger. It was beneath these old trees that he and Burk had walked, stood and talked, master and workman. Here they had closed the first deal whereby Thomas Strayton was to supply sand to the Damon Glassworks. What had intervened between that day and this? An era; everything and nothing. Where was the victory unless he could stand as he had stood on that day with the blood chugging in his veins like the engine in a tugboat and his huge hands itching to get back to three men's work?

He stepped out of the buggy as if he were a young man—a well man. His stick clattered to the ground. His bad leg sank under him and he would have fallen flat if Janie had not thrown her arms around him and supported him in a grotesque position, one knee on the ground, the other leg straggled out to one side. Torquay leaped down so suddenly that the horses took fright and bolted. A moment later came the sound of the buggy smashing to splinters on one of the stone pillars of the gateway, but none of the three heard it.

"Torque!" bellowed the old man. "God damn that leg! Put it under me again."

Mega and Jim came running from within the house to help carry Thomas to the room that had once been Burk Damon's. They laid him on the great mahogany bed, propped him high on the pillows and straightened him out. He asked for his stick, and when it was brought to him, before anyone could guess what he meant to do, he hit his bad leg a tremendous blow.

"What are you doing?" cried Torquay angrily.

"It's all right," said the old man quietly as he laid the stick aside. "I just wanted to make sure the thing was there, and it isn't."

To his other ills he had added a broken ankle. The doctors speculated as to whether the fracture would ever knit and within a few days he became a subject of closer human interest than in all the years he had passed in Hopetown. Mega acquired a helper of her own choosing and nurses followed each other in rapid succession, for he was still an enormously heavy man and otherwise mean to handle. But at last came Miss Ball, and from the moment she entered the room he was content. He saw that here was a woman who could give him a fight any time he wanted it, even if he should get back the use of his withered leg. Within two days she rang for Mega for twenty minutes on end. At last the colored woman flung open the door and came in, her face gray with anger.

"The girl's out; what do you want?" she asked with measured insolence, her glaring eyes fastened banefully on Miss Ball.

"I'll tell you what I want in a minute; but first let me say this: You're a colored woman, a servant, and you're growing old fast. You've had an easy time in this family and you can keep on having it to the end of your life if you answer that bell as fast as your legs will carry you. If you don't I'll throw you out myself and your rags after you."

"Did you hear her, Mr. Strayton?" whispered Mega. Her voice was as sibilant as the sharpening of a knife on a stone.

"I did," gasped Thomas, shaken with Herculean mirth, "and I guess you did too."

"Well," said Miss Ball sharply, "will you stay or won't you?"

A long pause, and then Mega answered quietly, "I'll stay, Miss Ball."

There was another who had heard. Attracted by the violent ringing of the bell, Janie had slipped out of her room and stood listening. She saw Mega come out walking very erect but with the blank look of a somnambulist in her once baleful eyes.

"Oh!" thought Janie with a sharp constriction of her throat. "Why couldn't I have done that long ago?" But it never entered her head to serve Miss Ball as Miss Ball had served Mega.

The big house had produced a strange effect on her. She knew all its rooms and they had remained so unchanged that she remembered them as if she had been absent only for a day. And yet she was more than a stranger; she was an interloper. She flitted from apartment to apartment and from floor to floor like a wraith. She would take up some lovely book to read and sink into a comfortable chair. Presently she would hear Gwen scream in a tantrum or Robert cry out with pain. She could even imagine Mrs. Jake Damon entering in the glory of her trim bonnet and tight bodice above an ocean of billowing skirts, to stand transfixed at finding her sitting in that chair. She could hear her amazed yet modulated voice—"Why, Janie, you seem very much at home. Did you think you were in a lunatic asylum?"

That's the sort of thing she would have said, thought Janie, up on her feet without knowing how she got there, her legs trembling and the book fallen from her lap to the floor. She forgot she was a woman almost forty years old. Indeed, she looked like a girl as she ran up the stairs to what had once been the nursery, and then higher and higher until she climbed into the attic.

She had gone there to cry in the first fit of homesickness she had ever known. The attic, too, was unchanged. She looked hopefully toward a corner, where a huge bag made of ticking into which generations of Damons had been wont to thrust discarded costumes had half stood and half hung from a low rafter. It was still there. As on that other day, she ran to it, to her knees and threw her arms around it.

CHAPTER XIV

WHEN the shutters were closed at the old Damon place on Lion Hill everyone jumped to the conclusion that Thomas Strayton was at last dead. Even before the undertaker's rig, bound on a preliminary call to make arrangements, had turned in between the two red stone pillars which supported the huge balls of half-baked glass, the news had reached Striker's drug store, the heart of the city.

"I thought so," said Chet Griswold. "When I seen Bert Blakeley dressed up in his black hat and Prince Albert, I could tell by his smile he hadn't no pauper funeral on his mind."

"Well, if it's really Thomas is dead," said Ed Bristol thoughtfully, "I can tell you where he's gone."

"So can I."

"Me, too!"

"You're all wrong," resumed Ed testily, "Quick guessers generally is wrong. Where he's gone is to pick on Burk Damon. If Burk went to heaven, that's where Tom has arranged to go—at least for a spell."

They all laughed.

"I guess he'll get back as good as he sends, wherever they come up with each other."

The talk continued in this strain for half an hour, and then came to a stop so abruptly that the silence was almost as violent as a thunderclap. Nobody had had time to call the attention of anybody else to what all saw simultaneously through the large show window which was never used to display goods to an extent that would obstruct the view.

Bert Blakeley, returning from his preliminary professional call, was driving by and beside him sat Thomas Strayton himself. He had been laid up for a long while, and yet no one had ever spoken of him as an invalid, perhaps because the public mind had a premonition that when he was thought dead he would do some such stunt as this.

The old man was looking particularly spruce in spite of the loose hang of his rough tweeds and the age of his flat-topped hard felt hat. With these long-familiar objects as an index, it was easy to remember his square toed congress boots and his frosty blue eye—no frostier, however, than the foam of snow-white whiskers which covered his chin and jaws, increasing the redness of his cheek bones.

Theirs was no surface color. It glowed from deep beneath the skin as if it had been burned in, annealed, and then glazed. At the moment of passing, his shoulders were squared and his hands folded over the head of his stout stick—more of a club than a cane. He knew quite well that the group of men in Striker's would be talking about him; he even knew what they had inevitably thought and had just been saying. It was for no other reason that he had forced Miss Ball to dress him early in his best attire and had sat waiting for a long hour, ready to accompany Bert Blakeley back through town.

"See 'em, Bert?" he murmured through tightly held lips. "They thought it was me that was dead. That's what they thought."

"You fooled 'em again, Tom," agreed Mr. Blakeley cheerfully.

There was no note of hope long deferred in his voice. He was thinking the old man couldn't last forever for all his bluster, and that the totally unexpected demise in the big house on Lion Hill had been something in the nature of a windfall to the Blakeley establishment; almost in the class of unearned increment. Over and above that, it contained such a titbit of news as seldom drops in the path of even the most select undertaker. So this was why nobody had seen Janie Tilwell for five months. Eighteen years married, and then this. Though she had been Mrs. Torquay Strayton for all that time, he still thought of her as Janie Tilwell.

Black clouds were piling up in the west and then sweeping in an even gray blanket high over the town. While the buggy was headed east Mr. Blakeley did not notice the advancing storm; but upon turning to approach his establishment through Dean Street he was startled to find it almost upon them. "I got no curtains, Tom. I guess we'd better head straight back for your place."

"What for?" demanded Thomas. "Do you think a little rain can hurt me?"

"Yes, I do," said Bert frankly. "I've seen it hurt stronger and younger men than you."

"You never knew a stronger man than I am," said Thomas, and from the waist up he was telling the truth. "I could throw you out of this buggy with one hand."

"I know you could," agreed Bert hastily "but——"

He closed his mouth and eyes instinctively as a wall of dust, twigs, bits of shingles, leaves, branches, and even small pebbles swept down upon them. The horses reared and plunged until a deluge of rain steadied them with its familiar feel. In a moment both he and Thomas were soaked to the knees and the cushion on which they sat was rapidly becoming a puddle.

"Jump out!" shouted Ed. "Get into the office."

"I can't jump out, you fool," growled Thomas, "and it would take four of you to lift me. Take me home."

It was all Bert could do to turn the nervous horses in the narrow space, but once he had succeeded he gave them their heads. As they tore up Main Street in the teeth of the storm the rain drove into the buggy in a solid mass and drenched its occupants from head to foot. Cold to the marrow of his bones, his teeth rattling in spite of all he could do, Thomas was lifted out and carried to his room. A mustard bath, followed by a steaming toddy of double strength, hot water bottles and three blankets topped by a down quilt soon restored him to the point of absolute comfort. But the core of strength within his great frame was broken and he knew it. When the others had left the room he motioned to Torquay to remain.

Torquay was just coming out of a daze. Never had he received such a numbing blow as Janie's death in childbirth; not even on that day when his father had swung him off his feet and knocked him unconscious against the sycamore tree. Of course he had known of her condition, but only vaguely. Suspicion had scarcely hardened into conviction. In a manner of speaking he had deliberately put off knowing about how it was with her, yielding to a false shame. Ostrich-like he had hidden his head and fooled himself into thinking the planets would stand still in their courses while he kept his eyes shut.

She herself had done much to blind him to the passing of the days. Only in that house where everyone, servants and masters alike, minded their own business in a state of perennial silence, could Janie, unnoticed, have gone about her amateurish preparations for an event which should usher in the apotheosis of all her daily visions.

Totally ignorant of the danger she was incurring, and unconscious of one of the commonest of the phenomena of human life, she looked upon her delayed fertility as manna sent from heaven in answer to her prayers. Her attitude before the miracle was a pitiful mixture of childishness and sublime mysticism. By a single stroke she was to be lifted out of nonentity into prominence. In the small world which had all but ignored her presence, she was to be raised on a pinnacle whence she could look down disdainfully on Mega, Miss Ball, and even on the terrible Thomas. Torque himself must at last step out from the shadow of a lifetime of confused misconception and behold her crowned as the mother of his child. She was going to surprise everybody as thoroughly as mysterious forces had surprised herself.

These thoughts, strongly tinged with the simplest elements of revenge, came first; but they were succeeded by others which raised her bodily out of the plane of vindication into the rarified atmosphere of a living dream. More than ever she became an unseen person, withdrawn into herself and wrapped in absolute comfort and an indescribable sense of peace. It had been easy to stay out of Torquay's way, for since the day she had seen Mrs. Jake going to his workshop and had realized what he had suffered from her allusions to Malcolm, she had refrained from arousing him.

Inevitably Miss Ball had suspected the truth, but all her experience had not been enough to warn her of the imminence of the event. She resented what she took for reticence in Torquay and regarded Janie's secretiveness with scorn. Let them put it off as long as they dared, they would both have to come running to her in the end. It never entered her head that these people, outwardly so mature, were as ignorant as two children throwing stones at a landslide.

Perhaps the greatest single factor in Janie's utter content during those secretive days was the change which appeared to her to have come over the house. From the moment she knew she was going to have a baby it had become her friend. Whenever she wandered through its quiet rooms, wherever she sank down to rest or to work in secret on small articles of wear, it seemed to put its arms around her. She was no longer a stranger, an interloper; she was a possession. It owned her as some day her child would own every corner of its vast extent. She could not look anywhere without seeing a baby crawling, drawing itself erect on table leg or chair, learning to walk, crowing with delight and occasionally weeping at a fall. The house seemed to be looking forward to the coming of a child as definitely as herself.

When Miss Ball awoke with a shock to the true state of affairs her monumental efficiency was shaken to its bases. For an instant she stood aghast before the evidences of Janie's abysmal ignorance and Torquay's stunned amazement. She recovered promptly and threw all her expert forces into action, summoning to their support the best surgical assistance available. But events moved too swiftly for artifice to keep up with them or for Torquay to be posted as to what was happening. He was still blundering hopelessly in his mind over the news that the moment of fatherhood was actually upon him when Miss Ball hurried out in search of him.

"You'll have just a moment with her, Mr. Torquay."

"What?" he asked stupidly.

"Come quickly if you want to see your wife before she goes."

"Goes where?" he asked, frowning; but he followed her.

Janie had always been pale, but now she was white to the verge of transparency. One glance was enough to tell him he was looking on a body drained of blood. Her blue eyes were huge, dark and strange. As they fell on him, standing awkwardly beside the bed, a smile curved her lips into familiar outline and brought back a face he knew.

"Good-bye, Torque."

There was no mistaking that voice; it came from beyond the world.

"No!" shouted Torquay hoarsely. Rage and terror came to grips in his mind, stirring it into a turgid whirlpool. "Janie, wait a minute! Don't leave me!"

He stood staring blindly at the place where she had been until one of the doctors came into the room and led him out. He walked in a trance, started up to the third story and stopped halfway, with his hand on the banister rail. He shook it to see if it was strong, his brain leaping back to the night when his father had crashed through the balustrade at the old house. That was the moment when he had first taken Janie in his arms and fallen beneath the insidious spell of her body. He remembered how he had carried her out beneath the trees and he frowned at the sudden sound of her voice—"I love you, Torque; indeed I do. I'd do anything for you—anything." He turned and went slowly down the stairs and out through the front door. He could see himself standing there, with Janie behind him, asking Burk Damon for her things, challenging Jake to step out.

He walked around to the side of the house as if he were looking for Janie's trunk. Miss Ball came to him and talked rapidly for several minutes, stopping abruptly when she realized he heard not a word she said. He saw her run down to the stables and almost immediately, it seemed to him, she was in a buggy with Jim driving Thomas' best team at their fastest clip. He was no good to anyone and it never occurred to him there were certain things, never attended to before, which demanded his immediate decision. Mega brought one of the doctors out to see him and after a moment the doctor went back into the house and assumed Torquay's duties.

Torquay was not overwhelmed with grief or choked with regrets. He was simply stunned and lost like a man staggering from a blow delivered by an unseen hand. He knew something radical had happened that made him feel as if his body had been terribly beaten, tangling all his emotions with broken bones; and because he could not give it a name, he was filled with a smoldering rage. That he could not centralize his anger on Janie or his father or himself made it all the worse. All he knew was that some hidden force had dealt with him so foully that he could neither speak, move nor think, and was consequently barred from going about the business of living in his ordinary direct way. It was outrageous that he should have come to such a pass when he had never meddled in anyone's affairs but his own.

He continued in this mood for hours, wandering about the garden or the house and occasionally going to the edge of the hill where he could look down on the spreading plant of the glassworks as well as on his private shop. He wanted to get back to work, and yet he dared not go. What would he do? How would he give an order? He saw his father being helped into Bert Blakeley's buggy and felt as little surprise as if the old man had not been laid up for months. He saw Jim drive up to the front door and let out Miss Ball, accompanied by a young woman who carried a large bundle of clothes, wrapped up hastily. She was crying silently, her red cheeks were wet with tears; but he did not stop to wonder who she was or why she was there.

It was the storm which first began to bring him to his senses. The terrific wind, the hurtling of branches through the air, the crashing of a great limb from an oak at the back of the house seemed to him the only reasonable sounds he had heard since Janie had said, "Good-bye, Torque." They were understandable, they fitted in with the turmoil of his mind, setting a pace for his racing thoughts and giving them something as disordered as themselves upon which to seize and steady themselves. That was natural; if you were on a bolting horse you couldn't steady yourself against anything fixed. You had to have something traveling as fast as the thing under you. Then Miss Ball had caught his shoulder and shaken him wide awake when his father came back, drenched, chattering and ponderously helpless.

"You've got to get your father out of that buggy and into bed," she shouted. "We can't do it alone."

Now the others were gone and he was standing looking down at the bed where Thomas lay. He experienced none of the sensations which the sight of Janie had inspired. He was quite calm because here there was nothing to fear, only his father and himself, two men who had never had to lean even on each other.

"Well, Torque," said Thomas, a spasmodic smile twitching at his lips, "I told you, didn't I?"

"Told me what?"

"I knew she'd do it," continued the old man, forcing his mind along old channels and even attempting a croaking laugh. "I always said she'd leave you, and she has."

"Can't you think of anything else to talk about?" asked Torquay angrily.

Thomas' face sobered, but he went on stubbornly:

"Anyhow you put it, they can always find a way. They're in the house today, washing the dishes, tidying things up, getting ready to cook another meal, slapping or kissing the kid for something he done or didn't do, and then tomorrow they're gone clean away."

Torquay's anger evaporated as he realized his father was rambling in his talk. He dragged a big rocking chair which had been Thomas' last favorite to the side of the bed and sat down.

"They leave you like that," muttered Thomas, "and you walk out alone with the kid sitting on your shoulder, holding on by your hair, steering you by the beard, learning to swear and hit and be a man. That's the milk I fed you on out of my own breast, and look where you are today."

"Well," murmured Torquay, "where am I?"

"You're at the head of the Pine Tree Glassworks, that's where you are. You're the master of every stick and stone the Damons ever owned. If you were to walk out with all you've got, there wouldn't be anything left here but a spot on the map where a town used to be."

"Since when was I the head of the works? You aren't dead yet, are you?"

"Yes; I'm dead—I'm as dead right now as I'm ever going to be, and you know it. I'll never get out again. I'll lie here like this through morning, noon and night shift, thinking how the worst of it is they never leave you even when they're gone. You ought never to of married, Torque, because they hang around even when they're gone. You'll see. You'll hear her talking, saying things, holding a grip on the cake she wouldn't eat."

Miss Ball came into the room. Two spots of red shone brightly on her cheek bones, for she was still professionally angry with herself for having been duped by Janie's false calm. She had a conscience as mechanical as the works in a chronometer and it had driven her to superhuman efforts to make good her fault so far as it was possible to do so. Her business was to prolong human life, and having failed with the mother, she was doubly determined to succeed with the child. She had scoured the country for a wet nurse. She had been to every doctor in town in search of a clue and had finally succeeded through the superintendent of the works in finding what she wanted. She had brought back Elsie Dunhill, who had just lost her child. It was this woman Torquay had seen getting out of the buggy.

"I wanted to tell you, Mr. Torquay, that all arrangements have been made. The funeral will take place day after tomorrow. I have also been successful in finding a nurse and I believe the baby will live."

The old man made a movement on his pillows as if he tried to throw himself out of the bed. He succeeded in turning so that his eyes rested directly on his son's blank face.

There was a long pause before Torquay asked in a low voice, "What baby?"

"Yours," said Miss Ball, apparently unmoved by the strange question. "The doctors managed to save the child."

"Ask her if it's a boy or a girl," whispered Thomas, his eyes lighting up momentarily with an odd gleam, half bantering, half malignant. "That's the usual thing, Torque. You say, 'Is it a boy or a girl?'"

"It's a girl," said Miss Ball.

Thomas attempted a derisive laugh and gagged. Presently the coughing spell passed, but only to usher in a fit of hiccups which persisted in spite of every known remedy. In his weakened condition he could not resist the strain long, and died early the following morning.

The double funeral affected Torquay in a strange manner. With the works shut down for the day, all the men were left free to attend or not as they saw fit. They came in a body, not awkwardly or from a sense of duty, but quite simply, as to the burial of one of their own. That should have reassured him; but the presence of certain bankers and others whose interests demanded that they stand well with the new head of the Pine Tree Glassworks forced him into a prominence for which he was totally unprepared. He felt ashamed throughout the ceremony. It seemed to him a waking nightmare to be endured with clenched teeth. All these people looking at him, wondering what he was feeling inside! Well, he wasn't feeling anything. He was just thinking that once the whole thing was over he could get back to the familiar round of his work.

One of the hardest feats known to man is to turn from what is uppermost in his mind by deliberate calculation, but Torquay accomplished it during the days that followed Janie's death. He told part of his brain to cease functioning and another part to attend carefully to the details of business. By this means he succeeded in actually holding his sensibilities in abeyance for several consecutive weeks and could have hoped to dull them until they became permanently atrophied if it had not been for the living reminder which Janie had left behind her. There was the point of danger and he knew it instinctively. As long as he could avoid seeing the baby he could keep himself from plunging into the whirlpool of doubts which threatened to engulf him the moment he permitted himself to think. As he had been blindly ashamed at the first suspicion of Janie's conception and again at the funeral, so he was ashamed that he had a child.

He used his home as a boarding house, coming to it merely for meals and to sleep. Food had to be ready when he wanted it and the door always on the latch, for he irked at any delay. His life was more than ever in the works, except that they did not only absorb his time; they offered him a refuge. Consequently he felt a tremor of apprehension when Miss Ball interrupted one of his hurried departures and demanded a hearing. There was no denying Miss Ball. She was an unsmiling woman, squarely made, with small eyes in a rather wide face above a firm jaw. She was as impenetrable as Mega, but with a vast difference. Mega was only ominously impassive, while Miss Ball was as direct in speech and action as had been Thomas himself.

"What is it?" asked Torquay, frowning impatiently.

"There is no reason why I should stay any longer," replied Miss Ball promptly. "I am going at the end of the week."

Torquay was profoundly shaken and his mind, released from control, leaped into action. If she had only been less successful in her efforts to keep the child alive, he thought, he would have let her go without a restraining word. The inhumanity of the unspoken and only half-formed wish did not even occur to him. He was concerned only that he was at last brought face to face with the realization that if Janie had gone completely, life would have become a simple matter, stripped of every complication. He could have devoted it with absolute content to his work, and in a manner part of himself would have painlessly ceased to breathe. But she had not gone completely; she had left just enough of herself behind to trip him up and throw him headlong into unsounded waters.

"I can't spare you," he said, choosing his words carefully. "I want you to run things just as you have been running them ever since you came here. I want most of all to be left alone. Think it over and you can make your own conditions and name your own price."

CHAPTER XV

MISS Ball stayed, but she was held by something far more subtle than money or the assurance of a permanent home. The sense of power had crept into her veins. She had not only a large and well-appointed house for her dominion but a human being had been delivered into her care from the hour of its birth. This extraordinary event moved her in a peculiar way. It was unprecedented in her varied experience and one might have thought it would have stirred her maternal instincts or aroused an access of pity, but it did neither. It appealed directly to the efficiency which had become the mainspring of all her thoughts and the key to all her actions. The longer Torquay Strayton ignored his daughter, the better she would be pleased.

Throughout his life Torquay had led a haphazard existence, sleeping when he pleased and where he fell, eating what was set before him and wearing what came first to hand; but from the day Miss Ball assumed control, all was changed without his knowing just when or how. An atmosphere of order supplanted disorder. It closed slowly around him like one of his own molds around a parison of molten glass. But once he had taken its form, he breathed more easily than ever before. System became a hard shell interposed between himself and all possibility of disturbance. Paradoxically, never had he known more freedom or felt greater security. But one day Miss Ball, driven by her allegiance to the straight lines of deportment, came to him in regard to the naming of the child. All people, including children, were cases, each under a regime fixed by authority. There were certain hours when some were given pills and certain times when others were given names.

"It's time the baby was christened, Mr. Strayton."

"Name her anything you like," he cried, like one abruptly awakened from a dream, "and don't bother me again."

He was angry because he had been startled into the realization that he was not alone in his shell after all. The bit of herself Janie had left behind would grow into a girl, become a woman, and ask him all those questions against which he had resolutely turned his mind. If he once let down his guard she would get a grip on him as her mother had done. She would move him to do horrible things. She would stir up a mess inside his mind that would drive him blind and set his whole body to aching as if it had been hurling itself against the four walls of a stone cell. He did not want to see her and his blunt fingers burned at the thought of touching her. If he saw her carriage being wheeled out of one door, he always went out through another.

Never did child, not excepting Torquay himself, open its eyes on a more curious world. The baby was the daughter of Torquay Strayton, master and sole owner of the Pine Tree Glassworks, but she was also the daughter of the Damons' ex-nursemaid. She was born into all the comforts money could buy and the care of a woman who was something more than an expert in hygiene, for Miss Ball had turned her back on school-teaching to become a graduate nurse. On one side there was a father who wished never to come near her. On the other there was Miss Ball, fanatically ready in that one matter to further his wishes. Behind the two of them there was Mega the inscrutable, a dark background, unseen at first, then vague, and finally looming like a black cloud on the horizon of childhood.

For a time there had been Elsie Dunhill, tender of heart and flesh. But she had faded out quickly, for there was no room in Miss Ball's philosophy for the peculiar influence and attachments of a foster mother. Elsie had cried much harder on going away than she had at her coming. In her wake followed a succession of nursemaids, all better trained and dressed than Janie had been in the same capacity, all vigilantly watched by an eye that missed nothing and all disciplined only by dismissal. Miss Ball knew better than to argue with servants.

When the baby carriage had been definitely stored away in the attic, Torquay could still avoid seeing his daughter through the care of Miss Ball. She kept the child in the nursery until he had gone to work, saw that she was having her noonday nap when he came for lunch and had her tucked away for the night before he returned in the evening.

On Sundays there was the special treat of two hours in the park for the baby, to make up for imprisonment during the rest of the Sabbath. On Sundays also the house seemed to take its one long free breath of the week, for Miss Ball went regularly to church.

But system cannot triumph forever over chance, and there came a day when Torquay left at the house important papers over which he had been studying half the night, only to forget them in the morning. He had locked them in a drawer to which he cared to give no one else access, and consequently retraced his steps at an unaccustomed hour.

The shortest way from the house to the works was through a gap in the cedars, directly past the gardener's cottage and down the road along which he had been traveling on the day of his last encounter with Jake Damon. Torquay habitually avoided this route, but not through any fear of meeting Jake, who had stubbornly drunk himself to death after the blow of seeing the home of his fathers sold to the archenemy of the house of Damon. There had been times when Jake's bull-like voice had penetrated the premises from which he had been exiled.

"Drink myself to death! What if I do? Who fixed it so I could? You did!"

Hearing those words brutally spoken, Torquay could see Eloise Damon's thin body lean forward tensely, courage in her face, scorn in her eyes. He could imagine her low voice—"Hush, Jake! Do you want them to hear you?"

"No, I won't hush. Let 'em hear and be damned. It was you took their dirty money. It isn't drink that will have killed me; it's you, damn you!"

The reason Torquay avoided the road to which he had a legal right of way was that he was apt to run into Eloise Damon. He had never forgotten the unusual sensation of being at ease in the presence of a woman which had come over him during their one encounter, but his pride prevented him from appearing to invite a renewal of the contact. There was a wall between them and they both knew it. The same sense which had led her to recognize that their honor was of the same brand was strong enough in him to make him respect her territory as he knew she would respect his.

Consequently he had worn a path around the stables and across the remains of an old orchard where eight old apple trees spread their limbs in a wide canopy, niggardly of fruit, but prodigal of blossoms and shade. Under these trees the grass was unusually thick and soft and in one corner there had recently been placed a large sand box flanked by a diminutive teetering board Torquay realized vaguely that the sand pile and seesaw had something to do with his daughter and must be indicative of her age; but never having seen them occupied, they had not troubled him.

On this day, as he hurried back from the works, he saw a round white moon on top the sand heap and a nursemaid seated on the ground with her back against one of the trees. A book had fallen into the grass at her side and she was sound asleep. While he was still looking at her the round white moon straightened up into a child of three and turned to stare at him. With her short skirts pushed down instead of up, she became at once an exceptionally presentable little person, wearing all the marks and graces of the offspring of the idle rich. He paused to look at her curiously for a moment before the realization swept over him that he was face to face with his own child.

Except for her eyes, which were as dark as his, there was no mistaking who had been her mother. She was copied in delicate miniature from all his recollections of Janie—yellow hair, pale skin, thin-boned limbs. Even the quick upward movement of her hands as she started toward him was stolen from Janie. She tripped on the board of the sand box and fell into the soft grass with a sound such as some dolls make under pressure. It was neither a cry nor a laugh; it was a grunt. The nursemaid awoke, saw Torquay, and promptly scrambled to her feet. The baby, recovering from her fall, solemnly renewed her progress toward him.

"Janie!" cried the nursemaid.

It was as though she had shot a bullet into Torquay's heart. His body grew instantly cold as he turned mechanically on his heel and started away with rapid strides, deaf to a loud wail of disappointment. He actually did not hear it. Suddenly the blood poured back into his veins, swelling them with fury at Miss Ball, at himself, at the blundering fate which had perpetuated the name of Janie. Under the first shock of his discovery it seemed astounding that out of all the names in the world that one should have been chosen; but as he cooled down he realized how natural the choice had been and that the astonishing thing was he had not known of it sooner. His brows settled into a black frown.

He hurried into the house; but when he had the document in his hand in search of which he had returned, all sense of haste left him. Reminding himself insistently that he was Torquay Strayton, master of the Pine Tree Glassworks, and at no man's beck and call, he went into the hall, took his father's heavy cane from its place in the corner, left the house through the front door and started down the driveway, headed for Main Street and a mile walk to the near-by works. Though he did not permit the thought to form in his mind, he was running away from the full moon on top the sand heap which had straightened into a girl three years old.

An accident may make a habit. From that day on it became a common sight to see him walking through town past Striker's and along the river to the old works beside the lone pine tree. There he would sometimes pause, but never stop for long before going on to cross the footbridge to his office in the main plant. At first the habitues of the drug store would glance at the clock as his figure loomed by the window; later they came to setting their watches by his passage. At noon and again at six o'clock Jim would drive down by the back way to fetch his master. If it were summertime Torquay would occasionally take the reins himself and guide the fast team for miles along deserted roads all others seemed to have forgotten.

Ever since his wife's death he had been letting his beard grow because he begrudged the time it took to shave, and there were romantic bosoms in the offing ready to see in this change of habit

147

a lasting sign of mourning. In addition, he was wearing out some of the rough tweed suits and congress boots his father's long illness had permitted to accumulate. Then there was Thomas' familiar cane. All these chance items enabled Ed Bristol to air his Biblical lore in a saying which precipitated the vague surmisings of his companions in sloth.

"Moses' rod could put out a crop of buds, but I'll be switched if Thomas' stick hasn't bust into the bloom of himself. Look at Torque, and you say to yourself, 'Hello, Tom!' "

The man who heads every subscription list in a community as a matter of course is seldom frowned upon. A cordial nod of the head was hung on the slightest hook of acquaintance as Torquay walked by, and those who could call him familiarly by his nickname had come to be looked upon as among the specifically elect. The proudest ladies half turned their heads as if they wished they knew him and wondered how Eloise Damon had acquired the right to give him her best bow on the rare occasions she was downtown early enough to pass him. But social acceptance had come too late to Torquay. He may even not have realized it was his for the asking, and if he had he would not have known what to do with it.

At the age of forty-six, he was already assuming the status of the old bottles on a shelf in his workshop—admired by connoisseurs but never touched. There was a sturdy Booz bottle and a light-green calabash he had brought down from the Hetney works. Those were his favorites. There were two flasks showing the bust of Washington turned out in Hopetown itself a generation before the Damon Glassworks had come into being. Going back still further, there was a Wistarberg pitcher with a ball cover, exceedingly rare; and one of those scent bottles by the same maker for which the colonial belles had abandoned carrying an apple, stuck full of doves. There was a freak container in the shape of the Baltimore Monument, and finally there was the first bottle to carry the Pine Tree brand. The mold which had fixed its shape had long since gone to the scrap heap, but the unalterable bottle remained. So it was with Torquay. He stood established, high on the shelf of admiration, and wearing the lable:

Do Not Touch. There was one person, however, within his immediate circle, who was not old enough to read.

On a Sunday he was sitting in the study which had veiled the inception of Jake Damon's solitary drinking bouts. Before that it had been Burk Damon's retreat through his long torment, and in the dim past it had witnessed the meditations of other Damon heads weighted down beneath curled-brimmed beaver hats. In a word, the room was sacred to the privacy of the dominant male. He heard an unusual noise and looked up to see that the knob on the door had become mysteriously animated and was making the motions of a horse trying to roll over but never quite succeeding. Just as he was about to rise and investigate, it did succeed.

The knob made a complete revolution and the door slowly opened. Torquay sank back in his chair at the sight of an apparition which most evidently should have been in bed. His daughter stood with one hand still raised to hold the door knob and the other unconventionally crumpling upward a diminutive hemstitched nightdress. Her yellow hair hung straight to her shoulders. It was glossy, freshly brushed, and with the rest of her small person seemed to exhale a suggestion of fragrance. He stared at her without moving and she stared back with the placid perseverance which makes the gaze of a child indomitable. "Where is Miss Ball?" he managed to ask at last. To himself, his voice sounded like a murmur, but to her it was doubtless a fearsome rumble. She resisted the impulse to look curiously at his beard, held her ground, working the knob back and forth, and answered at her leisure, "Gone to church." There was another long pause during which the two pairs of eyes, so much alike, never wavered from their locked grip. It wasn't right, he was thinking, for her to have eyes like that; they should have been blue.

"Where is your nurse?" he asked.

Again she took her time before she declared, "I threw my dolly in the tree."

Some moments passed before Torquay could fathom all the depths of that answer. This morsel of human flesh could already think and plan. It could watch for Miss Ball to go out and then lay a deliberate trap for an unsuspecting and too obliging nurse. It could even calculate the vital difference between throwing its doll into a tree and dropping it on the ground whence it could be more quickly retrieved.

"How old are you?" he asked vapidly. That was a too familiar question, requiring no rumination.

"Four years old," she recited at once, robbing him of what already he had grown to look upon as a statutory grace of time. As if she realized her advantage, she abandoned the door knob, stepped out into the room and stood poised, swaying forward and back, deliberately tempting equilibrium to hurl her toward him. His tongue grew dry in his mouth and his forehead wet with sweat. With a hastily premeditated effort, he gathered his brows into a scowl, but astonishingly it only made her laugh.

She lowered her head for the plunge and was already tottering when her nurse sprang in through the open door and swept her up, crying in horrified tones, "Janie! Why, Janie!"

Torquay, left alone, sat for a long time staring at his knees. If she had run forward and cast herself upon them, what would he have done? Perhaps he would have bellowed at her. Perhaps he would have pushed her away. But perhaps he would have caught her up and broken her in his arms before he knew what damage he was doing to himself as well as to her. To him she was not a small child who was making him ridiculous. She was far more. She was the emblem of persistence, the visible symbol of a domination he had never once admitted. She was the unheeded voice of his wife, gasping on her wedding day, "Oh, Torque, I'll never leave you, never!"

He jumped up, hurried out to the stables and hitched up the horses himself. The buggy made the turn out of the evergreens that masked the driveway on two wheels, barely missing the vanguard of the throng of people coming from church. Some of the men bowed to Torquay, but those behind them, seeing that he was blind to salutations, could give their entire attention to estimating he was moving at a twelve-mile clip and to wondering where on earth he was going at that pace without a hat.

Ordinarily Torquay was careful to answer every greeting, but today he saw nothing before him, not even the road or the horses on which his eyes were fixed. He sat erect, holding a firm rein instinctively, and let them tear along the Salem pike. At the Halfway House, nine miles out of town, he came to himself long enough to draw them up for the right-angle turn which would plunge them into the solitudes, the deep sand and the hidden mudholes of the Barrens. When they came to the Buckhorn road he turned them once more and then dropped the reins with a profound sigh.

He had known all the time which way he was headed. He had been making from the first for this narrow unused road. It meandered in a straight line, so to speak, as a man walks from his cradle to his grave. It climbed slowly and it went down fast. To turn from it was to realize sooner or later that the road itself was the only way out. Whoever left it had to come back as Thomas Strayton, bone weary, balancing his drowsing boy on his shoulder, had turned back through a long night from one vain excursion after another. In a fuller sense, he, Torquay Strayton, had come back to it twice, once when his father had first laid violent hands upon him, and now again.

In some half-mystic manner this road was wound into his life, bound into the fiber of all the questions a man asks about himself and gets silence for an answer. He let the horses follow it at will, dragging the buggy over hummocks, through sand and an occasional mudhole, and finally up the sharp rise which brought him face to face with the great brick house at Babylon. There he drew them to a stand and they were glad enough for the breathing spell.

When last he had seen it the house was deserted, and now it was a budding ruin. Several hinges had rusted quite through and let rotting shutters fall to the ground. There was a gaping black hole through the roof of the penthouse and some vandal hand had made a target of the panes of glass in the graceful fanlight. On one side a great straggling patch of flowering almond had burst into bloom, emphasizing solitude. The tired horses started on at a walk and he let them go until they came abreast of the spot where his father had broken open the rotten apples. He stopped them again and looked in vain for the fence on the top rail of which his father had smashed the one sound apple. The fence was quite gone and the high grass hid even its remains.

He was childishly disappointed.

For some indefinable reason he had wanted to examine the spot where a dark stain had spread on the gray wood.

But his journey had not been altogether in vain. The unbroken quiet of the Barrens, the profound silence of places once inhabited and now abandoned, had soothed the fever from his brain. Without curing him, their peace had permeated his veins so that his blood ran cool as he turned the horses over to Jim to be rubbed down, blanketed and discreetly fed. He was full of a new strength and through with running away.

To stand one's ground was not surrender.

He went into the house, sent for Miss Ball and waited for her in the study.

CHAPTER XVI

TORQUAY had never considered Miss Ball a woman in the terrifying sense of the word. The very characteristics which made others afraid of her set her definitely apart from the rest of her sex. Figuratively speaking, he would have felt at more liberty to knock her down than to employ his strength against a man of average weight. As far as he was concerned, she had been a neutral from the first hour he laid eyes on her. He respected her, but he was not afraid of her even in the sense his childhood had feared Mega. She came into the room and stood before him for a moment, while he hesitated over how to begin.

"Is the baby awake?"

Miss Ball was taken aback. She cast a quick glance at his face, but he was not looking at her.

"Do you mean Janie?" she asked. He frowned and nodded his head. There was another considerable pause before she continued. "She should be by this time. I'll go and see."

"Just a minute," said Torquay. "Let her come in here alone." There was a pregnant silence during which Miss Ball did not move. "There's another thing," he went on. "I think she's old enough to come to the table with you at noon, and that reminds me it won't be long before she'll have to be taught her letters."

"You needn't worry about that, Mr. Strayton. I was a school-teacher before I became a nurse."

"That's lucky." His frown deepened as he continued. "I've never talked to you about her before, Miss Ball, and I may never do it again. It's enough to say that she's to have all the breeding and training money can buy."

"I can assure you she'll have more than that," said Miss Ball sharply. "Is there anything else?"

"No; that's all. Perhaps it's too much."

He sat staring at nothing until the door was opened by an unseen hand and closed again. He looked up. Janie was standing just within the room, dragging a rag doll by one distorted leg. He braced himself for a repetition of all the stages of approach which had been inter-rupted on her previous visit by the arrival of the nurse, but he had failed to take into account the fact that his daughter was now fully dressed in her best Sunday frock. She was necessarily a very different person, perhaps struggling with the thought that manners were more welcome in this room than nightdresses. She advanced directly to him, dropped the doll and held up her hands to be lifted to his lap. For the first time in his life Torquay became genuinely absurd even to himself. He was like a beardless suitor who, having thought out the sequence of all the things he is going to say in an interview, finds himself thrown hopelessly off the track by the unexpected opening of the other side of the dialogue.

As he stared down into puzzled dark eyes the calm he had bor-rowed from the peace of the Barrens began to desert him. He could feel the sweat gathering on his forehead. It prickled and he would have liked to raise a hand to rub it away, but he dared not move. Not knowing what to do, he did nothing so completely that his immo-bility inspired confidence. The puzzled look left Janie's eyes and she laid investigating hands on one of his knees which turned instantly rigid. She shook it and seemed pleased to find it as immovable as the great limb of a tree. She cocked her head and began to examine him curiously, but from the neck down only. Her angle of vision made him a colossus and her fingers assured her he was hewn out of rock. The whole of him became a place to play. She threw her arms over his thigh and dangled her legs. With the tips of her toes just touching the floor, she tried to squirm up, but could not make the grade without help. Then she found his huge foot and discovered she could stand and even dance on it as if it were a platform. From that elevation she felt much taller. She turned, got a grip on the slack of his trousers and started up the incline of his shin bones. With a shrill laugh of triumph she landed upside down in his lap, lay kicking for a moment and then righted herself.

154

Torquay had begun to quiver imperceptibly from the moment she first touched him. By a superhuman effort he avoided watching her; nevertheless, he could see her clearly through the feel of her movements. He knew he must remain still at all costs, or crumble. He kept reminding himself of the calm he had felt when he had sent for her. He went over in his mind step by step the road which had led him to the resolution he was through with running away.

He remembered the rock on which he had determined to make his stand—to hold one's ground is not surrender. All in vain. As far as Janie was concerned, the universe began to tremble violently. Her playground was alive! She scrambled to her feet, threw her arms around her father's neck and pressed herself against him. The sudden warmth of her body was like a thunderbolt from the past.

"Don't do that!" He thought he had shouted, but he had uttered only a hoarse whisper. He unfastened her hands roughly, lifted her clear and set her down. She stared at him gravely, showing neither amazement nor fright.

"Go away," he ordered. A tiny frown wrinkled her forehead. She looked aside from him and slowly studied the strange room, filing it away in memory. Her eyes fell on her doll.

She pounced upon it, hugged and kissed it and then started for the door, once more dragging it cruelly by one foot. She glanced up at the knob she had succeeded in turning that morning, driven by the incentive of discovery. That incentive was now lacking. Without raising her head, she uttered a piercing scream. Torquay half rose from his chair as if lifted by an explosion, but before he could get to his feet Miss Ball had thrown open the door. She stood nonplussed by the calm of the author of the scream. The child caught her skirt, turned and gave Torquay a long level gaze before Miss Ball recovered sufficiently to pick her up and carry her out. Torquay stared with bulging eyes at the spot where she had been.

"Janie!" he whispered. "Wait a minute! Don't——"

Then he came to himself and sank back with a sigh of relief. He was safe. The test was over and he had passed it, without honors. He had endured torment and had not retracted. From now on he could

155

see his daughter without fear. He could have her at table, watch her grow and even call her by name. He could buy her a pony, but he realized Jim would have to pick her up and teach her to ride, for there were natural limits to security. In short, he had stood his ground and could face the coming years with an equanimity surpassed only by the unalterable calm in Janie's eyes as she studied him from time to time from within her own mysterious seclusion.

She was seven years old when Torquay, having passed the battery of eyes at Striker's, was stopped by a youngster who stood his ground.

"What do you want, boy? A job at the works?"

"Don't you remember me, Mr. Strayton?"

Torquay was even more at ease with boys than he was with men, perhaps because his own boyhood lived on so vividly in his mind. Besides, he had worked as a boy among boys and now employed them in large numbers. But he could not place the specimen before him. He was a lad of fourteen who wore a bridge of freckles on his nose and an outgrown coat with an equal air of impudence, which at the moment was slightly modified by uneasiness.

"No; I don't remember you," said Torquay. "Whose boy are you?"

"But you do know me just the same. It was me busted a mold in your workshop."

"When were you in my workshop?"

"With my mother."

"Oh," said Torquay, realization sweeping over him. "That was a long time ago."

"Yes," said Ralph. "I was only a kid and I've lived next to you ever since."

It was true, thought Torquay, and yet he had never consciously seen the Damon child in all that time. It made him wince to think ten years could become as a day if it were not that the unaging world kept on hand a steady supply of children as markers.

"I remember. Your name is Ralph. What can I do for you?"

"Perhaps you'd give me a job for the rest of the summer," said Ralph; but Torquay could see the idea had come to him only in the few minutes they had been talking.

156

"I could get you apprenticed to one of the men," he said, "but that isn't what made you stop me." Ralph looked up with something of the expression his face had assumed when he had smashed the mold. He turned red, started to say something, and then changed his mind. Having scored to that extent, Torquay tried a little guesswork. "Of course, you'll have to bring me your mother's permission in writing."

"Oh, that will be all right," said Ralph promptly, and Torquay knew he had guessed wrong. If he had been at the back of his house half an hour earlier he might have read correctly the impulse which had led Ralph to come to him. Janie was busy with a trowel and her small spade, digging in the bed which had been assigned to her as her own garden. From the other side of the cedars Ralph spied her. He had his pockets full of apples which frequent tests had persuaded him were too green to eat.

There are only two things a boy can do with an apple, eat it or throw it at something. The first one he threw went so wide of the mark that Janie did not notice it. The second struck the wall in front of her and bounced toward her. She straightened quickly and looked up, puzzled, directly away from Ralph. The third apple described a high arc over the tops of the cedars and descended majestically to strike in the exact center of her back. She cried out with fright as well as pain and turned just in time to see Ralph's triumphant face framed in the gap in the hedge.

"Oh!" she screamed. "You bad, bad boy!" And only then burst into a paroxysm of tears.

Torquay reached home in an unusually reflective mood. The encounter with Ralph Damon had done more than remind him he had lived for nearly half a century. It had led him to review all his life from the time he had started gathering parisons from the ringhole at just Ralph's age to this day, when he had offered to take on the youngest of the Damons as a boy helper in the Pine Tree Glassworks. That little fact alone was the true measure of the distance he and his father had traveled, but he did not see the matter in that light.

All he could think of was that thirty years over pots, furnaces and continuous tanks had brought him not one inch nearer to tearing the secret he sought from the fusion of glass. He was considering his life as a waste. If it had not been for the few minor improvements developed through his experiments, he would by this time be popularly thought a madman.

At times he shrewdly suspected that, even as it was, there were those, among them Miss Ball, who could have described to their own satisfaction the nature and degree of his insanity in scientific terms. He could shake that sort of thing off his mind with a shrug of his broad shoulders; but there was one other matter which would soon have to be faced squarely with all the resources at his command. Rumors had reached Hopetown of an automatic bottle-making machine which was destined to do to the industry what Mount Pelee had just done to the island of Martinique—shake it to its very foundations.

He was scowling as he stepped in the door, and his frown deepened when he heard a suppressed altercation between Miss Ball and Janie, who was sobbing persistently.

"What's the matter?" called Torquay.

It was the first time he had ever had to ask that question of Miss Ball. She came down half carrying, half dragging Janie, and in a few words told the story of the well-aimed apple. So that was what the boy had had on his mind, thought Torquay.

"Well," he asked finally, "what do you want me to do?"

"She's been saying over and over again that the boy was wicked. I don't know what will make her stop crying unless you can think of some way to have him punished."

"Do you think that would make her stop?" asked Torquay skeptically.

Almost before the words were out of his mouth, Janie nodded her head, choked her sobs and fastened on him a grave expectant gaze. He was troubled, caught on the horns of an absurd dilemma. There was no escape from a choice of two evils and no mistaking the look in Janie's eyes. Either he was her man in time of trouble or he wasn't, and this moment was going to decide it.

"I'll write a note to Mrs. Damon," he promised, "telling her what her boy has done—that's all."

Janie accepted the words as addressed solely to herself. Not even whimpering, she turned to leave the room. A quirk of satisfaction came to Miss Ball's straight mouth as she followed. Her reading of the omens had been correct. They left Torquay to the most difficult composition he had ever attempted. After destroying much paper, he evolved a bare statement of the occurrence and sent it to Mrs. Damon. Ten minutes later Ralph himself arrived with the answer and insisted on delivering it in person. Torquay felt sorry for him. The boy was evidently as frightened as he was determined not to show the white feather. There were smudges on his cheeks, but one knew they had been left by tears of rebellion. The note was the personification of Eloise Damon in three lines.

"A Damon should be able to take punishment from a Strayton by this time," read Torquay. "You may whip Ralph yourself."

Torquay's cheek bones flushed a deep red; he was angry, but it was the kind of anger that turned him calm. He tore up the note and dropped it in the wastebasket.

"You won't throw any more apples at my girl, will you, Ralph?"

"No, sir."

"Then that's all right. You can have a job at the works whenever you want it, with or without permission." Ralph did not move. "You can go now." Ralph licked his lips, swallowed and stared stolidly at Torquay, who finally asked impatiently, "Well, what is it?"

"Mother sent me over for a licking and said for me to be sure and get it."

Torquay was infuriated.

"Tell her to go to hell!" he roared.

"All right, sir; I will," muttered Ralph. "Between the two of you, I can see I'm bound to get a licking and I don't care much which one does it."

CHAPTER XVII

O N a day in August, 1903, Torquay sat at his desk, staring at a clipping from a trade journal which he had pasted on a square of cardboard and propped against his inkwell. It read as follows:

> "The machine settles completely the problem of mechanical bottle and jar production, lowers the cost to a vanishing point and cannot fail to revolutionize the industry, displace the can as a fruit package, and by providing a cleaner and cheaper vessel will greatly increase the use and demand for glass bottles and packers."

What the article failed to add was that the invention would give pause to boards of directors of the strongest bottle companies, bring sleepless nights to the heads of every successful proprietary concern and send many a less fortunate establishment to the wall with a crash. Almost overnight, credit became the key to life or death of every bottle-making glassworks in the country. Torquay was placed between the alternatives of admitting outside capital with its consequent interference or staking everything he owned to raise the funds for a drastic remodeling of the entire Pine Tree plant.

It was not in him to brook interference. His sledgehammer manner was becoming to a man who was master of all he surveyed, but it was poor equipment with which to go into an enforced partnership. He took his decision and began to lay his plans accordingly. Between his first reading of the circular and the day when he installed the first leased automatic bottle machines to reach Hopetown, five years elapsed. During all that time his inner life remained suspended, for he was in such a death grapple as he alone could measure. There were hours, days, when the very existence of all he and his father before him had wrested as spoils on the battlefield of trade was threatened with a wipeout. He had no thought for Janie; he was not even conscious of her presence. Nor did he once go near his experimental workshop.

Certain weaklings would have liked to see him totter and fall, however general the resulting ruin, but their hopes were destined to disappointment. At fifty-six years old he emerged a winner from what most people, including himself, regarded as the greatest battle of his life. There were a few gray hairs in his thick mane and beard, but not a scar on his reputation as a mighty fighter. He was still Torquay Strayton, master and owner of the Pine Tree Glassworks, the captain of his own ship. With almost as big a rush as it had poured out, money now began pouring in and from the moment he took up the first of his notes he realized he need never lack funds again.

That fact alone was enough to bring about a sort of pause in his life, a breathing spell which was bound to usher in some radical turn. But he himself did not sense his situation. If he had he would doubtless have put his will in command of his actions and resumed at once the habit of his workshop. Instead he took an interest in trivialities. On his desk lay a letter from Alfred Polperro, his companion on Hensbarrow Hill, asking him to find a situation for Albert, one of his three sons. Torquay had had the letter for almost a year and had never answered it. Now he felt suddenly expansive. He wrote offering to give Albert a start and inclosed a draft for his expenses large enough to create a sensation in Roche. After this magnanimous act he left the office an hour before Jim could be expected with the horses, crossed the bridge and walked toward the house.

There was no chance of his meeting either of the Damons, as Ralph was in college and that morning's paper had told of Mrs. Jake Damon's departure on an extended visit to her married daughter. He took the opportunity to look at the gardener's cottage for the first time in many years. Tucked away from the main street and cut off from his own house by the flourishing cedars, it had the air of a secret dwelling attended by fairies. There were narrow flower beds and window boxes. There had recently been a fresh coat of white paint on the clapboards and of leaf green on the shutters. Only the old shingle roof showed signs of needing attention. The gap in the cedar hedge was all but closed. He managed to push through it and came face to face with a total stranger, a slim young girl in tight-fitting riding clothes and boots. He drew back startled and so did she. They stared at each other.

"Janie!" he whispered.

"Yes: oh, yes!"

Her face seemed to break into light. She threw herself against him and buried her head on his breast, her arms half around his waist. In an instant he was shaken as no moment of the battle for the life of the Pine Tree Glassworks had been able to move him. She was his daughter—and he did not know how to hold her. He seized her elbows and his hands closed on them with a viselike grip—neither of acceptance nor repulse.

"You're the strongest man in the world," she whispered, but Torquay scarcely heard her. He was listening to his father. He was muttering his father's words aloud without knowing it: "You can't catch up with a woman. She can travel for weeks and months without moving her body. She can leave her body fussing around the house and all the time she's traveling, getting a start on you before you know she's gone."

"Oh, father, how can you say that! I'll never leave you, never!"

He could not remember how he had broken away from her, but long afterward he still felt as if her hands were clinging to his coat. He took to watching her at table and for the three hours she was permitted to stay up after supper. She was a pale girl, like her mother, but with that indefinable refinement which comes with expert care of the body and everything on it. Miss Ball was more than content with a nurse's uniform and two or three street dresses for herself, but all her aborted sensuousness seemed to have found a vent in clothing Janie. It was a cold sort of passion. It gloried in the chance to despise money and throw every emphasis on texture and line.

The result to Torquay was an added barrier and a defense. He saw Janie as living across the wall from himself in that faction which had all his life been an enemy camp. She belonged with Eloise Damon in her youth, or with the high-headed young ladies of the Misses Kinkead's school. She was of the quality but not of the body of the elect. But she was his property—a hostage which he could hold by force on his side of the wall. When Miss Ball confessed she had taught her pupil all she knew, reminded him that Janie was sixteen and suggested reluctantly that she should be sent to a finishing school, he burst into a rage.

"What for? There's only one finishing school and it will find you wherever you are. What you do is what teaches you. Who knows more about glass than what I do, and where did I learn it? What good has your schooling ever done you? She'll stay here, and if you're tired of watching her I'll get somebody that isn't."

Miss Ball was not offended. The moment was upon her when one throb of love in her heart might have lifted the scales of professional efficiency from her eyes and shown her herself as she was—a woman whose joy consisted in feeding her own and Torquay Strayton's suppressed fires. She had done her duty. She had suggested that Janie be sent away. But now her mind leaped to find pathological excuses which would justify her in perpetuating her domination. There was the vague legend of old Thomas Strayton's days of madness. There were her own conclusions as to Torquay's attitude to his wife and his extraordinary behaviour ever since the birth of his child. "Unnatural" was too loose a term to apply to him; he ought to be in a psycopathic ward.

"Janie should never marry," she murmured.

"What?" cried Torquay.

His attention was seized and turned from his wrath. His eyes narrowed as he read accurately the workings of Miss Ball's brain, and then suddenly opened and gleamed. What did he care what she thought as long as her motives would work to the same end as his? In a moment his vague desires as regarded his daughter were crystallized. He wanted her never to leave him. She was the Janie of his youth perfected, lacking the storm spots that had turned her mother black. He wished to have her always where he could watch

163

her. He wanted to sweep the room with a swift glance and always find her face with its strangely dark eyes. When she was immobile, as the older Janie had so often been, he tasted the forbidden fruit of idolatry without knowing he sinned.

Albert Polperro arrived out of a clear sky; Torquay had even forgotten sending for him. He was a pink-and-white youth of twenty-two with the beauty of a half-ripe cherry and the heart of a counter jumper. The size of Torquay's draft had already prepared him to show deference, but when he saw the size of Torquay's house and of the Pine Tree Glassworks his servility became abject. He ignored Mega by turning his own eyes to the texture of glass when she was present, but he groveled to Miss Ball with the astuteness of his kind. Perhaps he would not have cleaned Torquay's boots, but he would gladly have licked them. He never missed a chance to sir him.

Combining in his sleek person every quality which Torquay despised, he became oddly enough a godsend. Just as the monarchs of old had their court clowns, so Torquay now had his private buffoon. He invented for Albert the job of glorified errand boy, with the official designation of secretary. When they were alone he ignored him utterly; but when others came into the office he would call him Albert with a plaintive drawl and revel in otherwise humiliating him. But the cream of delight was to bait him after supper in the presence of Miss Ball and Janie. The streak of cruelty which in Thomas Strayton had made a victim of the older Janie broke out in Torquay and led him to seize on Albert as a sacrificial goat. What added spice to the pastime was that when the lash of his tongue fell on Albert's thick skin it was Janie who winced.

Next to herself, Albert was the youngest thing in the house. His youth made her feel vaguely that there should be an alliance between them against everything that was old, set and unyielding. But he could in no sense become her playmate because of the implacable rule of Miss Ball and the demands her father made on Albert. Every moment of Janie's waking day was pigeon-holed to certain employments; and Torquay, whether from abstraction or malice, absorbed Albert to his own uses. Sometimes he kept him up unconscionably late and again he would make him ridiculous by ordering him to bed at some absurdly early hour. On only one occasion had Albert rebelled weakly, spurred by a faint look of wonder in Janie's eyes and the scornful twist of Miss Ball's narrow mouth.

"I think I'll read for a while," he said nervously, looking around for a book.

"The hell you will!" roared Torquay. "I said go to bed and I meant it."

Janie felt a queer constriction of her throat at seeing Albert obey. She was at the age when a girl is apt to pin her affection on any man within her reach, and she would doubtless have come to idealize Albert if some such incident as the foregoing episode had not infallibly cropped up just in time to nip her dreams in the bud. Sometimes she suspected her father of a deliberate intention, and she would think perhaps if Albert were only planted like a tree out in the lawn, with plenty of room about him, he might grow into something beautiful. But whenever he spoke with his odd mispronunciations, always saying "denner" for "dinner" and "dhree" for "three" and "tike" for "take," she awoke with a start from her self-deception. She could forgive him for being made ridiculous by others but not by himself.

Instead of his being company for her, his restricted presence only troubled her fancies and made her more lonely. In addition, illness fell on Miss Ball, suddenly eliminating her from the ground floor of the house. In common with the generality of the medical profession with which she was so closely allied, she had no fear of sickness in others. But when it threatened herself sound judgment deserted her. She refused childishly to believe she was ill until the day she could not bend her legs to walk downstairs. The doctors diagnosed the malady as rheumatic fever, acerbated by her stubbornness, and predicted a long confinement. Torquay assigned her to a great room whose last occupant had been Mrs. Burk Damon, then dead some forty years.

Miss Ball did not resign the management of the house. Propped high on the pillows which she sometimes crushed in her arms to smother her agony, she received every morning not only Mega but the girl who helped in the kitchen, the housemaid and even Jim. She did not always have orders to give, but she wished to see them. Without suspecting it, they were the tentacles by which she kept in touch with every corner of the large dwelling and every activity of its occupants. After the servants came Janie, with her work or a book. She was not required to read aloud or to talk. It was enough that she should be steeped for two hours of every day in the influence which had laid out her life with the precision of a builder's blue print.

Janie neither loved nor hated Miss Ball, but she was permeated by her, and Miss Ball knew it. Mother love may be a mere accident, as dependent on individual characteristics as any other brand of affection; but the habit of a lifetime is a definite force, immeasurable in its power. Janie had had the habit of Miss Ball from the hour of her birth, and far from wishing to break away from an unchanging pillar in her life, she would have trembled at the thought of having it suddenly withdrawn. She came to the sick room not as one under orders but to receive something she could not name and yet would not know how to do without. Consequently she felt a sinking of the heart when she entered one day to find Miss Ball with a strangely stricken face, staring at one of her ankles. It was startlingly puffy and swelled.

Janie withdrew instinctively and went up to her own room which faced the overgrown cedars. They were stiff trees, but she loved them because she had grown up with them. She could remember when their tops had been on a level with the sash of her window, and now some of them were out of sight even when she was lying on her bed. She went to the window and stood looking out absently, wondering what she would do if Miss Ball should die. The evenings with Albert and her father were growing terrible. Her father had always looked at her strangely. Now he had become like a huge gray oyster shell. If she should touch him she knew she would cut her hands. When Albert spoke, or more often when he only looked at her, the jaws of the shell would open and close on him as her father's hands had once closed on her elbows.

Suddenly a voice came from so near it was like a slap in her face. "Do you dance?"

"No," said Janie, and stared about wildly as she had done when the apple the Damon boy threw had seemed to come from nowhere.

At the moment she had come to her window Ralph Damon had been crouched in sneakers on the roof of the gardener's cottage, seeking where he should fix his last shingle. He had seen her first only as a ghostly form appearing through the thick top of the biggest cedar. He had crept noiselessly to one side until he was able to see all of her and he felt more than repaid for his pains. He forgot the solemnity with which he had recently taken his degree and thought only of how much he would like to dance with so slim and erect a figure. But perhaps she did not dance. He asked her.

Janie moved to the side of the window and found herself on a level with a young man sitting with his feet hunched under him, a shingle in one hand, a hammer in the other and a nail in the comer of his mouth. Her first thought was wonder as to how he could have spoken so dearly, her next was one of shame that she had answered, her third was red-hot anger. All these thoughts were painted in her face by succeeding waves of color which, in combination with her blazing eyes, made of her a breath-taking spectacle.

Young Damon wished with all his heart he had not spoken to her in banter. He stood up impulsively to make some sort of amends. His feet slipped from under him. The hammer flew one way, the shingle another. He slid first on his back and then by a superhuman effort on his stomach down the steep slant of the roof. The cedars cut his falling body off from view. Janie felt faint. She caught the window jamb, leaned far out and listened for a thud, but heard nothing. The silence became too much for her.

"Are you hurt?" she called.

"No."

The voice sounded quite calm. She drew back and closed the window noisily just as Ralph let go his double hold on the eaves trough and fell lightly to the soft flower bed below. The next morning he appeared in Torquay's office.

"Would you have remembered me, Mr. Strayton, if I hadn't to send in my name?"

"Yes," said Torquay, after a quick glance at him; "I would have remembered you all right. What do you want?"

"You promised me a job whenever I came for it, with or without my mother's permission."

"That was a long time ago," said Torquay, "and we've quit taking on boys."

"A promise is a promise," said Ralph pleasantly. "Crawl out of that."

"What particular job would you like to have?" countered Torquay.

"I specialized in chemistry at college but I'd like to start in where you started, as a carrier-in."

"You're almost as clever as your mother."

"If I were," said Ralph, with his first show of temper, "you could put me in charge of your works and take a holiday."

Torquay was enjoying himself. He rested his blunt fingers on the edge of his desk, caught his toes beneath it and leaned back in his swivel chair until his huge body from the shoulders down was horizontal. "I suppose you'd do anything—anything at all. That's what they all say."

"Anything in reason."

"A-a-albert!"

Albert arose hurriedly from the small desk where he tended a telephone and typed telegrams.

"Yes, sir."

"Sweep out the office," ordered Torquay.

For an instant Ralph thought that the formula meant he was to be thrown out and he looked curiously at the man who was expected to do it. But Albert was not advancing on him. He was going to a closet from which he took out a broom and started sweeping the immaculate floor.

"Would you do that?" asked Torquay.

"The white-bellied slug," murmured Ralph. "I'll do it if you let me use him instead of the broom."

The instant the words were out of his mouth he regretted them, for Torquay's chair and fist came down with a simultaneous bang as he shouted, "A promise is a promise! Sure I'll let you!"

"You're even cleverer than my mother, Mr. Strayton," said Ralph, with a smile." I could do it, but you know I won't, promise or no promise."

"Now I'll give you a job," said Torquay, "because I damn well please."

CHAPTER XVIII

THAT evening Janie grew desperate. She, her father and Albert were sitting in the large drawing-room which the Damons themselves had used with much more ceremony than Torquay. There was something too big about him to bend to saving a room or even a suit of clothes for special occasions. What he wanted he bought; what he had he used. The left side of the house was divided in three. The drawing-room opened with a wide arch into the library, which in turn opened on the dining-room through folding doors. Except in the library, there were tall French windows which gave directly on the lawns and trees that bordered a broad veranda only a step high whose flat roof was supported by fluted pillars. The expansiveness which resulted gave the whole place an air of having been built to fit Torquay.

Janie, especially in winter, would have liked to curl up in one of the big leather chairs before the open fireplace in the library, but her father prevented her. He did not speak to her, but he would walk up and down and around her until her passive resistance was exhausted. She had learned that as soon as she moved into the drawing-room and formed one of a group around the big lamp which stood on a mahogany table in one corner, her father would not only settle down at once but leave her more or less to her own devices. It was as though Torquay could feel at home only in a reconstruction of the triangle of the old house above the flats—his father, himself and Janie's mother.

He did not altogether leave Janie alone, for there never was a moment when he was not conscious of her presence. He would stare at his outstretched feet, propped on another chair, at Albert, at the furniture, and then shoot a glance at Janie's face. Sometimes she would look up uneasily to find his eyes engulfing without recognizing her. Again he would talk at her through Albert.

"Well, A-a-albert, tell Janie what they call you down at the works. Speak up. Don't be afraid. Perhaps that's what she calls you herself."

"They call me Peaches, sir."

"Did you hear that, Janie? They call him Peaches. I wonder why. Perhaps it's your lovely skin, A-a-albert."

Ordinarily Janie paid no heed, but that evening she felt she must find some escape at all costs. Like her mother, she seldom offered conversation, for though neither she nor her father was conscious of the fact, Torquay had ground silence into the warp and woof of her being. Consequently merely to hear her speak was always something of a sensation, and now, unknowingly, she was about to let fall a bomb.

"I saw Mr. Damon yesterday."

Torquay's hands gripped the arms of his chair and his whole frame grew rigid.

"You saw Mr. Damon," he repeated softly; and then exploded, "What Mr. Damon? Where?"

"Why, Mr. Ralph Damon," said Janie, staring at him in amazement. "He was on the roof of their house. He slipped and fell off. That's what I was going to tell you."

"Did he speak to you?"

"Yes," said Janie, flushing at the memory.

"What did he say?"

She shook her head.

"What did he say?" roared Torquay.

"He—he asked me if I knew how to dance."

"By God, the first time a man sees you, you let him ask you if you know how to dance, eh? Where were you? You were in your room, that's where you were! You were in the window of your room. What did you have on? I'll change your room. I'll put you on the other side of the house. I'll teach you to make a show of yourself to every man that wants to climb on a roof to look at you."

A pink flood poured over Janie's neck and face and then receded, leaving her as colorless as paper. Her dark eyes looked steadily at Torquay, but there was no emotion in them, no fear and no grief.

171

They seemed to have become suspended, to have ceased to see, feel or reflect the thought in the brain behind them. They were severed from herself.

In the end they defeated Torquay. His torrent of words stopped as abruptly as it had begun. He sat back in his chair and looked from Janie to Albert and from Albert back to Janie. Every movement of his eyes stood for a lot of rapid thinking. His brain was in the grip of a fever, but it was a fever which brought with it no blindness. It merely sharpened his wits to the verge of insane cunning. He arose, plunged into the hall and left the house, slamming the door loudly behind him. For the first time in their two years of living in the same house, Janie and Albert were left together alone.

Albert glanced over his shoulder instinctively to see if the curtains were drawn. He straightened in his chair, leaned forward and started to speak, but his lips had gone suddenly dry. He wet them with his tongue.

"Janie!" he whispered, hut as if she had not heard him her eyes remained fixed on where her father had been sitting. "Janie!" he repeated more loudly, and she turned her face slowly to him.

"What is it?"

He leaned far toward her and talked rapidly, with one ear cocked at the front door.

"Only this: It's something I've always wanted to tell you. You're the most beautiful girl I ever saw."

"Why, Albert!" gasped Janie, recovering abruptly from her abstraction. "What's come over you?"

"Only you—that's what's come over me. I've never had a chance before. I—I think you're the most beautiful girl I ever saw."

It did not occur to her to tell him he had said that already. Her mind was in a turmoil and she could think only of how changed he was and of how profoundly she had misjudged him. He jumped up, glanced at the door and then dropped on his knees, beside her. She thought he was about to propose to her in the old-fashioned manner, but before she could catch her breath he picked up her hand, kissed the tips of her fingers and hurried back to his chair.

"I've been wanting to do that for ages-just kiss the tips of your fingers."

She sat looking down at her hand without speaking. It seemed impossible that only five minutes before she and her father and the old Albert had been sitting in the dead air of all their intolerable evenings together. Somehow the room had become vibrant, and it was the new Albert who had brought about the change. The blood tingled in her veins as she listened for what he would say next. But it was not he who broke the long silence.

"Janie!"

The voice was thin, muffled, and came from far away. She straightened tensely and listened.

"Janie!"

"It's Miss Ball," whispered Albert, aghast. "What do you suppose— Why, she couldn't——"

Janie arose and went slowly into the hall. As she started up the stairs the front door opened and her father came in.

"Where are you going?" he asked.

"Miss Ball called me."

"She must have shouted pretty loud."

"I just could hear her. She didn't seem to be shouting."

"Go back into the drawing-room," ordered Torquay.

"Oh, I can't do that," said Janie. "I must go to Miss Ball."

"You're not going to her now," said Torquay, "because that's where I'm headed myself. You go back or to bed."

"I'll go to bed," said Janie, and went quickly up the stairs before him.

But she did not go all the way to her room. She stopped halfway, leaned on the rail and listened. She heard her father rap sharply on Miss Ball's door and enter, closing it behind him. They began to talk; but though she had heard Miss Ball from the drawing room, she could not make out a word they were saying, now that she was much nearer. She saw Albert come out into the hall and start up the stairs cautiously. His room was a small one at the back of the house on the same floor as Miss Ball's. He hesitated when he got to the top of the flight and she thought he was looking for her.

"Albert!" she called softly.

"No, no!" he whispered hastily. "I can't come up to you."

"I just wanted to say goodnight," explained Janie.

"Oh, yes. Good night, dear. Don't tell anything."

He hurried to his room. She had a feeling of disappointment in him, as if he had changed back into the old Albert while she was not looking. She fixed her mind on his sudden boldness in the drawing-room and tried to think that if she had been present he would not have turned soft again. It was her influence that had made him into a man and if it had happened once it could happen again. If she truly loved him and he her, she might make him into anything she wished. She went on slowly up the stairs, dreaming.

Both Torquay and Miss Ball were of the sort who can be violent without noise. Torquay had come into her room prepared for a battle and it chanced that he found her in the same mood. He stood by the door for a moment, getting his bearings. There was a great bay window overlooking the lawn at the front of the house, and facing it, against the opposite wall, stood a bed of equally vast proportions whereon lay Miss Ball. Her head was illumined by a reading lamp placed on a stand, but the rest of her showed only as a blurred and bulky outline. Her hair was neatly dressed and she wore a bed jacket over her nightdress, for night and day had become one to her. Pain and its momentary absence were the only divisions of her hours.

Near the bed was a large chair placed for Janie's convenience, but Torquay did not immediately make use of it. He strode up and down, doing something with his hands he had never done before and that he had never seen anyone do except old John Polperro. He was cracking his knuckles one after the other.

"Stop that," said Miss Ball. "If you want to pull your fingers out by the roots, go somewhere else to do it."

She spoke quietly, but with the authority of one who has finished with all servitude. She thought she had no desires left for herself. Food, clothing, shelter, life and death had assumed an equal insignificance. No one and nothing could assail her.

"Janie has got to marry Albert," said Torquay.

In an instant Miss Ball's assurance crumbled into consternation. "You're mad!" she gasped. "I always knew it."

"I can do anything with Albert," he continued as if she had not spoken. "He'll stay where I put him. He'll do what I tell him. It's like I'd been training him for this all the time, but I never saw it until tonight."

"Janie should never marry. If I thought so before, I think it more now. You're mad. Your father was mad."

"And you're a sick old woman," retorted Torquay brutally, "with only one thought left working in your brain. A lot I care whether you think I'm mad or not as long as I know you're an old fool! If she marries Albert she stays here, don't she? I can watch her and so can you and Mega. But if she marries that Damon lad, he'll tell the lot of us to go to hell."

"That Damon lad?" repeated Miss Ball in a whisper.

"Yes; that makes you think a bit, don't it?" He began cracking his knuckles again, this time unnoticed by Miss Ball. "He'd take her away if it was to live in a barrel. He'd empty this house. I wouldn't ever see her, and you wouldn't. She'd not be Torquay Strayton's daughter; she'd be Mrs. Ralph Damon and all his mother's hoity-toity friends would fall over themselves to call on her in a backhouse. They'd make a ring around her, with you and me on the outside."

"Why do you think she'd marry the Damon boy? She doesn't even know him."

"Oh, yes, she does. She's known him to talk to for two days. She showed herself to him in her window when he was on the roof of his house."

"I don't believe it," said Miss Ball, clutching one of the pillows beside her and twisting a corner of it in her trembling hands. For a time her body was wrenched with spasms of pain. She did not utter a sound, but agony was written large in her face and in the slow contortions of her limbs. Finally she emerged from the actual struggle and lay panting, her forehead shining with sweat. Some moments elapsed before she murmured with closed eyes, "Send Janie to me."

"You admit she's got to marry Albert?"

"I don't admit anything until I see her."

Torquay laid his hands on the back of the chair and leaned on it. It cracked in every joint with his weight. He stared belligerently at Miss Ball, but she would not open her eyes.

"All right," he said at last; "but let me tell you one thing: If you meddle with my plans I'll lock the door on you and bring in your food myself. No one will come here, only me and the doctor."

He twirled the heavy chair as if it were a thumb top. It tottered groggily and settled down with a thud as he left the room. Presently Janie came in, still fully dressed, and sat down.

"Yes, Miss Ball."

Miss Ball turned her head slightly, suddenly opened her eyes and fastened them on Janie. It was almost as if she had taken a mechanical grip on her with a pair of forceps.

"Well, Janie?"

"I went for a ride yesterday," began Janie presently. "Along the river and across the meadows, and then over the hills to Lower Hopetown. It was lovely. In the afternoon I read the Third Epoch of Jocelyn. It's longer than the second, and there were two words I couldn't find in the dictionary. The evening was just the same as they always were—before tonight."

"Is that all?" asked Miss Ball, tightening the forceps.

"No. After I came in here I went to my room. I was standing at the window thinking how terrible it would be if anything happened to you. I wasn't looking at anything. All of a sudden a voice quite near by said something and I answered before I knew what I was doing." She paused, but Miss Ball did not speak. "It was Ralph Damon, the same one that hit me with the apple. He asked me if I knew how to dance and I said no. He had a piece of board in one hand and a hammer in the other. He must have been mending the roof. Then he tried to get up too quickly and he slipped and fell all the way down. I tried not to be glad; but I had to ask him if he was hurt and he said no."

"And this evening," murmured Miss Ball.

"You mean when you called me?"

176

"Yes."

"Father went out. Perhaps you heard him slam the door. Then Albert surprised me. He changed all of a sudden. He said I was the most beautiful girl he'd ever seen and he kissed the tips of my fingers. Then we heard you calling." Miss Ball made no comment. There was a longer silence than before. Finally Janie asked, "Is that all, Miss Ball?"

"Yes; you may go to bed."

CHAPTER XIX

WHEN her father called to Janie to go to Miss Ball she had responded so quickly that he had seen her come out of her room before he turned. In the half light she looked exactly as her mother had looked when she had stepped out of Torquay's bedroom at Thomas Strayton's command. That was the night of the broken banister and the crashing fall which had maimed Thomas for life. If he had minded his own business he would have saved his leg and it might never have occurred to Torquay to marry. His father had driven him into marriage and through marriage into a shadowy realm of half-seen demons where no man could plant his feet. He would never have known an hour of torture if he had kept on living in and for the Pine Tree Glassworks.

He left the house and hurried down to his workshop. Why had he turned his back on it? He stood on the oyster-shell mound and stared at the black shed which looked as if it were on the verge of crumbling into a ruin. The sight of his daughter Janie came between him and the dark building. He forgot the five years of his battle for the life of the Pine Tree Glassworks. All he could see was two pale women in one, twisting him this way and that, tormenting him with things beyond the reach of a man's hands, making a mockery of the strength of Torquay Strayton. By thunder, he'd show Janie, and he'd show his father! If she wanted to leave him, she'd have to take the same road her mother had traveled.

He plunged beneath the low eaves of the shed to get away from himself, but the darkness did not soothe him. He struck a match and lit the flares; to his surprise, there was oil in the lamps. He went to the furnace, thinking of the hard work it would be to start it up unaided; but the bed of kindling, logs and coal was already carefully laid. That was the way his plant was run, he thought with a touch of pride. His men knew what ought to be done and nobody had to ride them.

He set the drafts, turned the water cocks and lit the fire. It burned with a roar, for it had been laid and seasoning for five years. He left it for a while, went to his desk in the mold room and lit the double student lamp with green shades whose brass base weighted down a sheet of yellowing paper. On it was written the last of a long sequence of formulas. The stubborn hope of years burst into flame in his heart. Perhaps this was the combination he had sought all his life. Throughout the night he sat in the mold room, going over older experiments and rushing out every half hour to stoke the fire and bring the tank up to fusing heat.

In the weeks that followed, Albert was almost stunned to find that not only was his time his own for much of the day but that Torquay had found something to do besides bait him and watch Janie in the evenings. Albert had once gone as far as the oyster-shell mound with a message he thought important, but he had been met with such a torrent of invective when he ducked his head to pass under the eaves that he had scarcely had time to catch a glimpse of a fantastic Torquay in blue overalls, backed by Ralph Damon, naked to the waist and handling an old-fashioned blowing iron as lightly as if it were a trout rod.

"Get the hell out of here," roared Torquay, "you fruit salad, you pink-cheeked bladder, you soap ad, you breakfast——"

But Albert waited to hear no more. He hastened away, wondering vapidly how Torquay Strayton, who had flown into a rage at the mere mention of Ralph Damon's name, could be making of that same Damon the companion of his weird orgies. He could not understand that he had stumbled on a master key to that inner Torquay who was so big he could lay a mark and boost a good man on one side of it as readily as he was prepared to knock him down if he crossed it. Ralph Damon never went up the hill from the works as far as Torquay was concerned, but in two months he had become as much a fixture in the plant itself as one of the huge new bottle machines.

Albert was puzzled in the extreme by Torquay's contradictory attitude. He seemed to be treated more abominably than ever, and yet he had come to be trusted enough to be left evening after evening alone with Janie. The fact that he felt he was betraying the confidence placed in him somewhat weakened the style of his courtship, but it did not put a stop to it. His plans were definite. He wished to win Janie's heart to the point where she would declare for him and no other. Failing that, there was a darker road along which he might ride roughshod over Torquay and Miss Ball's objections. He was coward enough to shrink from his own conception, but rascal enough to force his mind to cling to it as a last resource.

As for Janie, she was living with one foot in a dream world and one foot out. Sometimes she found herself standing on one leg, sometimes on the other. There were days when she was sublimely happy in the thought that only a man of great strength of character could have hidden his love for two whole years. There were other times when the creak of a door or a distant footfall would make Albert start guiltily, drop her hand, or leap up from her side and pick up a book. At such moments her brows would pucker into a frown. She would lose her illusion completely and sit dazed, wondering what had become of the man her fancy was so quick to build up again when she was alone. It astonished her to discover she could love Albert best when he was out of sight. He in turn had an occasional spark of scorn for her gullibility. To him she seemed a fool and the game almost too easy. He could not conceive that she had grown up in an atmosphere from which the idea of avarice had been eliminated.

Like most supreme dictators, Torquay was genuinely democratic. He liked to have the best food, clothing and service obtainable and he took pride in always owning the fastest road horses in the county; but for a person of his wealth and position these were simple needs. He had never felt the slightest impulse to make a splurge, and if his older workmen continued to address him as Torque, it was because the man in him persisted as something big enough to eclipse his money. Janie may have been a simpleton in never once thinking of herself as the outstanding heiress of the locality, but her simplicity was merely a tribute to a quality in her father too large to be ticketed and hung on a peg.

The effect on Albert can be easily explained, but scarcely measured. He had been torn from a setting where a shilling bulked so tremendously in the exigences of daily existence that perspective was reversed. To him, love, courage, family, children and every other form of human development were things to be glimpsed around the edges of a coin. Naturally the most important thing in life was to be assured one could eat to the end of one's days. The next important thing was shelter. After that came raiment, which offered the first bridge from necessity to luxury. When one was once sure of warmth one could pass on to display. Finally the man who married money was a genius, worthy of the envious esteem of his fellows. In a manner of speaking, Albert was as straightforwardly simple as Janie herself.

All went smoothly for the lover of sudden ease. He was ready at any time to chance his luck with Janie, but there was one thing that gave him pause. Every time he thought of the moment of facing Torquay the marrow in his bones turned cold. What would the huge man say? More important still, what might he not do in one of his abrupt outbursts of rage? Albert had reason to ponder long on this particular point, for Torquay did not always go directly from the supper table to his workshop, and whenever he lingered it was to indulge in a new habit of cracking his knuckles while he shot glances like blows at Janie's impassive face.

"What's the matter with your father?" asked Albert uneasily one evening just after Torquay had gone out.

"I don't know," murmured Janie. "It has nothing to do with us. He's looked at me like that ever since I can remember." Albert frowned.

"Has Miss Ball been asking you any questions lately?"

"No; she never did exactly ask me questions. I just used to tell her things. But she's not the same anymore. She's changed. I mean her body is changing. There's something terrible the matter with her and I don't think she'll ever get well."

"I know," said Albert indifferently. "It's dropsy."

Janie · arose. "Oh, Albert, I'm so frightened." He sprang to his feet, threw his arms around her and drew her close. She sank against him with a sigh of relief and dropped her head on his shoulder. He began to tremble, but his arms only tightened their hold. Something told him that this was his moment as far as Janie was concerned.

"Don't be frightened," he whispered. "Kiss me." She shook her head quickly, but did not draw away. Instead she slipped her arms around his waist and clung to him.

Outside, Torquay had run into Ralph Damon, evidently on his way to the Strayton house.

"What do you want?" he asked sharply, making no attempt to hide his amazement at Ralph's daring to come to the house. Damon was taken aback.

"I had something to tell you," he half stammered.

"Let it wait," growled Torquay.

"It's an infusion of gelatin," blurted Damon, trying to seize Torquay's attention and justify his own intrusion. "It's not the real thing, but if you're going down to your workshop——"

"I'm not," interrupted Torquay. He turned on his heel and went back to the house.

He glanced over his shoulder to make sure Damon was not following, then he threw open the door and stepped into the hall. His eyes fell immediately on Albert and Janie, standing in the drawing-room locked in each other's arms. For an instant he felt as if the rush of blood to his head would burst his temples. He wanted not only to kill Albert; he would have liked to tear him limb from limb. He opened and closed his hands slowly, took a stealthy step forward and then stopped. Something passive in Janie's pose had arrested him and given him time to think. This was just what he had been playing for, wasn't it? A hard smile lit up his eyes.

"Well, A-a-lbert?" he drawled.

Albert's dreaded moment of the supreme test had come upon him so suddenly that he was robbed of any opportunity to vacillate. Just as it is sometimes given to the mouse to become a lion and to the worm to turn, so did he face Torquay with an indistinguishable imitation of courage. He even stood away from Janie.

"We love each other, sir," he declared in a full voice.

"We want to be married."

"Is that right, Janie?" asked Torquay, ominously calm.

Her eyes were full of Albert standing up to her father at last. He had not really asked her to marry him in so many words, but this was even better. He had been telling her of his love for many days, and now he was not only bold enough to face Torquay Strayton but dared take her consent by storm. She nodded her head, her eyes fixed full on Albert.

"You'll marry him?" persisted Torquay.

"Yes," she said clearly.

Albert turned his head to look at her, the gleam of a first triumph in his eyes. Torquay strode forward and slapped him on the back. It was a terrific blow and it did strange things to Albert. Interiorly it made him see stars and think every bone in his body was dislocated. Exteriorly it made his legs flip up at the knees and forced him to dash across the room and crack his shins against a heavy chair in his wild effort to save himself from a headlong fall. Never did suitor become more instantaneously ridiculous.

"Congratulations!" roared Torquay.

"What did you say, sir?" stuttered Albert, holding to the chair and one shin. He could hardly believe his ears, but Torquay looked more genial than he ever had before.

"What did you say, sir?"

"Congratulations!" repeated Torquay. "Blessings! You can have her."

"I don't want him now," murmured Janie.

"What do you mean?" demanded Torquay, turning on her with a frown. "You wanted him a minute ago, didn't you?"

"Yes," said Janie; "but not now."

"Nonsense!" shouted Torquay, feeling a first premonition that he had made a grave error. "Even a woman can't change as quick as that!" He wanted to say more, but stopped himself. "Fix it with her, Albert," he added impatiently as he turned to leave the room. "It's up to you now to shake the nonsense out of her."

The words were all Albert needed to turn him as constantly bold as he had once been cautious. Not only his manner but his fiber changed. The very next morning, upon arriving at the office, he took the broom from the cupboard, marched into the works, opened a furnace door and threw it in. At the house he assailed Janie on every occasion with a flair which sometimes nearly carried her off her feet. But every time her own knees weakened, the recollection of the way in which Albert's legs had flipped up as he started on his career across the floor of the drawing-room blinded her to his new qualities. Her mouth might be warm with the anticipation of a first kiss, but that memory was always enough to make it curl disdainfully, sometimes against a distinct effort of her will.

Torquay grew impatient and then nervous. He had several interviews with Miss Ball and took to spending time at home that he would far rather have devoted to the research to which Damon's inspiration had given fresh impetus. Ever since their unfortunate encounter on Torquay's grounds, Ralph had assumed a distant manner which would have galled any other employer; but it fitted in too well with Torquay's ends for him to quarrel with it. He encouraged the mental mechanism that worked in step with his own brain and accepted the total submergence of sociability without a word of protest.

He was cool and keen in Damon's company in the workshop, but at the house he became a chained beast. He would sit staring at Janie, his feet doubled under his chair, his hands locked and his heavy body leaning forward on his elbows.

"First you say you will, then you say you won't.

What kind of dealing is that? Empty as a woman's word—that's the name for it."

"Father!"

"Yes. Cuddle up in his arms, take a good taste of him, and then lick your lips and look around for the next."

"Oh, please, father——"

"Don't wrap your tongue around me. If I'd said you couldn't marry him you'd have slid down the vines to get at him. You'd have done anything for him—anything. Ha! Women! The blackness that creeps into them while you're watching every hour, every minute, and you don't see it go in! All you know, it's there and if you bust 'em open you'll find a black core."

"But I promised never to leave you, never!" Janie would cry wildly, torn between her present trouble and the memory of that breathless moment when she had cast herself into her father's arms. In those days she had thought that if he would speak to her, if it were only to curse, she would be completely happy.

"Who's asking you to leave me? Who asked you to leave Albert? Blackness—that's what it is. Nobody ever asked you to leave no one, only yourself."

After a series of these scenes, with Torquay roaring as loud as ever Jake Damon had shouted in his drunken outbursts against his wife, Albert made a show of his boldness one evening by bearding Torquay in the drawing-room which had so often witnessed his own humiliation.

"You want to look out, sir. She'll be calling you by the name Ralph Damon has given you down at the works."

"Damon, eh? What name is that?"

"Torquemada of Lion Hill."

"Who the hell was Torquemada? Speak up now! You started this! Spit it out!"

"Why, father, you know," said Janie quickly. She was up in arms to defend him against the supercilious smile growing on Albert's lips. "He was the head of the Spanish Inquisition—the greatest torturer the world has ever seen. You've just forgotten."

"Torturer, eh?" muttered Torquay, scorning to cover up his ignorance. His broad shoulders slumped and Janie sprang toward him.

"It's a horrible lie!" she cried, laying a trembling hand on his arm.

He stared at it, powerless to move. It was as slender and smooth as the other Janie's hand had been with the spot of black ink shining on its whiteness. He struck it away and plunged from the room. Presently Miss Ball sent for Janie. When she entered the familiar room it seemed to have changed. Everything appeared to have grown smaller in proportion as the snow mountain on the bed had risen. Even Miss Ball's bust had shrunk to nothing, leaving her head almost a disjointed thing inhabited only by her eyes. They were still alive. They fastened on Janie, led her to the old chair and made her sit down.

"Well, Janie?"

"Today I went for a ride. I——"

"Never mind that."

There was a long silence, prolonged far beyond the limits of any ordinary break in conversation. It was not a passive pause; it was more in the nature of a profound struggle, a combat of the unnamable forces which determine the intimate relationship between mind and mind.

"One man is as good as another," continued Miss Ball at last. "You'd better make up your mind about Albert."

"You mean——" whispered Janie.

"That's all," said Miss Ball, interrupting her. "You may go."

What had she meant, thought Janie, standing in the middle of her new room, which overlooked the growing town. Did she mean she was going to die and that marriage with Albert would somehow take her place? She kept on asking herself questions that could be put in words, but deep inside her there was a magnetic needle which pointed steadily to a frozen north. The hours seemed a blank that intervened between that moment and the next evening, when she found herself alone with Albert.

Her father was nowhere around. She had not heard him go out, but the open door showed her the study was dark. She went to Albert with grave purpose in her face. He put his arms around her and to his surprise she did not resist even when he drew her to the couch. She let him fondle her. With half-closed eyes she waited for a sign from within herself that she might some day find in him the man she loved. Her father stepped out from the dark study and stood glaring at them. His eyes were blood-shot and his fists were clenched at his sides. She broke away and sprang to her feet, a wave of color staining her cheeks. " 'More bitter than death the woman whose heart is snares and nets,' " rumbled Torquay. " 'Counting one by one, to find out the account . . . one man among a thousand have I found; but a woman among all those have I not found.' "

Albert would not have approached him in that mood for a clear title to the Pine Tree Glassworks and all the Strayton wealth, but Janie walked straight toward him. There was a look in her eyes that told Torquay he might strike her, strangle her, and she would not flinch.

He half threw up one arm to ward her off, but she slipped inside it, came close to him and laid her hands on his shoulders.

"Father, do you wish me to marry Albert?" His arms closed around her slowly as if they moved against his will, but there was no tenderness in them. They were like iron vibrating in unison with distant machinery.

"Yes," he muttered hoarsely.

"I'll marry him for your sake."

"Yes; for my sake," repeated Torquay dumbly.

She burst into tears, her face pressed hard against him. Her body seemed to melt and dissolve so that he was forced to hold it up. He stood staring blindly at the floor until she straightened and released herself.

CHAPTER XX

A T noontime on the next day but one, Ralph Damon, having finished his lunch, was reading the local paper.

"Well, I'll be damned!" he gasped.

"Why?" asked his mother.

"The Strayton girl is engaged to that Peach Blossom."

"You mean Mr. Polperro?"

"Peaches, Polperro, or Poll Parrot—take your choice."

"You seemed to be annoyed about it."

"Have you ever seen her?" asked Ralph, as if he expected an answer.

"Only from a distance. And you?"

"Mother, do you mind telling me why you never called there?"

Mrs. Damon laid down her book.

"No," she said, "I don't. It was because that sort of thing was specifically excluded in the price Mr. Strayton paid for our house and furniture. You can scarcely remember it, but he bought everything we had except our strictly personal effects and self respect."

"You knew if you didn't call, no one else would, didn't you?"

"Yes; I suppose I did."

"Well, now I'll answer the question you asked me. I've seen the girl and I think it's a dirty shame."

"I won't reprove you for your language, because it's so direct and to the point, but I can't resist reminding you the girl wasn't born at the time."

"But her mother was, wasn't she?"

"Her mother had been my nursemaid, but that wasn't why I didn't call on her. It was on account of something else."

"What?"

"You're sure you want to know?"

"Of course."

"It was because I was afraid I would fall in love—really in love—with Torquay Strayton."

"Merciful cats!" cried Ralph.

"Sometimes the only way to pay back an impertinent question," murmured his mother, "is to answer it. What particular interest have you in the Strayton girl?"

"Mother, you're clever—genuinely clever. You deserve your piece of cake. Except in the far distance, I have seen Miss Janie Strayton only twice, once when I soaked her with the apple and once when one good look at her made me fall off the roof."

"With fright?"

"No," said Ralph thoughtfully; "the other thing."

There was a pause; Mrs. Damon picked up her book. "Torquay Strayton," he continued, musing aloud.

"Well, I'm not so surprised as my cry of pain may have led you to think. He's a man all over. Twenty years ago I can imagine even you falling for him. Today he's a sort of wandering giant and he's lost his way."

"What do you mean?"

"You've heard him yelling, haven't you?"

"Yes," said Mrs. Damon, her mind leaping to other memories. "Is that all?"

"No. Any man who would give his daughter to that soap ad, that pink-cheeked bladder——"

"Ralph!"

"I beg your pardon, but those are a couple of the names I've heard him call his future son-in-law."

"Then you're betraying a professional confidence."

"Mother, do you believe Torque Strayton is mad?"

"No."

CHAPTER XXI

IF Janie had consented to marry Albert with the unspoken hope of winning some demonstration of her father's love, she was quickly disillusioned. It is true that Albert grew into more of a man day by day, sometimes not quite along the lines she would have chosen. But the more he assumed the prerogatives of a successful suitor, the more strangely did Torquay react. Though she could not know it, he was going through a hell of his own making. He had hung himself on tenterhooks above a fire and the one thing that kept him from treating Albert as Albert had treated his broom was the obsession that in Albert lay his only chance of keeping Janie within the range of his eyes. The sight of her tormented him; but her absence would drive him mad, to Miss Ball's complete vindication.

"Torquemada of Lion Hill!"

The name made him laugh grimly. It had caught on and he could feel its influence undermining the reputation it had taken so many years to build. No; that wasn't fair. He had never tried to build anything except the Pine Tree Glassworks and that stood as solid as a flourishing oak. His reputation had grown on him as naturally as the bark on a tree, and if there were any who wished to hack at it with their puny axes, let them hack and be damned. Instead of swerving to the storm, he drove straight along the way upon which he had set his feet. He would make no more false moves that might give Janie an excuse to dodge her marriage.

By day he sat in his office and from time to time passed unexpectedly through the plant. Never were his subordinates kept more constantly on their toes, and wherever a Pine Tree workman happened to pass his idle hours there was one defender to jeer at the gossip that Torque Strayton was getting a bit touched in his old age. Sixty-one was not really old, and with Torquay it merely represented the stormy equinox of dampening fires which comes to most men

190

much earlier in life. He was sound in wind, bone and body and he proved it by spending half of every night in his workshop.

The older hands, from among whom he always picked his night crew, would have grumbled if they had not been ashamed to let him best them.

Ralph Damon, the sole accepted volunteer from the younger set, had proved a deserter. He tended to his job in the main plant more assiduously than ever, but the shadow of the lone tree by the oyster-shell mound had not fallen on him since the hour he had read of Janie's engagement. He was well aware that his disaffection might be misread by all and sundry if they had the wit to link up one event with the other, but there were two people who would make no mistake as to his motives and the rest could go hang. One of these two was himself, the other was Torquay Strayton.

Two months was the maximum of grace that Janie could wrest from Torquay, Miss Ball and Albert for preparation for her marriage; but there was no limit to what she might spend on clothes. Torquay raised Albert's pay and advanced the money for such an engagement ring as had never before been sent to Hopetown. He shrewdly attended to the buying of it himself, having long since taken Albert's measure in matters of finance. Miss Ball dictated letters which brought sketches, models and implorations that Miss Strayton might appear in person for the selection of her trousseau. Torquay took her to New York.

It seemed to Janie that whatever the troubles life was holding in store for her, that journey would pay for them all. True enough, Torquay left her to sit in lonely state on the train while he retired to the smoker with the pipe which had become his inseparable companion; but once in New York, he chartered one of the few taxicabs then running and stood by her through every ordeal of a thrilling day. To sit beside him in the intimacy of a cab was joy enough, but to follow him across the broad sidewalks and into smart shops where the weightiest purse was apt to get light-headed was a revelation and a bulwark to her pride. He was as unconcerned as a rolling bowlder. Everybody looked at him with a sort of gasp of the eyes; he looked at nobody. When passers-by saw Janie they looked again, but she was too bewildered to realize her share in his triumphal progress.

"What a lovely suit, Miss Strayton! Did we do that for you?"

To Torquay shops were only stores and floor ladies were only store hands. As for the customers who looked up startled at so much bulk, he was attending to his business and he left it to them to attend to theirs. Where Janie planted him during her enforced disappearances, he came to rest on his two feet and took no more credit for patience than a rock. She would come out in glory from a cubicle and stand before him.

"Father, do you like this?"

His eyes would wrap her around for an instant and then look away.

"Do you like it, Janie?"

"Oh, I think it's lovely."

"We'll take that," he would say with a side nod to the saleswoman.

Janie was left alone for a moment with a parading model. The girl passed closer and closer until she was within easy speaking distance.

"Forgive me for telling you, lady," she murmured, "but you've got some father."

"Yes!" gasped Janie.

"This country ought to adopt him and have a live one for a change. He's big enough."

Janie laughed aloud. The saleswoman hurried to her.

"Excuse me, but did the model speak to you?" she asked crisply.

"Yes," said Janie, giving her a level look. "She said something that made me like the dress. I wasn't going to take it, but I will now."

On the way to the station the thought struck her that she was having her last moments alone with her father. A thickness came into her throat and her eyes began to smart. She half put out her hand to lay it on his arm, but he shrank into his corner.

"Oh, father," she gulped, "I've just got to tell you! You've been wonderful!"

"Wonderful?" said Torquay. "We came to get the things and we got 'em, didn't we?"

"Yes," said Janie, and turned her head to look out of the window through eyes that saw nothing. She was happy again long before they got back to Hopetown and all went well until the night she told Torquay she wished to give a reception. It was no sudden whim. As her wedding day approached, a cold terror seized her. A film was slowly lifting from her eyes. For the first time in her life she conceived of the great house as a prison guarded by grim jailers. Mega, still the dark inscrutable woman. Miss Ball, half dead and yet pervasively alive. Her father, watching her with a look that did not seem to see her. Albert, gradually growing into a sinister threat. She had never before felt she was caged, but now even her wings were going to be clipped.

"A reception!" rumbled Torquay, his heavy brows drawn into a black frown. "What for?"

"The people who come we could invite to the wedding," explained Janie.

"Who do you think would come?" asked Torquay roughly. "All the folks that have called on us, eh?"

"I've thought about it a lot," persisted Janie. "I think a great many people wouldn't dare not come."

"Have you made out a list?" demanded Torquay sharply to hide his growing nervousness.

"No; just the usual social notice in the paper. That would be enough."

He started to say he would see her further first, but he caught his tongue and a cunning light came into his eyes. She was right. There were a lot of men and their wives who wouldn't dare stay away from such a summons. There were other women who would jump at the chance to repair an error of long years' standing. They'd break down the wall. They'd sweep in on her and float her out into the camp where she belonged. It would be as bad as if Ralph Damon had married her. Janie was watching him gravely. Her lip trembled.

"Will you put the notice in the paper?"

"Yes," said Torquay, never suspecting how near the word carried him to damning his immortal soul.

Janie had a free hand as to the arrangements for her reception which had to take place at once or not at all. Mega followed her instructions with unusual meekness and slanted eyes. The maid did the extra work willingly but without enthusiasm. There was no time for any but local caterers and their resources were heavily drawn upon. Jim was sent on a tour of all the local hothouses. On the eve of the appointed day Janie was waiting for her father when he came up from the works for a hurried supper.

"The notice wasn't in the paper," she said. "You—you promised."

"It will be tomorrow," answered Torquay shortly.

"People won't know until almost noon," murmured Janie.

"Well, what of it? You said they wouldn't dare not come. It won't take 'em four hours to get here, will it?"

The next morning all Hopetown was having a laugh at the Straytons' expense. By lunchtime Ralph Damon was telephoning and sending wires broadcast to locate his mother who was away on a round of visits. Down in the town the habitués of Striker's were assembled in full force and Chet Griswold was saying, "Well, that's the tin hat! Any man dares say Torque ain't mad from now on is asking for a free ride over the hill to the bughouse."

Ed Bristol wrinkled his withered forehead and puffed huge clouds of smoke from his pipe.

"I'll take the ride," he muttered.

"What?" Everyone looked at him pityingly.

"If all of us was mad like Torque, and Thomas before him," continued Chet stubbornly, "we'd each own a bank."

"A sand bank, eh?" They all laughed at that.

"Even a sand bank was enough to eat up the Damons," murmured Ed, but no one was listening to him any longer; he spoke too low.

In the great house on Lion Hill the drawing-room, the library and the dining-room had been thrown into one. Never in the palmiest days of their social preeminence had the rooms looked lovelier. Masses of flowers brightened their shadows. Everything a smoker could desire was at hand in the library, while from beyond came the gleam of snowy table linen and shining silver. Janie was sitting very still amid the banks of cut flowers. She had read the morning paper. She looked as if her eyes would never move again. But when Mega came in and asked if she wanted lunch, she spoke quite clearly, though her lips scarcely stirred.

"No, thank you; and please don't come in again unless I ring."

On the other side of the cedars Ralph Damon was still haunting the telephone; it never occurred to him to go back to work. Occasionally he would pass through to the front window, from which he could see a short stretch of Main Street and the entrance to the big house where the curving driveway sprang out from the double thicket of evergreens. The telephone rang at last. He ran to it, knocking over a chair on his way.

"Is that you, mother?"

"Yes; what on earth is the matter?"

"Where are you?"

"In New York."

"God!"

"Ralph, what has happened? We were just going to the matinee, but if it's something important——"

"No, you can't do that! Please, mother, catch the first train and I'll have a car waiting for you at the Camden side of the ferry. You've got to travel down here faster than you ever moved before."

"Ralph, tell me at once what's the matter. I called you up the minute I got your first telegram, and two more have arrived while we've been speaking. All they say is for me to come before four or get in touch with you if I'm too far away. I can't possibly get there by four. Now tell me."

"There are some things you can't explain over the telephone. All I can tell you is there's a dirty lowdown murder going to be pulled here this afternoon and you're the only one who can spike the gun. If you can't come by four, you can by five or by six. But if you don't try your best I'll never forgive you and you won't blame me."

"I'm an old woman, Ralph, but I'll start for the station in five minutes. Good-by."

195

Ralph pored over time-tables. If his mother caught the one o'clock train, she would not need the car, as she could make a connection which would bring her to Hopetown by five. He glanced at his watch and saw that she could scarcely make it. He ordered a car by telephone to go to Camden and wait for her. If she had to use it she could not reach home before six. That would be rotten, but it couldn't be helped. He sat down to wait. Every time he thought of the notice in the paper his face would turn hot, his eyes glittered, and he would jump up to pace from one end of the small house to the other.

The notice had appeared just as Janie had written it:

> Miss Strayton and Mr. Torquay Strayton will receive their friends this afternoon at a reception to be held in the Strayton home on Lion Hill from four to six.

That was the way it read, but instead of being one of half a dozen social notes, it was headed NOTICE in large letters and had been placed in the advertising section along with other paid matter. What self-respecting man would obey that insolent order? What woman would see in it anything but a chance to damage her own prestige?

At four Damon went to his room and dressed immaculately in clothes he had seldom put on since an immemorial custom had given him the right to wear them upon becoming a junior at college. After that he spent his time hurrying backward and forward to keep watch on the road up from the works and on the main entrance to the Strayton place; the house itself he could not see. This occupation prevented him from going to the station on the chance his mother should come by train. At a quarter after five he gave her up, left a note for her pinned to the advertisement in the paper and started out alone. Not a single guest had passed between the pillars ornamented by his grandfather with the great balls of devitrified glass. What was worse, neither Torquay nor Albert had come up from the works.

Ralph was not in the mood nor was he dressed to push his way through the gap in the cedars. Carrying stick and gloves, he went down the narrow road and turned into Main Street. As he did so three youngsters spied him and for an instant were struck dumb; then one of them recovered breath and wits.

"Hey, you, Mr. Damon!" he shouted. "We don't want no grand dukes from the Grand Cañon this town!"

Ralph smiled, but did not turn his head. He was wondering if he was about to make a fool of himself to someone besides the boys in the street. He arrived at the big house and was about to press the bell when he noticed the door was wide open and unattended. Probably the maid, tired out with waiting for people who would not arrive, had gone away, forgetting to close it. As a baby he had been lord of this domain, he had ruled it for four years. It seemed absurd to ring. He entered, laid his things on the hall table, went to the drawing-room door and looked in.

Janie was sitting in a big chair directly facing him. She had on the most charming of her new afternoon frocks. It was slightly open at the neck and her throat and face rose from it like white marble from a chalice. She was looking straight at him, but to his amazement she did not move. He felt a flash of embarrassment before it struck him that whatever the reason she did not see him.

"Miss Strayton?"

She sprang to her feet with an indistinct cry and threw one hand to her throat.

"Oh!" she gasped. "I thought I was dreaming!"

"I know you were," said Ralph easily. "I could see it in your face."

"I don't meant that," said Janie, with something of her father's honesty in speech. "I mean I saw you come in quite plainly, but I was sure I only dreamed it. You are Mr. Damon, aren't you? Won't you sit down?"

If composure in the face of disaster stood for breeding, thought Ralph, she was thoroughbred from the toes of her slippers to the top of her yellow head. Her hair fascinated him. It was swept in a broad smooth band straight around her head, its ends hidden in mystery. What fools women were to pray for curly hair! Perhaps it was because they were too lazy to do this sort of thing.

"Won't you sit down?" she repeated.

"No," he said, coming to himself. "I'd rather eat if you don't mind. It won't be any trouble, will it?"

"Hardly," said Janie, leading the way toward the dining-room.

"You see, I didn't have any lunch," he explained.

She stopped in the middle of the library and turned toward him, surprised.

"Why not?"

He met her eyes squarely.

"Do you want me to answer?"

She looked down for a moment, her brows drawn in a thoughtful frown, and then up again.

"Yes."

"For the very same reason you didn't eat any."

"You shouldn't have said that," whispered Janie.

She reached out her hand, steadied herself on the back of a chair and then suddenly crumpled into it, buried her face in her arm and began to cry. He stood staring down at her, his jaw set and his clenched hands thrust deep in his pockets. "What made you say it?" she sobbed. "Why couldn't you have helped me play the game?"

"It's you who aren't playing the game," said Ralph sharply.

She raised her head, but not to look at him.

"You mean that," she stated.

"Of course I mean it. A lot of people never learn the only way to find out there are two sides to a table is to kick it over. Never be sore at a low-down trick. It will always help you. It's only another name for a boomerang."

"I can't understand all that—not just now."

"And I can't explain it; but my mother will as soon as she can get here."

"Your mother?"

"Yes; she's on her way from New York. She's the one woman who wouldn't have been stumped by that notice—and she had to be away!"

Janie arose swiftly and faced the hall.

"If she should come in that door, I would make a bigger fool of myself than I have with you. I couldn't stand it now."

"You're not the kind of person who can make a fool of herself. You'll never make a fool of yourself as long as you live. I'll tell you why—you're too real."

"It's strange you should say that. I've always wished I could be just myself."

"And what have you been?"

"I've been the shadow of something. I don't know of just what, but I've been a shadow. It must be that, because I've never been held and I've never held anything."

"You're thinking of your father."

She turned to him, startled.

"How did you know?"

"Haven't I worked with him day and night?"

Her eyes hardened.

"Yes; and you nicknamed him Torquemada of Lion Hill. How could I have forgotten? I'm sorry, but I can't be friends with you."

Ralph's face paled.

"If you stick to that you'll send your father rolling to the bottom of the hill."

"What hill? You'll have to explain."

"I'm the best friend he ever had. Look around you. I'm the only thing that stands between him and what he tried to do to you. If he had a knife at your throat instead of at your heart, perhaps you'd thank me for knocking it out of his hand."

"Please don't talk to me like that," said Janie, her lip trembling. "I don't know where I am or where I'm going, but I take back what I said."

"Don't think I blame you for sticking up for your father," said Ralph quickly. "I don't. I love you for it, and I'm glad I hit you with the apple, I'm glad I asked you if you could dance and I'm glad of that bit of foul play in the paper." She stared at him in amazement.

"Aren't you?"

"I don't know what you mean."

"That isn't fair. You do know. You know I was meant to come here in three jumps and nothing else could have brought me. Are you glad or aren't you?"

Her eyes gave way before his.

"I was terribly unhappy when you came," she said simply; "I'm only half unhappy now."

"So am I," said Ralph. "When I started over from our place everything looked as clear as could be. There was going to be at least one man at your reception, and a woman if my mother could get here. That's all I thought about. But now I'm half unhappy."

"Why?" asked Janie, smiling unconsciously at the puzzled look in his face.

"You've got to believe me when I say that was all I was thinking about," he continued. "Do you?"

"Yes; I do."

"Well, here's what's happened. I don't want to rush you or anything like that; but if you'll only give me half a chance, I know I'll love you back to the first day I saw you and ahead as long as I don't go deaf, dumb and blind."

"Oh!" cried Janie, throwing up her hands as if he had struck her. "You know I'm going to be married! You know it! You know it! And now you've said that!"

He stepped forward, caught her wrists and held them down. She looked at his set face with swimming eyes.

"Janie, you're not a big enough coward to marry that crawling slug."

"You don't know what you are doing!" she whispered, her head falling to one side. "I gave my word to my father."

"I knew it!" cried Ralph, tightening his hold. "Break it if you have any love for him. Don't mind me; I'll look out for myself, but your father can't." She straightened her head and looked at him, hanging her weight on his hands as if she wished to rest on them. "I mean it," he went on earnestly. "There's only one way for you or anyone else to win your father and that's to fight him tooth and nail for his own good."

"Win him?" said Janie, her eyes widening.

"Something's the matter with him. I don't know what it is, but I know you're the only person in the world who can cure him."

"You're frightening me."

"I can't believe you're really afraid——"

"No, no!" cried Janie. "Not of him—of you. You're talking to me as I've always longed to be talked to. Whether you're right or wrong, you mean what you say. Don't you?"

"I do, and because you're just a little afraid of me, as I am of you, I've got to ask you something. Why does your father want you to marry that—that——"

"I don't know."

"Did you ever think you loved him, that—that——"

"No; I only wanted to love him. I tried and tried, but I couldn't—I can't."

He drew her toward him so quickly her relaxed body had no time to resist. Before she could think she was in his arms. Her own blood betrayed her. It tingled in her veins and throbbed in her ears, telling her to let herself go. She was fallen against him.

"Oh, please! You mustn't! It's wrong! It's wicked for me to be like this—to feel like this."

"Janie, that's a lie," he whispered. "We both know it's a lie. Promise me you'll stand by me as I'll stand by you."

"I promise."

"Promise me you'll never give me up."

Torquay loomed like a black cloud through the hall into the drawing-room. Albert was at his side, his mouth wide open and gasping.

"I'll never leave you, Ralph," said Janie, her fingers creeping to a hold on his shoulders. "Never!"

A laugh like a thunderclap burst from Torquay. Ralph and Janie drew apart only enough to turn and face him. Albert's mouth still hung open and his pink cheeks had become blotches of brilliant red.

"Black inside!" rumbled Torquay, his blood-streaked eyes fastened on Janie. "Woman! Rotten to the touch! Perjured! There's a worm in you—a black core in your white body."

"It's you that's black inside and out," said Ralph quietly. "You're a great torturing bully chewing on your daughter and your own heart."

"Get out of this house!" shouted Torquay at the top of his voice, throwing both his clenched fists high in the air as if he were going to crash them down on Damon's head. Ralph moved Janie firmly aside and took a step forward.

"You're not dealing with that miserable pink-cheeked bladder there," he said with a short nod toward Albert. "You can beat me into a jelly and when you get through what's left of me will still be man enough to tell you what you are—even dead, I'd tell you what you are—as big a man as ever swung a sledge hammer and as big a coward as ever kicked a woman."

"No!" cried Janie piercingly. She rushed to her father, threw her arms around him and buried her face against his breast. "Father, I love you—I've loved you all my life; but I won't marry Albert; I can't marry Albert—not now—not ever."

Torquay's hands fell lax at his sides. Sweat sprang out on his forehead. A film seemed to spread over his dilated eyes, falling like a veil between him and Damon; but they still stared, looking at something beyond confining walls. He had forgotten Ralph. He had forgotten Albert. He was back at his old fight, barely holding his own ground with all the strength that was left to him.

Eloise Damon came quickly through the hall, stepped into the drawing-room and stood still for a moment, her eyes fastened on Torquay's back. Her hair was quite gray, but she was still as thin and erect as when she had gone to him twenty-three years before. In her gloved hands she was holding the small local paper, pleated and folded into a thin strip. She moved forward.

"Miss Strayton—Mr. Strayton——"

Janie threw up her head, then straightened quickly and drew away from her father. He revolved slowly, like a mass on a pivot, until he faced Mrs. Damon.

"I'm sorry to be so late," she continued, and turned with a smile to Janie. "If I'd been in town instead of New York I'd have come over on the stroke of four and begged you to let me help you receive."

The quivering answering smile that broke instantly in Janie's face came near to hurling Mrs. Damon from her pinnacle as a woman of poise. It was all she could do to restrain herself from throwing her arms around the slender girl who had the brains to render thanks as quickly as that. But she had other work to do. Her eyes caught her son's with that swift interlocking which binds two people who know and trust each other profoundly.

"Ralph, something pretty terrible has happened at the works. Better get down there at once."

Damon started immediately for the door, casting an involuntary glance of wonder at Torquay and Albert as he went. Neither of them seemed to have heard his mother's words. All Albert's attention was given to being nervous and awkward. Torquay did not move even by the flicker of an eyelash. He was staring at Mrs. Damon and seeing her. As soon as Ralph had gone she met his eyes and held them, while she drew the folded paper slowly through her fingers.

"I see somebody has already said to you what I came here to say."

She handed him the long strip like one surrendering a whip. He took it and without looking down began tearing off small pieces and dropping them on the floor.

CHAPTER XXII

OUTSIDE, Ralph ran into one of the foremen pacing impatiently up and down under the portico.

"My God, Ralph, I thought you'd never come! Where's Torque?"

"Never mind him," said Ralph, making for the gap in the cedars. "Tell me what's the matter."

"I guess Torque's crazy all right. Your mother stopped me from going in to drag him out. She promised she'd send you."

"Tell me what's up."

"We ran after Torque when he was coming up the hill to tell him the cap on old Number Two was looking bad. But he wouldn't even turn around, and now old Ed Waller is done for."

"Done for!" exclaimed Ralph, stopping in his tracks.

"Ye-ah. He was starting for home with all his clothes on and his dinner pail in his hand. Something made him look round from the steps and he must of seen the Number Two cap caving. He gave a yell, jumped for the runway, swung around a sheet of zinc and tipped her out with the hand that had the dinner pail slung on his wrist. He let her go. The dinner pail caught on the top edge of the zinc and it carried him with it. Just as the cap broke he shot down headforemost like he was diving off a dam."

Before he had finished speaking they were both running at top speed down the hill to the plant. Ralph knew well enough there was nothing he could do for poor Ed Waller; but there would still be disorder and danger of fire. The main works had a battery of six furnaces. Four of them were brand-new, constructed to feed the huge automatic machines from revolving tanks. The two others were part of the original equipment. They had been kept on for the manufacture of carboys according to the old system. It was the tank of one of these that had caved.

"Did they manage to cover the gap?" shouted Ralph over his shoulder.

"Ye-ah; they stopped it, and when I left they was skimming the scum to see if they couldn't find something looked like Ed."

"What was the heat?"

"Twenty eight hundred." He caught his breath and continued. "Ralph, a brick will float in melted glass; what about a man?"

"I don't know," confessed Damon.

"He went deep—like he was diving."

They arrived at the works and found them surprisingly quiet. A skeleton crew was looking after the machines. All the other men were gathered about Number Two, some of them ladling at the ringhole and some waiting their turn. Ralph joined the group. Hatless and dressed in his smart cutaway coat, and striped trousers over spats already smudged, he presented an incongruous figure. But no one noticed how he looked. The foreman in charge came to stand beside him.

"There's nothing to speak of in the scum, Ralph," he said quietly. "Shall we drain the tank?"

"Go ahead."

"Would a man float, Ralph?"

"I don't know," said Damon for the second time.

"It was pretty hot, wasn't it?"

"Sure; and there wasn't much glass. We knew the cap was going and we'd stopped feeding. We were heating her up for a clean-out. We've had to keep her hot, of course."

The emergency trap at the bottom of the tank was thrown open. The molten glass poured out into the flat receiving pan and began to spread. There was not much left. The men stood around in solemn silence, each one of them thinking about old Ed Waller—the same Ed who had given up his job as gigman on the railway because a voice from nowhere had shouted "Ed! Ed!" as the train chugged past the old house above the flats.

From time to time someone would get on his knees and peer in at the settling mass, illumined by its own glow. Presently the glow began to die and soon after the flow ceased. The pan was dragged out and set to cool. Its contents had been skimmed so clear it showed scarcely a flaw. One after another, the men went away. Some of them had stayed overtime to help, others had to go back to their work. But hours later Damon still remained. He would go away for a few minutes and then come back to stand staring at the sheet of glass. It seemed to be cooling evenly, but once as he approached from a short absence a spot as big as the palm of his hand appeared to show a different luster. He leaned over it. The difference disappeared.

He retraced his steps and came back again from the same direction. The spot was there. He repeated this performance several times before he tested the sheet of glass at its edges. It was exceptionally brittle, though still warm. He waited another hour for it to cool and then took a hammer and began breaking it up for the cullet heap. He came nearer and nearer to the spot which looked different from a distance and the same near by. It fascinated him, but he was afraid to touch it. Finally it was isolated, loosened—a bit of glass half an inch thick and as big as his hand. He heard someone coming. Impulsively he picked it up, stirred the broken fragments over the bare spot with his hammer and thrust the small slab in his pocket. For an instant he thought it was burning him, but it was only a trick of his imagination. The glass was cold.

Somebody spoke to him and he answered without knowing what he said. He walked out of the plant and started to go along the river bank, but the night was cloudy and pitch dark. He turned, crossed the foot-bridge and went along the familiar path toward Torquay's workshop which he had not entered since the hour of reading of Janie's engagement. It seemed years instead of weeks ago. For an instant he wanted to stop his mind and start it to rehearsing every moment and every sensation of his interview with Janie. But the glass, weighing heavily in his pocket, restrained him. Its unusual weight when he had picked it up had shot a prickling sensation through his veins to his heart. He came to the solitary pine tree and leaned against it.

The slower glass is cooled the stronger it is. Every bottle maker, under the pressure of large orders, chafes against this fundamental rule of the game; but he knows that to speed up his annealing leers would be fatal. A bottle, when it is hot, is made up of billions of extremely active molecules. Cold imprisons them. If the outside layer of glass is cooled faster than the inside, tension is created and the tap of a finger nail can make a bottle explode. Damon had not touched the piece of glass in his pocket since thrusting it there.

Now he slipped in his hand, and using his thumb for a fulcrum he pressed lightly on the other side with his fingers. He was prepared to have the bit of glass shiver into fragments, but nothing happened. He pressed harder and the glass bent. A full minute passed before he turned it over, still in his pocket, and bent it back.

He went home, walking with an odd absence of feeling in his feet. It seemed to him that his legs were gone, but that in some mysterious manner he was progressing at a slow pace past the sheds, over the bridge and up the hill. There was a light burning in the house and he found his mother waiting up for him.

"Ralph, do you know what time it is?" she asked.

"No," he answered out of a daze.

"It's after midnight."

He was astonished, but he did not let his surprise show in his face. He must have stood for an hour or more leaning against the pine. She asked him just what had happened at the works and he told her about Ed Waller's death.

"It was terrible, but there was nothing you could do, was there?"

"No."

"What made you stay so long? You knew I was anxious."

" I don't know. I guess I wanted to be there until things settled down. Anyway I'm glad I stayed."

"You seem to be very much upset," she continued.

"Perhaps it's the accident and perhaps it's worrying about the Strayton girl. Nothing much took place after you left us, but I saw enough to make me believe she'll never throw herself away on Mr. Polperro."

"I know she won't," said Ralph promptly, glad of something he could tell without reservation. "She's going to marry me."

"Already?" exclaimed his mother, with raised eyebrows. He did not seem to hear her. She frowned and then continued, "I've been prepared to have it come to that ever since she smiled at me, but don't you think there are apt to be flaws in anything that crystallizes as quickly as that?"

Ralph was as startled as if she had pricked him with a pin. He turned with a jerk to stare at her. Gradually it came over him that she had used a most natural figure of speech for a woman whose existence had once stood on a foundation of glass. It was the sort of thing Jake's wife or the wife of any other Damon for half a dozen generations might have said. Her face grew puzzled and then broke into quiet laughter.

"What are you laughing at?" he asked.

"You. There's always something funny about people in love, if you're far enough away to see it."

He was completely reassured.

"Laugh all you like, mother. You'll have lots of chances, because my troubles have only begun. Torque Strayton isn't the kind to admit he's beaten before the flowers begin to arrive for the funeral. As for Janie, she would never leave him and I don't want her to."

"Janie? Was it Janie and Ralph in half an hour?"

"It seems sort of fast, but it really wasn't. I don't know quite how it happened, but it did. The apple helped, of course, and my falling off the roof; but even without those things, I'd have known and I'd have had to tell her."

"Ralph, did you really ask her to marry you? Forgive me for appearing curious, but I had an idea the reception was given to announce her engagement to Mr. Polperro and——"

"—and you think I was extremely tactless," interrupted Ralph, only to be interrupted in turn by his mother.

"Tactless? Never! If you hadn't been made of tact from the feet up, including your brains, you would have telephoned to some of my friends to go to Miss Strayton's tea. That's what a tactless person would have done."

"But that wouldn't have helped!" exclaimed Ralph.

"I don't know why, but it would have been throwing pennies at a beggar, and she wasn't that! If you could have seen her sitting there— Well, anyway and however it happened, she promised to stand by me as I'm going to stand by her, and neither one of us had time to talk about stuff like marriage. . . . I'm going to bed."

"Don't forget to take a bath. Those clothes looked very fine this afternoon, but now———"

"Good night!" called Ralph from halfway up the stairs.

Once in his own room, he took out the bit of malleable glass, locked it away in a drawer and tried to forget it. If it had been the result of a formula he would have gone straight to his employer's house with it and waked him up at whatever the cost. But he knew it was no time to tantalize Torquay by waving his will-o'-the-wisp, imprisoned at last by so strange a stroke of fate, before his tormented eyes. The boldest chemist, taking into account the myriad elements involved in composition and the hair-line divisions of time and heat, would not dare say a secret had been discovered. All he could affirm was that the goal toward which Torquay had been striving for more than forty years was not a myth. Besides, the glass might discolor as their gelatine compounds had done. Ralph was more tired than if he had been engaged in exhausting labor, but he could not go to sleep. He lay awake, thinking disjointedly of what he ought to do and trying to form some plan which would give him at least a starting point in the morning. His mind slipped. Before he knew it he was reliving every moment of the time he had spent alone with Janie. When he came to the point where he had taken her in his arms and she had given him her promise never to desert him, he fell asleep. He awoke to find his path laid so clearly before him that he did not even feel amazement over the vanishing of his doubts. First he had a frank talk with his mother as to their joint resources. They came to an understanding almost without words. Then he went down for an interview with Torquay in his office. He knew he would find him there; he could even have predicted the sort of reception Torquay would give him.

In everything but his manner, Torquay showed evidences of

having passed a sleepless night. His clothes were the same as he had worn on the previous day and looked as if he had not taken them off, which was the truth. His eyes were sunken, still streaked with red, and he was indulging in his newly acquired habit of cracking his knuckles. But when he spoke, it was quite calmly.

"Well, Ralph, that was a nasty business about Ed Waller. Things turn out funny. I did him out of a job once. Shouted at him when he was gigman on the railway and he thought it was a ghost. The next day he asked my father to take him on. That must have been nigh fifty years ago. Ed was our oldest hand, wasn't he?"

"Just about," agreed Ralph.

"I suppose you thought it would have done no good to call me, and perhaps it wouldn't. But I wish you had. Perhaps I wouldn't have come down here any more than I'd turn back when they yelled the cap was weakening. But then again I might, and I could have stood around with the rest of you and thought about old Ed. I suppose in a way I'm to blame for his dying like that."

"It was an accident, pure and simple," declared Ralph. "It might have happened just the way it did if you'd been in the works shouting out orders. Ed's dinner pail caught on the zinc and pulled him in."

"I've heard all about it. You don't have to tell it over to me again. Ed had a married daughter. I wish you'd see her. Tell her I'm sorry and that I'm not dodging anything. Make it right with her. Whatever you arrange goes."

"Why don't you send your errand boy?" asked Ralph with a nod toward Albert.

"Him!" cried Torquay. "You must think I'm crazy like the rest of them thinks. I wouldn't send him to buy the coffin. I wouldn't trust him with a registered letter. I——"

"But you'd trust him with Janie, your own daughter," interrupted Damon.

Torquay had been sitting loosely. He gathered himself together into a compact mass and leaned forward, his blunt fingers spread on the desk. Gone was his easy manner; he was completely transformed.

"You want it now, do you?" he said hoarsely.

Ralph did not answer at once. He went to the door, opened it and turned to Albert.

"Get out. You'd better move quickly, because if you're here when I've counted three I'm going to throw you out. One—two—three!"

Before Albert had time to make up his mind whether he would obey or resist, Damon reached over, seized his coat by the collar, dragged him to his feet, turned him, planted a knee in his back and sent him flying into the hall. He slammed the door and faced Torquay.

"What's the matter with you and what's the matter with me?" he demanded. "Why do you want Janie to marry a thing like that?"

"That's none of your business," said Torquay. "My daughter isn't going to marry you. She's going to marry Albert, and if ever I catch you fooling around her again I'll serve you the way you just served him."

"You don't know her, and you don't know me. If you send her away I'll follow her. If you keep her here I'll see her. You heard what she said to me. She'll never go back on that."

"She went back on Albert, didn't she?" snarled Torquay.

"Inside of a week she'll go back on you."

"She never was for him. It was you rammed him down her throat."

"I had to," said Torquay, a sudden ugly gleam in his eyes. "I had to do it on account of their cuddling."

For an instant it was Damon's turn to see red. His fists itched to bruise themselves futilely on Torquay's clenched jaws, but his head told him if he let them do it he would be playing directly into his tormentor's hands. "Ask her," continued Torquay, quick to perceive his advantage. "I caught them at it not once but twice. I won't have her switching around from one man to another. You wouldn't like it yourself. In a way, I'm saving you from a lot of trouble."

"All right," said Ralph, turning on his heel, "I will ask her." At the door he stopped. "I came here to tell you I'm off your pay roll from now on."

"I wouldn't do that if I were you, Ralph." The voice in which Torquay spoke was astonishingly transformed. It was in no way wheedling; it was merely the difference between the voice of an obsessed mentality and that of Torque Strayton, master of the Pine Tree Glassworks. "There's no need for it," continued the kindly voice. "You're doing fine here. All you and me have got to think about to get along is for each one of us to mind his own business."

"That's very good of you," said Ralph shortly; "but I'm through. I'm going to take a holiday and when I'm ready I'll have a job with the Hetney people. I'm not worrying about that sort of thing. What I want to know is how it will strike Janie. I'm going up to see her about it now."

"Try it!" said Torquay calmly, sitting back in his chair. "Just try it!"

Ralph left the office and started up the hill with a puzzled frown on his forehead. He could not make out Torquay's moods. In some of them he was a man of views so fair and broad as to disarm his most bitter detractor. In others he was as narrow as a needle's eye. But broad or narrow, he never lost the power to make others feel that they were in the presence of great though unguided forces. What stumped Damon was the older man's attitude toward his daughter. He felt instinctively that if he could once read the motive behind it, he would have the answer not only to his own riddle but to all those crawling rumors which were gnawing at Torquay's foundations like grubs at the root of a tree. He did not attempt to see Janie at once; instead he went to his mother and stood looking at her, the frown still on his forehead.

"Did you have it out with Mr. Strayton?"

"I don't know. I told him I was going after his daughter tooth and nail. I chucked my job. I said I was on my way to talk things over with Janie."

"Yes—but what did he say?"

"That's just it. I haven't the least idea where I get off. He's two men. One half of him is as fair and big as all outdoors; the other is some kind of blackguard I don't know anything about. Mother, what's the matter with Torquay Strayton? I've got to know and you can tell me."

"I could tell you, Ralph, but it wouldn't be fair to him."

"Why not?"

"Because he doesn't know it himself."

"Do you mean to say you'd put his good before mine?"

"You know I wouldn't. There are two sides to telling anything—the tongue that says it and the ear that hears it. To me, Mr. Strayton has become the most natural man I ever knew. There's absolutely nothing puzzling about anything he says or does. But if I told you in half a dozen words what it's taken me twenty years to find out, there's no telling what twist your ear would give to the statement."

"You'll have to trust me, mother," said Ralph quietly. "I won't eat, drink or smoke till you come through."

"All right, take it—Mr. Strayton is in love with his daughter."

"In love with Janie!" gulped Ralph. "You mean——"

"I thought you'd make a fool of yourself," said his mother sharply. "The reason he wishes her to marry Mr. Polperro is that Mr. Polperro will stay wherever Mr. Strayton puts him for the rest of his life. If you went away from me, I'd miss you; but I could stand it. If Janie should leave her father he would wither and die in three months at the outside. I don't mean he'd fade; I mean he'd die and be buried."

"That's big; it isn't horrible."

"It's big and pitiful; but it's not horrible, because it's blind. Instinct tells him it would kill him to lose the sight of Janie—the same instinct that led him to play that cruel trick in the paper. Of course there's something hidden behind it all that we can't see."

"What sort of thing?"

"Now you're overrating my powers of perception. I can only tell you that whatever it was it has been strong enough to keep him from ever— No: I can't be absurd."

"Keep him from what?"

"From ever looking at me."

Ralph gulped again.

"Mother," he said as soon as he recovered, "the thing that keeps you everlastingly interesting is the way you threaten not to tell a thing and get a fellow, to drop his guard. Then you hand it to him like an uppercut to the jaw. Are you joking or would you have married Torque Strayton? That's not one of my asinine questions, because if you say

213

yes, I'll know I can take off my hat every time he walks by." "It's a strange thing to say to you, Ralph, but I'm in the mood to play fair all around. Since I've been free I'd have married him any time he asked me. He'd have given me one more life—a life I've missed living."

"That's enough for me. Will you forgive me for trampling?"

"You haven't trampled. I haven't said a word I didn't want to say. I'm not a girl—I'm even a long way off from when I was a young woman. The only feeling I have in regard to Mr. Strayton is one of having lost a life. I could never have been in love with him as you are with Janie. That's all of that. . . . Did he say you could see her?"

"He told me I could try it the way a man gives yon leave to take a bone away from his bulldog."

"In that case I think you're in for a hard struggle."

"Well, there's only one way to find out." He started for the door.

"Ralph!"

He turned; their eyes met and held.

"I understand, mother. I won't give him away to Janie or himself, and of course I won't give you away either. Was that it?"

"Yes," said his mother slowly. "Let your tongue hit once in a while, but never let it slip. It's a good rule."

A few minutes later Ralph opened the door to the Strayton house and only then rang the bell. When Mega answered he was standing in the hall. She had taken to wearing a mobcap to hide her grizzled hair. Age had begun to wither her body, but her arms still looked as if they could and would do battle with a man. Her eyes smoldered with fury as she asked him in her insolent drawl what he wanted.

"It was a bit cold outside," said Ralph easily, "so I stepped in. Will you tell Miss Strayton I'm here?"

"No."

"In that case I'll wait," said Ralph, and walked into the drawing-room. A glance showed him the library and dining-room were empty.

"You needn't look for her in there," said Mega deliberately. "She's safe enough where she is from you or any other man. She's in Miss Ball's bedroom that's where she is."

"How is Miss Ball?" asked Ralph politely. "I understand she's an invalid."

"Mr. Strayton will tell you all about how sick she is when he comes in for his lunch."

"That's a long time to wait," said Ralph, and sat down.

Mega shrugged her shoulders and went out. He heard the door through which she had entered the hall slam behind her. He knew she would be back again when she thought he would least expect her. He sprang to his feet at once and was halfway up the stairs when he felt her presence behind him. He glanced over his shoulder and saw her holding to the newel post and gazing at him with unbelieving eyes. He kept on. The first two doors he opened after a perfunctory knock showed him unoccupied rooms. Upon opening the third he stood transfixed and an icy chill rippled over his flesh.

He saw a huge bed with a malformed heap upon it which made the counterpane look like a snowslide. At one end of the mountain of bedclothes was a woman's diminutive head, bent at a sharp angle. Beside the bed was Janie. She was fallen on her knees, her face buried and her arms flung upward against the steep slope. Her shoulders were twitching spasmodically and she was uttering the faint dry sobs of one who has been weeping for a long time. He walked toward her slowly, glanced at the face on the pillows and stooped over quickly.

"Janie!" he whispered.

She did not seem to hear and he laid his hand gently on her shoulder. She turned toward him without looking up. He gathered her in his arms and in another moment was out in the hall. Still holding her firmly, he tried in vain to place her on her feet. Something besides strength in its ordinary sense seemed to have gone out of her. Not only her face and her body but her mind appeared to have been drained at the sources of volition.

"Janie, it's all right now," he whispered earnestly. "Please stop crying, won't you? Please try to stand." She looked at him curiously, studying his features one by one with a frown. "It's Ralph, dear. Everything's all right now." She put her arms around his neck, hung her weight against him and gave a long shuddering sigh.

"Of course it's you, Ralph. I'm so cold. I've never been so cold."

He shouted for Mega and was startled when she appeared immediately at his side. Together they carried Janie to her room, opened the blankets on her bed and laid her between them.

"Ralph," she sobbed, struggling to rise, "please don't go. Please don't leave me with Mega."

He put his lips close to her ear.

"I've got to go, dear," he whispered. "Don't be afraid, because it's only for a moment. But I've got to go."

He ran down the stairs, out of the front door, and plunged headlong through the gap in the cedars. When he got home he called loudly for his mother and she came down to find him already at the telephone giving Torquay's private number.

"What is it, Ralph?"

"Go over to the Straytons' as fast as you can make it. You'll find Janie in a bad way. Her room is the old nursery. Please hurry, mother." As she darted swiftly toward the door she heard him say, "Mr. Strayton? This is Ralph. You'll have to come up to the house at once, sir. Miss Ball is dead."

CHAPTER XXIII

TWO weeks later Damon would have been almost unrecognizable to his friends if he had left the house. But he did not leave it. He paced about interminably, climbed the stairs and stumbled around his own and his mother's rooms. Sometimes he took out the mysterious bit of malleable glass and stared at it fixedly as one stares, fascinated, into a crystal. Books meant nothing to him, for they had lost their power to seize his runaway mind. When he heard the door open he would plunge down the stairs and stand dumb before his mother. For fourteen days she had been almost continuously in Janie's bedroom, and her patience was rapidly coming to an end with her endurance. She had been robbed even of the rest she might safely have taken because Ralph's whole attitude drove her back to the Straytons' every time she sought her own home.

"Don't look at me like that," she snapped. "There's nothing the matter with you but your babyish mind."

"It's thinking about that slug Polperro makes me this way, mother," said Ralph rapidly. "I've been thinking perhaps he crawls into her room when you're over here and sits there looking at her. If I was sure of it I'd——"

"Stop that, Ralph. Come in here with me." She led the way into the front room, sat down and pointed to another chair. "Sit down there. Lean back and don't move till I've finished." He hesitated but finally obeyed partially.

"Ralph, I've told you over and over again that no one sees Janie but her father, the new nurse and myself. She's never unconscious and the doctors say she isn't even ill. Miss Ball had an extraordinary influence over her. That's gone. Sometimes it seems as if the bones had been drawn out of Janie's body with it. It does no good for you to act as you have been doing. Go out and take a long walk. Come back from it a man or I'll leave for Gwen's tomorrow. I think I'll go

217

anyway. You are so selfish I can't stand the sight of you."

"Mother!" cried Ralph, springing to his feet.

"Don't touch me!"

"I won't, dear. But if you'll just go to bed I'll bring you up some toast and tea myself. I'll sit by you until you go to sleep. When you wake up you'll forget you ever had to say that to me."

He was as good as his word, and as soon as his mother had sunk into the first profound slumber of many days he prepared to go for a walk. He was astonished to find he had left the slab of glass in plain view on his dressing table. He picked it up, sought for one of the calling cards he so rarely used, went over to the big house and rang the bell. Mega opened the door.

"Lay these on Mr. Strayton's desk, please," he said. He passed around the house but did not attempt to look up at Janie's window. As he walked mile after mile along the deserted paths which interlaced the woods bordering the park, he kept wondering what Torquay would do when he found the bit of malleable glass. For days Ralph had been obsessed by the idea that it comprised the powers of a talisman as far as his own fate was concerned. It might drive Torquay quite mad, but it was far more probable it would force him to come to terms at any cost for the possession of its secret. What those terms would be Ralph had not thought out. He had no plan, but he could not help thinking of the secret in his sole possession, such as it was, as a lever with which he might move a mountain. When three days passed without any apparent development he began to worry.

During two of those days Torquay did not enter his study. On the third Mega began to be troubled lest the spite she held against Damon react unpleasantly on herself. She went to find Torquay to tell him there was something waiting for him on his desk, without saying how long it had been there. He was sitting in Janie's room, as he had sat for hours every day since Miss Ball's death. His chair was set beside the window. With his back to the light, he leaned slightly forward, resting his folded hands on his father's stout cane, his eyes fixed on Janie's face. There was a strange intensity in their gaze, which was broken when Mega opened the door to murmur her message.

"Tell Mega to go away," murmured Janie, without opening her eyes.

"You heard that," rasped Torquay, turning his head to glare at the colored woman. "Get out and stay out." Mega was pleased. She had told him. She hoped he would forget her message and that much inconvenience might result. No sooner was the door closed on her than Torquay resumed his former position. He was watching for something—waiting for it.

"A woman can leave her body fussing around the house, and all the time she's traveling, getting a start on you before you know she's gone."

His father had been right, but he wanted to go him one better. He was straining all his powers of perception to see how it was done. What made them start and where did they go?

Suddenly Janie half rose in the bed and held her body up on rigid arms. Her hair was divided evenly and hung over her shoulders in two loose braids. Only the knowing eye would have recognized the fineness of her modest nightdress, girlishly yoked at the neck, short-sleeved and narrowly pleated by hand. Her face was not pale, it was flushed, and her eyes burned with too much light as they fastened on her father's unchanging gaze.

"I want Ralph," she said in a clear low voice for his ears alone. "I've told you over and over again I want Ralph."

"Why?" asked Torquay, as if to lead her on.

"Because he isn't afraid of me. He's not afraid to touch me or hold me. You're afraid of me. I never knew it before. You're afraid."

"Go back," whispered Torquay, clenching his hands over the head of the cane. "Lie back."

She relaxed, fell into the pillows as abruptly as she had risen from them, and closed her eyes. He sat on, watching her until she fell asleep. It was a healthy sleep. She was leaving him day by day, but not along the road her mother had taken. Each day she was stronger inside. He could see the strength growing in her and hear it in her voice.

"A woman can travel for weeks and months without moving her body. That's the way they're made."

He was a fool to wait any longer. He was free today—now. Janie, his daughter, was going away from him, leaving him. After twenty years his wife was lifting the grip of her hands. All he had to do was to sit tight, to hold his ground.

The nurse slipped quietly into the room, sat down beside the shielded lamp and began to read. He arose and went out, leaving the door open behind him. The nurse closed it softly and he stood for a long time in the dark at the top of the stairs. Presently Mega's message came back to him. He pressed a switch and the halls became flooded with light. A moment later he was in his study, staring curiously at Ralph Damon's card with the slab lying beside it. He could not distinguish what it was, as it took the color of the green blotter on which it lay. He stepped forward and halted sharply as he perceived it was a fragment of glass with peculiar edges; not sharp—rounded.

It was ten minutes before he moved again, and then only to walk forward slowly and pick up Damon's card. He read the name, studying the formation of each letter. He turned the card over, seeking in vain some written message. He bent it this way and that, and finally flipped it into the waste-paper basket. Still without looking at the glass, he sat down and tipped his chair back exactly as was his habit, with his toes caught under the body of the desk. His brows gathered slowly into a frown which tightened moment by moment. It was not puzzled. It was the frown of a man who is driving his brain with whip, knee and spur.

At last his forehead cleared and the chair settled forward abruptly. He reached out, picked up the slab, bent it this way and that, just as he had done with the card, and tossed it into the waste-paper basket. From that moment until the break of day he sat at the desk staring at nothing, living somewhere outside his body, and for every hour that passed some part of his great frame seemed to cave in. His size remained the same, but there was a hollowness in his face and chest, a flabbiness about his arms and a fallen slouch to his shoulders which made him look like the counterpart of the abandoned house at Babylon.

When the day streamed in through the uncurtained window he turned out the desk light, drew a pad toward him and began to write.

The exertion seemed to pull him together. He frowned, grunted, thought aloud in muttered phrases and occasionally swore. He filled a foolscap page, folded it and slipped it in a long envelope, which he sealed and inscribed with Ralph Damon's name in large round letters. Then he opened a drawer, locked the document away and left the study for the dining-room where Albert was sitting over a solitary breakfast. Torquay looked him over deliberately.

"Pack your things, Albert, then come down to the office and I'll see you get a year's pay instead of a month's notice. Catch the noon train out of town. I'm tired of seeing you around."

"Yes, sir," said Albert in a whisper, his pink cheeks turning blotchy and red.

He was wondering if it would be safe to sue Torquay for a large sum of money according to the custom of the country. His engagement to Janie was no secret; it had been officially announced.

Torquay did not sit down to eat. He stood beside the table, feeding himself with bread and milk from a bowl that looked like a garden bird bath and then drinking his morning coffee from a cup to match. His eyes never left the top of Polperro's blond head.

Between two sips he said casually, "If you did that I wouldn't think any more of killing you than I would of slapping a blood-sucking mosquito."

He set down his cup and presently started for the plant. After half an hour in the office, where he dictated a receipt for Albert's signature, he went over to the old works beside the solitary pine and stayed there until lunchtime.

"Where's Mr. Polperro, Mega?" he asked upon returning home.

"He left on the noon train," drawled Mega, "like you told him to."

"So I did. This house is getting emptier and emptier. Find Mr. Damon and ask him to come over here. Did you hear me?"

"Yes, Mr. Strayton."

He pushed his plate away, arose and went upstairs to Janie's room, but he did not enter. After looking at the door knob fixedly for several moments he turned and retraced his steps slowly, holding to the banister and shaking it from time to time as he descended. It was as strong as the day it was built, he thought, his mind wandering back to the old house above the flats. He entered the study and was sitting hunched behind the desk when Ralph was shown in.

"Have a chair, Ralph. I think you can take it better sitting down."

"I'd rather stand," said Damon.

"Sit down," ordered Torquay, and waited until he was obeyed. "Ralph, when Janie was a kid you plugged her in the back with an apple, and now you've tried to plug me in the back with a bit of unbreakable glass. As far as I happen to know, those are the only two mean things you've ever done."

Ralph's cheeks reddened and his eyes began to smart, but he kept them fixed steadily on the eyes that were watching him.

"You look like you did the day your mother sent you over here to take a licking," continued Torquay. "The only difference is that this time you're going to get it. You may not have known just what was in your mind when you slung that bit of glass at me, so I'm going to tell you. You thought that after forty years it might knock me so silly you could trade it in for Janie. Do you want to know what I did with it?"

"Yes," said Ralph through set lips.

"I threw it in the waste-paper basket along with your card. I'll tell you why. Because it made me kind of sick to think you'd slipped up on yourself and offered to trade with goods you couldn't deliver."

Ralph turned white around the mouth.

"Mr. Strayton, I've been a skunk. But don't think I'm crying off. I'm here to take all the licking that's coming to me."

"You've had it," said Torquay, slouching deeper into his chair and letting his eyes wander over Ralph's tense figure. "Sit back now and forget it."

"I can't. If you talk to me like that I'll make a fool of myself."

A gleam of humor shone in Torquay's sunken eyes.

"No need of that; you've tended to it already. Where did you think my brains were when you gave them only three weeks to forget about what happened the last day you were on the job? If you'd gone to the Hetney works now, and held your horses for a month——"

222

"Thank God, I wasn't quite as rotten as that!"

"Or as clever. The worst of it is, Ralph, we aren't much further along the road than we ever were. We've fingered the gold, but we don't know where is the end of the rainbow. You can't walk backward through fire. I mean you can't undo heat. You've got to start from the end that's nearest to you." He took out his watch and glanced at it. "That's all I've got to say to you at present, but I wish you'd come back here in an hour's time. Will you do that?"

"Yes, sir."

"Don't start on that sir business now. I've just got rid of Albert."

"Got rid of Albert!" repeated Damon, his thoughts leaping back to Janie.

"Yes; Albert pulled out at noon on a one-way track."

Ralph stood up.

"How's Janie, Mr. Strayton?"

Torquay slid down in his chair until he seemed to be sitting on his shoulders. His eyes turned glassy with staring at the blotter before him.

"You can have Janie whenever you want to take her," he said mechanically, without looking up. "But remember what I'm telling you. One way or another, she'll leave you as sure as it takes two matches to light a pipe, as sure as the best glass——"

His voice died away. He felt the draft from the open door and could hear Ralph going up the stairs two steps at a time. Immediately he came to life, opened the locked drawer, laid the letter he had prepared in the center of the blotter and hurried out of the house.

Ralph was kneeling beside Janie's bed. He was unable to utter a word, but it made no difference except to the horrified nurse. She spoke to him sharply and then to Janie. They did not hear her. Finally she seized his arm and shook it violently.

"Don't do that, please," said Janie, without taking her eyes from Ralph's face.

Hearing her voice released his tongue.

"Janie, it's all right with your father." She laid her hands on his shoulders.

"Where is he?"

"Downstairs somewhere. Janie——"

"Ralph, I've been thinking it out all the days I've been lying here. I'll never give you up, but I'll never take you either unless you can bring me my father. You've got to believe it. It isn't my fault. It's something I can't help."

"I don't want you to, Janie," said Ralph quietly.

"I'll go and get him."

"Oh, not that! Do you think I'm asking you anything so easy?"

"Let me try, will you? I'm not blind, Janie. I've never heard him talk in my life as he's just been talking. Something's come over him I never saw in his face before."

"You're hurting me. He hasn't been here today."

Ralph went down the stairs much more slowly than he had gone up. He knocked at the study door, and as there was no answer, he opened it. He glanced around the empty room and was about to turn, when his eyes fell on the large envelope, boldly addressed. Without realizing quite what he was doing, he stepped forward and read his name. He picked up the letter and weighed it in his hand for a moment before he opened it and unfolded the large sheet it contained. He began to read:

> Ralph, the cud-chewing gang that think I'm crazy will probably call this suicide but you and me will know the difference. I've been heading to find out one thing all my life and old Ed Waller showed us where it is. Now don't lose your head. You can't walk backward through fire. I mean you can't undo fire. But here's all the data we didn't have about Ed, set down so you can walk forward. You can figure on a basis of 2800 degrees of developed heat. Ordinary workman's clothing and dinner pail. In dinner pail——

Ralph's eyes began to skip.

> In pockets— Batch as follows— Timed from 11 A.M. sharp to——

The paper fluttered from his fingers. For an instant he stood quite still, then he rushed into the hall, turned toward the stairs, whirled and shot out through the door. He did not feel as if he were running fast, but presently every breath began to drag like a file through his lungs. He forced himself to slow down and think. Of course it would be the old workshop and he must go in from the rear. The next thing he knew he had passed noiselessly under the eaves and was looking up at the back of a looming figure. There was no mistaking Torquay. Grotesquely illumined in the glare from the broken furnace cap, he was standing on the runway, holding his watch in one hand. From the wrist of the other hung a dinner pail, caught on the edge of a sheet of zinc which was slowly tipping outward. Ralph crept forward stealthily, seized Torquay's ankles and snatched his feet backward from under him.

Two weeks later Torquay was still in a daze, and the broken wrist which had made Ralph a match for him was still in splints. A freak spell of warm spring weather seemed to stir his blood and his mind. He demanded to be dressed in the first words he had uttered since his bellowing curses during the fight in the glasshouse had brought the men streaming from the storage sheds three hundred yards away. They had been in time to drag the two combatants to a place of safety, but had come too late to save the remnant of the old works from going up in flames.

It was Ralph who got him up and helped him with his clothes and Janie who fastened his collar, arranged his tie and made a sling for his disabled hand. She was careful not to stir him with anything like an open caress, but her fingers tingled every time she touched him. She held her breath when she found he did not shrink from her. Even though his tolerance seemed little more than apathy, it brought her nearer to him than she had ever been before. Her eyes shone and her face looked as if it might break any moment into a shower of smiles. A long chair, padded with rugs, was placed for him on the low veranda and Janie was about to sit down on the step near him when he motioned her away with his left hand.

"Wouldn't you like me to read to you, father?"

"No," said Torquay impassively.

"Is there anything you want to hear about the works?" asked Ralph, trying a different tack.

"Nothing," said Torquay, and frowned. "I think I'd like to be left alone as much as anything."

He sat quietly all that day and the next, his face an unreadable mask. When food was brought to him he ate it without comment, but never asked for anything on his own initiative. He was so completely passive that he seemed to have become a fixture. It was as if for some reason known only to himself he had reverted to the immobility of his childhood which had won him admittance into many an unfriendly roadside school. So lulled were the senses of all those about him that when he disappeared during the morning of the third day the blankets were sprinkled with leaves before his absence was discovered.

The search for Torquay Strayton has become one of the epics of Hopetown. It began at the scorched pine tree beside the oyster-shell mound, spread up and down the river, and swiftly widened its lines until even the ruined brick house at Babylon came within its scope. By midafternoon Ralph had driven more than a hundred miles. Passing through town to strike out in a new direction, he stopped at the Strayton house for a word with Janie. He found her walking up and down on the veranda, and while they stood looking at each other, neither wishing to speak first, a small boy came across the lawn. He was playing with a ball, which made his progress decidedly uneven. Janie was glad of the diversion.

"What do you want, boy?" she asked, as a crooked bounce of the ball brought him near with a rush.

"Nothing." He tossed up the ball and caught it. She turned from him and was starting into the house when he added, "Your father's sitting in the old State Street Church."

"Get in the car, Janie!" cried Ralph, as soon as he could collect his wits, but he was too late. She was already halfway across the lawn. He ran after her, realizing as he went that the short cut across the school grounds and the cemetery would more than equalize the difference in speed.

The old State Street Church was located on a knoll as high as Lion Hill. Sheltered by towering trees, it stood in the center of a graveyard a block square. It had long since been condemned as unsafe; but the true reasons for its abandonment probably lay in its worn red-brick aisles, awkward rectangular pews and precarious bird's-nest pulpit, perched high against the front wall. It was still sturdy and by far the oldest, most airy and loveliest house of worship in the city. Oddly enough, it faced away from the street and the town, which added to its aloofness. Only the oldest inhabitants knew that this strange position was due to the fact that geography had changed while the church had remained fixed. The roadway which now forms a right angle at the back and side of the edifice once passed directly before its front door.

Janie had never before entered the old church, and she caught her breath at the first sight of its exquisite proportions; but the next instant her eyes fell on her father's broad back. It was bowed over almost level and his forehead rested on his right arm, laid along the pew in front of him. A cold chill seized her heart as she rushed down the aisle and stopped beside his still figure. She was struck dumb with terror and stood trembling until Ralph was at her side. Then she reached out her hand and laid it gently on Torquay's shoulder. He raised his head at once.

"Well, Janie—and Ralph too! I suppose it's dinnertime." He arose and stretched, slipping his game arm from its sling and opening it almost as wide as the other. Never before had his massive limbs seemed to demand so much space. He dropped his hands at his sides and braced his shoulders. He filled his lungs with the cloistered air, raised his head and looked around with a possessive eye. "I've found the church that was made for Torquay Strayton—it's back to the world and no preacher but God, no sinner but me!"

They stood aside to let him pass and followed him up the aisle, pressing against each other to make sure they were awake. They walked slowly, fearing to catch up with him, but out under the trees he waited for them.

"Who's afraid now?" he said to Janie. She rushed to him and looked up into his face, her eyes still questioning and her lips twitching nervously. "Janie," he went on, his arms closing slowly around her, "I've got to tell you a couple of things it's taken me sixty-two years to learn. One of them's this: It isn't good for a man to be alone, and I've been alone all my life."

"Father! Please don't! I—I can't stand it!"

"And this is the other," whispered Torquay, tightening his arms. "My dear girl, your mother was a good woman, white through and through to the last breath in her body. She loved me, Janie. She loved me the way you love Ralph. Not my father, nor God, nor the devil in myself—not even dying—was strong enough to make her leave me."

THE END

Man Alone

George Agnew Chamberlain

Colophon

Ash Cole, Gabriela Marroquin, Gabriella Verducci, Shannon Wilson, editing interns at Stockton University, assisted with establishing the text, design, and typesetting of this work.

Additional preparatory work was completed by Dontae McFadden, Nicole Lanzoni, Mariyah Black, Hunter Blair, Lyndsey Clarke, Maddy Connelly, Anisah Dean, Emma Marsico, Suzanne McConlogue, Autumn Mcgaster, Shannon McGivney, Victoria Orlowski, Emily Siriano, Madison Szucsik, Alice Watt, Frank Wendling. Final proofreading was completed by Gianna D'Andrea, Matthew R. Dietrich, John A. Guttschall, Hunter Lynn, Rain Miller, Dickson Moreno, Megan Marroquin, Esmeralda Rivera, Diamond Rogers, Choo Still, Elena Suarez, Jibreel Tompkins, Gavin J. Wyllie. The body text is 12 point Garamond. Heidi Hartley designed the cover.

This is a publication of the South Jersey Culture & History Center. Our mission is to foster awareness within local communities of the rich cultural and historical heritage of southern New Jersey, to promote the study of this heritage, especially among area students, and to produce publishable materials that provide a lasting and deepened understanding of this heritage.

South Jersey Culture & History Center

ADDITIONAL GEORGE AGNEW CHAMBERLAIN
TITLES
PUBLISHED BY SJCHC.

Highboy Rings Down the Curtain.
The curtain rises on a horse like no other, noble to the end. This
short novella is Chamberlain's first work set in New Jersey.

47 pages, paperback.
ISBN: 978-1-947889-17-0

The Lantern on the Plow.
Set in southern New Jersey, *The Lantern on the Plow* follows the trials
and tribulations and the ultimate triumph of the Sherborne family
as they struggle to find there way in a changing landscape.

338 pages, paperback.
ISBN: 978-1-947889-19-4

www.ingramcontent.com/pod-product-compliance
Lightning Source LLC
Chambersburg PA
CBHW041604240626
47164CB00008B/172

* 9 7 8 1 9 4 7 8 8 9 3 0 9 *